More Adventures of Thunderfoot

Dan Bomkamp

Lovstad Publishing
Poynette, Wisconsin
Lovstadpublishing@live.com

ISBN: 0692490019
ISBN-13: 978-0692490013
(Previous ISBN: 0615750567)

Printed in the United States of America

Books by Dan Bomkamp
The Adventures of Thunderfoot
More Adventures of Thunderfoot
Thanks, Thunderfoot
The Gosey
Big Edna
Voyageur
Lost Flight
Tag
Spirit: the Castle Rock Cougar

Cover design by Lovstad Publishing
Cover photo by Dan Bomkamp
On the cover: Tyler Cole & Belle
as Thunderfoot and the dog.

DEDICATION

This book is dedicated to my Mom. She has been there for me through all these years. She has never faltered in her support for me and our family. Through everything that life has thrown at her, she has been our strength and the rock that we have relied on.

Foreword

I have been lucky to live my life in a very beautiful broad valley, surrounded by steep forested hills that stand like sentinels watching over the last one hundred free flowing miles of the Wisconsin River.

It is a valley teeming with wildlife of many kinds and offering opportunities for all outdoor people. Quiet and peaceful, it's a five-minute drive to a river full of smallmouth bass, or a backwater slough that is home to northern pike and large mouth bass, or schools of bluegills. The hills abound with deer, turkeys, grouse, and many other species of game.

I've also been very lucky to make my living doing something I enjoy for most of that time. As far back as I can remember I wanted a bait shop. I went to college and got my degree, but still the bait shop called, and finally I started a successful business that lasted 15 years and loved every minute of it. Now, I'm involved in the sporting goods industry on a different level, but I still do something that I love to do, and feel very lucky to have a job that allows me to work with all the "big boy's toys" of the outdoors.

A sporting goods store is a magnet for kids, and I enjoyed helping kids get started with an interest in the outdoors. A kid who is fishing is much less inclined to get into trouble than one standing on a street corner. I lost my own father much too early in life, but in our few years together he taught me a love of nature and a respect for it. After he died, I relied on neighbors, relatives and friends to help me keep my love of the outdoors alive. Once I became an adult and had the means of doing it, I began helping kids find an interest in fishing and hunting. Of course, fishing and hunting have their dangers too, but a hook in a finger is pretty minor compared to some of the things that can ruin the young life of a kid with nothing to do and no interests.

My life changed for the better the day Thunderfoot and I

became friends, and without him, I wouldn't be writing this book. James Buroker is one of the best friends I've ever had. He was a mischievous boy, and he became the idea for the character of Thunderfoot. He is still a great friend and a mischievous young man with a lovely wife and beautiful young son of his own.

Of course, many of the adventures in the book are things that he and I actually did together, but no two people could do so many goofy things. Thus, many of the story ideas are things that have happened with other outdoor buddies or one of my twenty-one exchange students. After the real Thunderfoot grew up and moved on with his life, things were pretty dull, so I began hosting foreign boys, and have had many great adventures with them also.

I have hosted boys from ten countries and almost all of them have fished and hunted while living with me, providing me with a treasure of funny happenings that make great stories. I owe much to all of my "sons" and my many great friends and hunting and fishing partners, who, over the years have provided me with a wealth of funny stories. I hesitate to try to name them all, fearing that I might miss someone. So I'll just say thanks to all of you for the fun, friendship and great times we've had together. You'll all recognize yourselves in the stories.

As you get older, sharing the excitement and wonder of the outdoors with a young person makes it all new and exciting again for someone who's "been there, done that." There is a special happiness that kids bring to everything they do, and the outdoors really makes that true.

There is nothing as important as our natural world. We must do everything we can to keep it in good shape for the kids that will inherit it. By teaching young people the joys of being in nature, we insure its future. We are but caretakers of nature and we must leave it as good as or better than we found it.

I have had some memorable times with Thunderfoot, and hope that everyone has his own hunting partner to share memories with. After all, when it's all said and done, reliving that hunt or fishing trip is just about as good as experiencing it the first time around. And, you usually find that the fish are bigger and the shot that took the deer or turkey was longer and more difficult each and every time the story is told. I hope you will see something of one of your own adventures in this book.

~~ Dan Bomkamp ~~

More
Adventures
of
Thunderfoot

It Seems Like Yesterday

I had put a little too much force into my cast, and before my popping bug had even hit the water, I knew it was going to be much too close to the brush pile. I was right, the bug landed too close to the log jam, and the current whisked it toward the logs very quickly. It took me a couple of precious seconds to strip the loop of line off the water so I could get the bug moving, and in that short time the swift current quickly caught the popper. I tried to strip the line a second time, but it was already in the log pile. With a quick snap of the rod, I tried to lift it to safety, but the hook snagged a log and my bug was hooked solidly. I snapped the rod up and down a couple more times, trying to get the hook free, but finally I resigned myself to the fact that my bug was a goner. Taking hold of the line and pulling, my leader soon snapped just a few inches up from the popper. There sat my little Bumble Bee imitation on the log, like a real insect, that had just landed and was taking a rest and watching the world go by.

I turned and began to wade back to the sandbar where the canoe was beached, and as I did, Thunderfoot stepped into the water and began wading toward me.

"Get a little close?" he said, with a twinkle in his eyes and a big grin on his face.

"Yeah, just a bit. I suppose you'll go and catch all of the fish while I tie on another bug."

"I'd consider it my duty," he said mischievously, and began wading toward the bank.

I sat down on the canoe and opened the tackle box, trying to decide which popper to try next. As I sat there, I watched Thunderfoot wade out to the drop off which was about twenty feet from the riverbank. There the water dropped into a channel that ran right along the bank. We had pulled up on the sandbar farther out in the river, so we could fish the brush piles along the bank for smallmouth bass.

It was the middle of the summer and the water was warm, so we were both wearing shorts and tee shirts, and wading barefoot, in the sandy-bottomed river. He waded to the edge of the deep water and then stripped off several loops of line and snapped his fly rod up, made one false cast, to feed some line out, and then expertly dropped the bug within a few inches of the bank and about three feet above the log pile ... He stripped in the excess line and twitched his bug across the upper side of the logs, just a few inches from the uppermost branches, and a nice smallmouth smashed it just as it got about half way past the brush pile. He raised his rod up quickly to set the hook and pulled the smallie from the dangerous, log infested waters, and then took his time and fought the fish in dose. His fly rod almost doubled over when the fish made a hard run and then jumped high out of the water, shaking his head, trying to get rid of the hook. Finally the fish tired, so he dipped his hand into the water, and grabbed the bass by the lip and held it up for me to admire.
"A beauty," I said, looking at the bronze fish, with drops of water dripping off its sides, like little diamonds shining in the sunlight.
He just grinned and took the hook from the fish's lip and slid it back into the water, and began fishing again.

It seemed like only yesterday when I had met Thunderfoot, and now three years later, here we were, best friends. I sat there watching him fish and thought back to the first time I'd seen him.

I owned a sport shop, and like most sport shops, it was a magnet for kids. There were always a few kids hanging around, looking at the rods and reels, or talking fish stories with me. On this particular day, a couple of new kids came through the front door. The older one was about 12 or 13 and introduced himself as James, or "Jamie" as his mom called him. His younger brother was Caleb, "like in the Bible." They looked around for a while and then Jamie mentioned that they had just moved to town and were living just down the street, so we were new neighbors.

Well, it didn't take long, and we became friends. His parents had recently split up, so his hunting and fishing trips were few and far between, because his dad lived in another city.

A short while later, I suggested we go and do some squirrel hunting, and that trip was the first of many adventures we had together over the next years. It was also on that squirrel-hunting trip that I had nicknamed him Thunderfoot.

I had lent him some hunting clothes and boots, which were all a bit too big for him. We had to roll up the pants cuffs and the shirtsleeves, and the boots fit just fine with a couple of extra pairs of socks. As we started walking up the ridge road to the woods, he kept stumbling and dislodging rocks and stepping on sticks, and making such a racket that I told him he had feet that made noise like thunder. And, somehow that got changed into Thunderfoot, and stuck.

When I first met him, he was fairly tall and skinny, with a shock of light brown hair and the bluest blue eyes I'd ever seen. He was a real likable kid with a smile a mile wide. Now, he had matured into a handsome young man. He hadn't grown much taller, but he had filled out nicely. Instead of a tall skinny kid, he was now a tall young man ... He still wore his hair fairly short, and in the summer time, it turned to a dishwater blonde color from all the time we spent in the sun. He had grown into the hand-me-down hunting clothing I had given him, and his feet had caught up to me, so now my shoes and boots were always being borrowed by him for one activity or another.

He still had those incredible, sparkling blue eyes and combined with his perpetual grin, he was a good-looking kid, who was as likable as they came. Except for an occasional very early morning "wake up," he never complained about anything and always could find something good in everyone and everything. Along with maturing physically, he had matured a lot in his adeptness in the outdoors. He was a safe, compassionate hunter, and a very skillful fisherman. All in all, he was a delight to spend time with, hunting, fishing, or just hanging around together.

I was sitting there in the canoe watching him fish, and kind of forgot about tying a new bug on my line.

He pulled another smallmouth out of the log pile and then moved down the bank a short way and began working another brush pile.

"Are you taking the afternoon off" he said, as he looked back and saw me just sitting there.

"No, I was just sitting here thinking."

"Oh, I see. I thought I could see smoke coming out of your left ear. Solving the world's problems or trying to figure out which popper to try."

I ignored him and tied a new bug on my line and then waded down beside him. We fished the brush pile a while longer and then decided to get the canoe and continue on down the river.

We had started just after daylight, and had conned his mom into leaving her car for us at the boat landing, while we drove upriver about 20 miles to another landing in my pickup truck. There we launched the canoe and the plan was to fish the whole day and end up back at the lower boat landing. Then we could pick up his mom's car and drive back up river to get the pickup. Finally, we'd go back to the lower landing and load the canoe in the pickup and the day would be done. It was kind of complicated, but the only way to fish the river from a canoe without paddling upstream.

A mile or so downriver, we beached the canoe again, and began wading toward the bank to fish, when we heard a honk. Instinctively we both looked up toward the sky, looking for the goose that was honking. We looked and looked but couldn't pick out any geese, when we heard the honk again. This time it was close, and not up, but down. We looked down and there was a Canada goose standing about ten feet away, looking at us.

"Holy cow, look at that," Thunderfoot said.

"He must be lost," I said, "or, maybe he's hurt and can't fly."

We crouched down and the goose waddled over to us. He wouldn't let us touch him, but he seemed to be happy to have some company. We waded into the water again and began fishing, and soon the goose was swimming around us while we fished.

"This is pretty cool," Thunderfoot said, as the goose swam and preened himself.

We fished for a while, caught several fish, and then decided to move on again. We got into the canoe, and began paddling, and the goose swam alongside the canoe with us.

"Come on Gordon," Thunderfoot said.

"Gordon?"

"Yeah, I think he looks like a Gordon. Don't you?" he said.

"I thought maybe Gloria, but probably Gordon is fine," I said.

"I wonder if he can fly. Let's paddle fast and see if he tries to fly to keep up."

We began paddling as fast as we could and soon the goose was falling behind. When we got about 50 yards ahead, he honked a couple of times and then he took off and flew up to join us.

"Well, I guess that answers that question," I said.

We pulled up on the next sandbar and decided to have some lunch. Soon, the goose was honking and waddling around begging for food. Thunderfoot shared his sandwich with him and then threw him some corn chips, which he seemed to like very much. He was making a grunting sound as he ate them and kept begging for more like a pet dog.

The rest of the afternoon slipped by too quickly. We caught quite a few fish, took a swim with Gordon, enjoyed the warm sun, the sparkling white sand, and the swift current as it carried us downriver, and all in all had a pretty fine day.

As we got to the boat landing, the goose swam to a sandbar a short way away, and watched as we pulled the canoe up onto the landing. Then he began walking back upriver across the sandbar toward where we had met him.

"Gosh," Thunderfoot said, "I hope he's gonna be OK."

"Oh, I think he'll manage all right without us. He must have just thought it would be fun to see how humans are for company."

"I wonder if he's going way back up river?" Thunderfoot said. He was obviously sad that the goose was leaving.

"I haven't got a clue, but I guess we should think that we were pretty lucky to have such a neat experience of sharing that time with him," I said.

Thunderfoot nodded. "Bye, Gordon." Gordon honked.

We got into his mom's car and took off up the road to the upriver landing to get the pickup. He was driving since he had just gotten his driver's license and would have no part of me doing the driving. I held my foot to the floor, helping brake on every turn, and there were permanent indentations in the armrest where I held on for dear life. The road ran along the river for a while, and then followed along beneath the bluffs. The river bottoms were on the right side of the road as we drove along, and suddenly, as we came around a curve, there were two emus standing by the side of the road. As we got closer, they trotted down over the bank and into the river bottoms.

We drove for another mile and neither of us said a word. Finally, Thunderfoot looked over at me and said, "Did you see those ostriches?"

"Emus."

"What?"

"Emus, they were emus. Yeah, I saw them, but I wasn't sure if I was going nuts or what."

"If you're nuts, so am I," he said. "What were those things doing there?"

"I have no idea. I know there are some farmers who raise

them, but there isn't a farm for miles along here."

"Whew," he said, "I thought I might have gotten too much sun and baked my brain when I first saw them." We both were quiet for the rest of the trip. The shock of seeing the emus after our encounter with Gordon, made us wonder what was next.

We got to the boat landing and I got into the truck and Thunderfoot stayed in his mom's car. Since he had gotten his driver's license he was always pestering to do the driving, and I didn't expect him to wait for me, but instead to take off right away. But, he waited for me to get the truck started and then motioned for me to go first.

"You lead," he said.

"Why? You usually say I drive like a granny. Why don't you go first?"

"Mom's car is smaller than your pickup, and the way today has been going with strange critters, we'll probably see an elephant or rhino on the way home and it's better if you go first to clear the road."

We both laughed at the joke, but I think he was serious. It had been quite a strange day, but that's what you get sometimes when you get to spend a lot of time outdoors. You see things that you just wouldn't see any place else, and sometimes the rules just don't count. Just in case, I planned on driving really carefully all the way.

Thanks, Thunderfoot.

Charlie Brown

"Did you call the marina yet?" Thunderfoot asked as he came through the front door.

"Yup, and I didn't get the answer I wanted."

"Oh, no! What are we gonna do now?" he said, slumping down into a chair.

The fuel pump on the outboard motor had died, and I had taken it to the marina for a new one, and, of course, they didn't have the right part, so they had to order it. They had guaranteed me that it would be ready by the weekend, but the weekend started tomorrow, and the part wasn't in yet, so we were without a boat.

"You know," I said, "we could go over to the Barge."

"Where?" Thunderfoot asked.

"The fishing barge, the raft below the dam. I used to fish there all the time before I got my boat," I said.

"Is the fishing good there?"

"Yeah, great. It's right below the dam and there's lots of room to fish. It's a big raft that's anchored there. It's about twenty feet wide, and about three hundred feet long, and shaped like a backwards capital L. There's a bait shop and restaurant on the shore. The people who run it are old friends of mine," I said. "I haven't seen them in a long time. It would be nice to go over and spend the day visiting with them and fishing."

"Well, let's go for it then," he said, much enthused.

We packed a couple of rods each and some tackle and decided to leave early in the morning, so we could have a full day of fishing.

"How about lunch?" he said.

"Adeline has real good hamburgers on the fishing barge," I said.

"We can eat out there."

"Adeline?"

"Yeah, the people who own it, Chris and Adeline. Chris runs the boat and takes care of the fishermen and Adeline runs the restaurant and feeds the fishermen. They're real nice folks, you'll like them," I said.

The barge was anchored at the dam, and the boat landing was about a mile downriver, so Chris drove his boat down to the landing every hour to pick up fishermen who were waiting to go out to fish. He also hauled back those fishermen who were done for the day at the same time. Chris and Adeline charged a few bucks per person for the boat ride and your day of fishing. The boat was about twenty feet long and had a large open deck for tackle, and then a cabin for the customers to sit in, to keep warm and dry. He could haul twenty people at a time, and it was a pretty neat set up. The bait shop/restaurant was run by his wife who served up lots of good burgers and fries, gallons of soup, and some chili that would take the chrome off your car bumper.

I had known Chris and Adeline for many years and had become friends with them. They were both in their sixties, but you'd never know it, as spry as they were.

Thunderfoot and I left the next morning and somehow got to the boat landing about ten minutes after the hour, so we had missed the boat. Now we had a fifty-minute wait.

"Well, let's go up to the bar and have a pop and a snack while we wait," I said, motioning to the roadside tavern up on the highway above the landing.

Of course, Thunderfoot, who was always hungry, was in favor of that, so we walked up, went in, and ordered a pop each and some chips.

I was visiting with the bartender and noticed an old friend coming toward us. I turned to Thunderfoot and said. "I'd like you to meet my friend, Charlie Brown."

Thunderfoot turned and looked and then looked one way and then the other way and saw no one. I motioned down with my finger and there was Charlie Brown, a full figured beagle, sitting on his haunches with his paw up waiting to shake.

Thunderfoot broke out in a big grin and grabbed the dog's paw.

"Hello, Charlie Brown," he said as he shook with him. Charlie Brown then raised his paw to me and we shook also.

I gave him a couple of chips, and he looked at Thunderfoot expectantly.

"He would appreciate a taste of your food," I said.

Thunderfoot gave him a chip and he got back down on all four legs and walked back to his rug behind the bar.

"He's cool," Thunderfoot said.

"Yeah, he's been here forever. You can see that he's a bit chunky from all the mooching, but everybody likes him," I said. "He goes out on the barge every day to visit, too."

We finished our pops and went back to the landing to wait for the boat. We could see it pull away from the barge and start down to us about five minutes before the hour.

Just as the boat was almost to the landing, I looked up the road and saw Charlie Brown sauntering along toward us. I poked Thunderfoot. "Here comes Charlie Brown. It looks like he's going over with us."

Thunderfoot began grinning and knelt down to pet him as we waited for the boat to dock. There were four other fishermen this trip, and we all put our gear on the deck of the boat and then filed down the steps to the cabin. I introduced Thunderfoot to Chris and then we took off for the barge. Charlie Brown sat in the middle of the floor, keeping an eye out for anyone who might have something to eat for him.

When we got to the barge, Chris slid the boat along side the railing and then cut the motor and jumped off onto the barge with the bow rope, and secured the boat. Charlie Brown waited until we were tied up, and then jumped off the boat onto the barge and began his appointed rounds.

He would start at one end and work his way to the other end.

The barge had a wooden railing all around it, to keep people from falling off, and it also made a good place to prop up your fishing pole, while waiting for a bite. There were little wooden benches all over the place to sit on, and many of them were occupied with fishermen of every size and shape and age.

Charlie Brown would walk up and sit down next to one of the benches and watch the person fish that was sitting there. Most people knew him and talked to him like he was a person. Of course, most also gave him a part of a sandwich or cookie, and that was his real motive. He would then get up and move to the next fisherman and work his way all around the barge until he had visited everyone.

We picked out a couple of benches and I walked up to the bait shop and said hi to Adeline and got some minnows. Then we fished for a couple of hours and had some pretty good luck catching quite a few walleyes and saugers.

"I'm beginning to get a bit gant," Thunderfoot said.

Gant was his word for starved, hungry, famished, whatever. It meant he needed food, and he used it a lot. Gant was getting hungry, faminished was really hungry, and he was one or the other all the time.

"Well, reel up and we'll go up and have something to eat," I said. Adeline made each of us a burger and we both tried the chili.

Thunderfoot almost tipped off his stool as he put a big spoonful of the red hot stuff in his mouth, but managed to get it down.

"Wow, that's hot," he said, but added quickly, with a big smile to Adeline, "but really good, too."

Adeline smiled.

We finished our lunch and Thunderfoot took a bite of hamburger with him for Charlie Brown, who by now, was almost done with his daily rounds.

A while later, he walked over and sat by the boat, waiting for a ride back to the landing.

11

"When he was younger, he would swim back sometimes," I said.

"No kidding?" Thunderfoot said.

"Yeah, he would just jump off and swim across the river and go home. But he got hit by a car a few years ago and has a bad hip now, so he waits for a ride."

Pretty soon, Chris came walking down the barge toward the boat, to make his hourly run, and Charlie Brown jumped on and disappeared down into the cabin.

We fished a couple of hours longer and then decided to call it a day. We went up to say goodbye to Adeline and then loaded our gear and fish onto the boat. Chris took us back and Thunderfoot thanked him for such a good fishing trip.

Chris smiled as he pulled away from the bank and gave us a wave.

"They sure are nice people," Thunderfoot said.

We loaded the gear up and started down the road from the landing. "This has been a really good fishing trip," Thunderfoot said.

"Yeah," I said. "I kind of forgot how pleasant it was to go out there fishing."

As we got to the highway, Thunderfoot looked over at the bar where Charlie Brown lived and grinned. "Gosh, he's a cool dog."

Just then Charlie Brown walked out through the open front door and looked our way.

Thunderfoot looked at me and grinned. "I think he's got ESP, too."

Could be.

Thanks, Thunderfoot.

Bogus Bluff

I was just finishing breakfast when Thunderfoot came through the front door.

"Have you ever heard of Bogus Blum" he said.

"Yeah."

"How come you never told me about it?"

"I don't know, I guess it never came up. Why the sudden interest in Bogus Bluff?"

"The gold," he said. "The buried gold is there someplace and maybe we can find it."

I began laughing, and he looked a bit peeved at me. "There's no gold there; that's just an old story that's been handed down for a hundred years."

"One of the guys at school said that his grandpa had told him about a shipment of gold that was being hauled down the river on rafts in like 1832 or something like that, and the Indians attacked them at Lone Rock and they went ashore at Bogus Bluff and hid the gold in a cave, and it's still there because nobody's ever found it so far," he said.

"And where did this grandpa get all of this intimate knowledge?" "I don't know.]eez how am I supposed to know," he said. "I just thought it might be a fun thing to do, to go and look for it."

Right away I felt bad throwing cold water on his idea, but I'm just not the kind of a guy who sees crawling around in a cave as some kind of exciting recreation. I've never felt real comfortable in tight places, and being a bit "full figured" never felt the need to squeeze into some hole in the ground, just for fun.

"I really think that gold story is mostly fiction," I said. "Besides, if the gold was there, somebody would have found it by now. The counterfeiters were there for months and never found it." Right then I knew I had said too much.

"Counterfeiters? What counterfeiters?" he said, his eyes wide and excited.

"Oh, there's an old story about some counterfeiters who held up in the cave back in the early 1920's, about 1922 I think. They were counterfeiting 1913 liberty head nickels up in the cave."

"Oh, that sounds like a money-making enterprise," Thunderfoot said. "1 know a nickel bought a lot back then, but I don't think you'd get rich by making nickels."

"Well," I said, "this nickel was worth a lot more than a nickel. You see, in 1913 the mint changed the design of the nickel to the buffalo head, but a few nickels were struck in the old liberty head design with the date 1913 on them, before the change order got to the mint, so there were a few liberty head nickels made. These counterfeiters made some plates to forge fake nickels and then were planning on selling them to collectors for about a thousand dollars apiece, which was big money back then. All they had to do was sell one here and there, and they would make a lot of money.

"Well, supposedly, the Treasury Department found out somehow, and surrounded the cave, but the counterfeiters snuck out a back entrance and snuck down the hill to the river, where they had a boat hidden, and took off down the river to get away. The Feds chased them and started shooting at them and finally caught up with them, and the counterfeiters threw the plates that made the nickels into the river to get rid of the evidence.

"Of course, the Feds had evidence anyway, because they caught the guys with a whole sack full of bogus nickels. And, that's where Bogus Bluff got its name, from the bogus nickels that were made there."

"Wow, that's a cool story. Did they ever find the counterfeit plates?" Thunderfoot asked.

"Nope, they sunk into the sand and are probably still out there someplace."

"Cool. Now I know we should go up there and see it. Do you know who owns it?"

"Yeah, I know whose land it's on."

"Do you suppose he'd let us go see it?"

I knew I should say that the owner didn't let people into the cave, but that was a lie, so, against my better judgment, I said I'd look into it and see if we could go and explore it. I was hoping that some other hot topic would come up in the next few days and he would forget about it.

That weekend, Thunderfoot came over early Saturday morning, dressed in what looked to be caving gear. He had on long pants, boots and a sweatshirt, even though the weather was warm and humid. He also had a flashlight in each pocket of his pants.

"Are you wearing that?" he said, looking at my shorts and tee shirt.

"It depends on where we're going."

"We're going spelunking, doncha know?"

He hadn't forgotten. I was trapped, so I went into the house and changed into some bib overalls and a sweatshirt and some old hunting boots.

We drove across the river and up the north side, to the hill where Bogus Bluff overlooked the river valley. I parked the truck and we got out.

"See up there, on the face of the hill?" I said, pointing to the opening of the cave. "That's it."

"Wow, I've seen that before, from the river, but never thought it was anything but a dent in the rocks," he said. "That's pretty steep and high up. Do you think you can get up there?"

"Of course. I'm old, not dead. I'll be right behind you."

Boy, was that the wrong thing to say.

He took off up the hillside, and we followed a cow path for the first fifty feet. Then the hill became real steep, I mean almost vertical. There was a narrow path that ran right along the rock wall of the hillside. fu we continued on up, the hill became steeper and the path became narrower. Soon, we had to hang onto cracks in the rocks and grab hold of brush and roots to pull ourselves up along the narrow track.

"Are you OK?" Thunderfoot asked, looking back down the hill at me.

"Yeah, I'm coming. What's this, a race?"

"Sorry, I'll wait for you to catch up."

I slowly worked my way up to where he was standing on a little wide spot, and stopped to catch my breath.

"Wow, this sure is steep," he said. "How come the front side of these hills are so steep?"

"The river did this," I said. "Back when the glaciers melted, there was some kind of huge flood that came down through here and formed this whole river valley."

"Wow, you mean there was water way up here?"

"Yup, from one side of the valley to the other, the water was all the way up these hills. That's what scoured all of the dirt and rock away from the fronts, and made these cliffs. It's probably what made the caves, too."

We stood looking out across the river valley. It was at least four or five miles to the hills on the other side. In between, on the valley floor, the farm fields were laid out in squares. The dry flat ground gave way to the river bottom sloughs that extended for several hundred feet on each side of the river. The river bottoms were made up of ponds, marshes, and swamps that bordered the river itself. Now, the river was only a trickle of what it once had been. While it still was several hundred feet across, thinking of the time when it reached from bluff to bluff was a sobering thought. The sun sparkled off the water and the sandbars looked like little patches of gold on the blue water as it meandered through the valley for as far as we could see.

"Awesome," Thunderfoot said.

"Yeah, it sure is," I said, leaning back against the rock.

"Well, are you ready to go on?" he said, "or are you going to give me some more geology lessons, to stall for more time?"

"Let's go, smart guy."

We climbed another twenty-five feet, and the track leveled out, and we were at the entrance to the cave.

It was larger than it looked from the road, and there were names carved into the sandstone at the entrance and as far as you could see back into the depths, before it got too dark to see.

"Well, it looks like somebody's been here before us," Thunderfoot said. "I guess the gold's probably been found by now."

"You didn't actually think you'd find gold here, did you?"

"Well, you never know," he said, grinning. "Let's go inside."

"You want to go in there?" I said.

"Well, that's where the cave is, so I guess we'll have to if we're going cave exploring."

He handed me one of the flashlights and we started in. I switched my light on and it didn't work. "This light is dead," I said. "Looks like we'll have to go back down."

"You have to hold it straight up and down and shake it and it'll come on," he said.

I held the flashlight like a candle and shook it and it came on, but as soon as I turned it horizontal, it went out.

"Oh, this is nice," I said. "I'll trade lights with you."

"No way," he said. "That one works fine, just be careful with it." So off I went, into the darkness, with my light held so it shined on the ground in front of my feet.

The entrance went back for about 30 feet and then began to narrow and the ceiling started to get lower. The walls were black, and slick with moisture. Soon, we were stooping and then the opening became larger and we came to an area where the cave split into three tunnels.

"Now what?" I said.

"Well, let's take the left one and see where it goes, and then come back and try the other two," he said.

We started down the left tunnel and it stayed about the same size all the way to the end. It was about twenty-five feet long and came out to another entrance on the side of the hill.

"I bet this is where the counterfeiters came out," Thunderfoot said, looking down the hill.

We turned back and got back to the starting point of the first tunnel, and tried the middle one. It went back about twenty feet and then the ceiling got low enough that we had to get down and crawl for another ten feet. Then we came to a hole that opened into a large room. The room was about ten feet wide and twenty feet long with a ceiling that was at least ten feet high. The ceiling was black with soot, and the walls had names carved into them from people who had been there before us. Some of the names were back into the 1800's. Brad and Becky, June 1896. Dave was here, 8/23/51, and on and on. "Wow, this is probably where they counterfeited the nickels," Thunderfoot said. "Look at the ceiling, their candles and torches probably made all that soot."

"Imagine working in here, though," I said, as a shudder went up my back. "And sleeping in here. Not me."

I was starting to get a closed-in feeling and wasn't at all comfortable in this dark, cold place.

"Let's go try the last tunnel," Thunderfoot said.

"Oh, let's leave it go. It's probably just another short side tunnel."

"Aw, come on, let's look," he said. "As long as we climbed all the way up here, we might as well get our money's worth."

We crawled back out to the entrance to the middle tunnel and looked down the third one. Thunderfoot shined his light down it and it went for a long way, as far as we could see.

"Wow, this one goes a lot farther," he said. "You go first."

"Why me? You're the one with the thirst for knowledge and the good flashlight."

"Yeah, but think of this. We get back there and say, you get stuck, and I'm ahead of you, and I can't get out because you're blocking the way, so we both starve. This way if you get stuck, I can get out and go for help," he said, shaking his head yes.

I shook my flashlight to life and started down the tunnel. We went for a long, long way, and the end was still a long way off. The floor of the tunnel was damp clay, and soon our shoes were covered with it. After a while, the tunnel became lower, and we had to crawl. We crawled for what seemed like hundreds of feet, and then it became smaller yet. Now, the sides were about thirty inches apart, and the roof was only about two feet high. We now had clay smeared over our clothes from head to toe, and our hands and faces were covered in it also. "Boy, this is sure fun," I said, sarcastically.

"Just keep going and quit griping," came Thunderfoot's reply. "This is getting smaller and smaller. I think we should turn around and go back," I said.

"How are we gonna turn around? There's no way to turn around.

Do you want to crawl backwards all the way out?"

"What if there's animals or snakes in here?"

"What would a snake or animal be doing in here?" he said.

"There's nothing here but rock and mud."

Just then my flashlight went out for about the fiftieth time. With the light off, it was as black as black could be. I shook it back on and began thinking about the millions of pounds of rock and dirt that was above me and how dark and cold it was in the cave, and decided that I was not particularly happy about being in there. But, the only way to fix the situation was to keep going.

I began crawling on my belly, and by pushing with my elbows and toes, could move forward about a foot at a time. Soon, I could see that the tunnel turned to the right a short way ahead. As we got closer to the corner, my light fell on something just at the side of the wall to the right. I looked in horror at the rattles of a rattlesnake's tail!

"Oh my God, go back, go back!" I shouted, and began backing up as fast as I could go. Thunderfoot wasn't moving as fast as I was and I quickly overtook him and began crawling right over the top of him.

He couldn't go fast enough to stay ahead of me so we piled

up about ten feet from the snake. We were wedged in tight between the mud floor and the rock ceiling.

"Whoa, whoa, what the heck is wrong with you?" he shouted.

"A rattlesnake is up there. Get back out of here! Get back! Get back!"

"Wait, wait, are you sure?" His voice was muffled because I was halfway on top of him. "What would a snake be doing in here? Think about it."

I took a couple of deep breaths. "Give me your light," I said as I slid my hand back between the wall and my side. His hand came up from under my legs and handed me the light.

I was afraid to shine the light up the tunnel to see if the snake was after us, but I had to before we could keep on going, so I finally shined the light ahead and cautiously pointed it up the tunnel. The snake hadn't come around the corner. I shined it up to the corner and the snake tail was still there. I looked closer, closer. Now I wasn't sure it was a snake tail after all. Now it looked more like a corncob. I crawled a couple of feet closer, and now it really looked like a corncob.

"Well," Thunderfoot whispered, "is it a snake?"

"Uh, no, I think it's a corncob."

Silence.

Then, a snicker, then a laugh, then all heck broke loose. "Good Lord, you almost had a heart attack over a corncob?" His laughter echoed down the tunnel walls.

I felt a bit stupid, but now I had the good light and was keeping it, so I crawled a little closer to the corner and could see the corncob and some oak leaves lying on the floor of the cave.

"I think we're near the end. There are some leaves laying here too," I said.

"You better make sure there aren't any poisonous scorpions or something lurking under them."

More laughter.

We turned the corner and then you could begin to see a little light up ahead, and the air became warmer and fresher. We were at the other end of the tunnel. We crawled out of the hole and were amazed to find ourselves on top of the hill.

"Wow, we came out clear on top," Thunderfoot said, squinting in the bright light. His face was covered with clay from being pushed down into the floor when I tried to climb over him.

"I had no idea we were going uphill all that time," I said, sitting in the grass, so very glad to be out of the darkness.

We sat there breathing the fresh air and enjoying the view of the river and the valley far below us for a long while. We were both covered with mud and clay and it felt good to just sit in the sunshine and soak up the warmth after the chilly dampness of the cave.

"You know, it's hard to believe that so many people have come and gone here. All those names in the cave, and this valley, just think how much it's changed in the years. It kind of makes you feel that you're just passing through during your time in history," Thunderfoot said.

"Wow, that's pretty philosophical for you," I said.

"That's me, a pretty philosophical kind of guy," he said, grinning and wiping the mud and clay from his hands onto his pants. "Well, shall we hike down hill or go back through the cave?"

"It's a real nice day for a hike."

"I thought you might say that," he grinned and slapped me on the back."Come on, old man, let's go."

Thanks, Thunderfoot

Losing Lucy

"Lucy, you get back over here!"

I heard Thunderfoot yelling at my golden retriever. They were out in the yard where he had taken her on a potty break.

Lucy was just a year old and had grown up with Thunderfoot. He had gone with me and picked her from her nine littermates after my old dog, Sophie, had died of cancer, so she was a special friend for him. He had named her that same day that we got her, and now, she was full grown and a beautiful girl. She and Thunderfoot played and goofed around together all the time, and when he stayed over at my house on a night before a fishing trip or hunting trip, she slept with him in "his room."

He had commandeered my spare bedroom shortly after we began fishing and hunting together three years earlier. Many times, we came home wet or covered with mud, and he often had brought a change of clothes with him for just such an occasion, so after a while, he had a pretty good selection of clothes which I had washed and stored in the spare bedroom. Plus, it was more convenient for us and his family, if he stayed in the extra room on the night before a trip. That way I didn't have to go to his house and wake up the whole household in the middle of the night. So, eventually, the spare room became his room, and Lucy was ready to snuggle with him in his bed when he stayed over.

I had just gotten new living room furniture when Lucy came to live with us, and she wasn't allowed on it, unless she was on someone's lap. Of course, Thunderfoot always coaxed her up on his lap and when he wanted to take a nap on the couch, she lay on top of him and took one too. As she got bigger and bigger, they made quite a sight, a great big dog lying on top of a boy on the couch.

He came into the house just then, and she was right behind him, panting and jumping up and down, waiting for him to give her a cookie.

"You're a bad girl. I shouldn't give you a cookie," he scolded. Lucy looked properly repentant, so he went to the dog cookie can and gave her a treat, which she gobbled down like she hadn't had a thing to eat in a month.

"She ran across the street again, and almost got hit by a car," he said to me.

"I'll go borrow Tim's shock collar," I said. "That'll take care of it." I really didn't want to go to the shock collar as a way of keeping Lucy out of the street, but we had tried everything else, and nothing had worked, so I called my friend and ask if I could borrow his collar, and drove over to his house to get it.

When I got home, we put the collar on Lucy and decided to give it a try. It was a plastic dog collar with a small plastic box on it, and two metal contacts which protruded from the box and were held against the dog's neck by the collar. There was a battery in the box on the collar that gave power to the contacts. The other half of the system was a hand-held control device with an antenna. When the dog was doing something that you didn't want them to do, you told them to stop and pushed a button on the control device. It signaled the collar to fire the contact points which gave the dog a mild shock. It didn't do any harm, but really scared the dog. Once or twice was usually enough to get them to quit a bad habit.

We went out in the yard and just turned our backs on Lucy, so she would go for the road. Sure enough, it didn't take long and she was trotting over to the neighbor's. Just as she got to the street, I yelled, "Lucy, No!" and pushed the button on the remote. Lucy stood up on her hind legs and yelped and turned and came running back to us.

"Wow, that works good," Thunderfoot said, consoling his friend.

She wasn't hurt, but was scared and didn't know what had happened to her.

We went about our business and it wasn't long until she snuck off toward the road again. This time I yelled, "Lucy, No!"

and she turned around and came back without a shock.

"Hmm, maybe she learned her lesson in one try," I said.

We kept the collar on her for the next few days and she was as good as she could be. She would go near the road and then turn around and come back as soon as we called. Now we had to make her stay off the road without us being with her, so we let her out and then went back into the house and watched from the window. She wandered around the yard for a while and then started drifting toward the road. She got to the edge of the road and stopped, as if she was waiting for something to happen, and then started across. Thunderfoot opened the door and stuck the transmitter out and pushed the button, and Lucy yelped and sprinted back to her own yard as fast as she could go.

"That did it," he said, smiling.

For the next couple of weeks, Lucy didn't go near the road, so we figured she was cured. We took the collar off and I returned it to my friend and thanked him for letting us use it.

The next day, we were out in the yard, and suddenly Thunderfoot looked up and there was Lucy on the other side of the road.

"Lucy, get back here," he shouted. Lucy looked at us, and casually trotted back to her own yard. Somehow, she had figured out that the collar was what was keeping her home, and without it, she could get away with crossing the street.

"Well," I said, "I guess I'm going to have to get a collar and keep it on her all the time."

The very next day, Thunderfoot and I were working in my shop, cleaning up the place, and Lucy was there with us. She was in the way all the time, and it was getting hot and dusty in the shop, so we opened the door and let her out into the yard. Thunderfoot checked on her and she was lying in the grass chewing on a stick, so we went back to work. A few minutes later, he stuck his head out the door and she was still lying in the grass.

"She's being a good girl today," he said.

It wasn't two minutes later that we heard tires squealing on the road and a dog yelping. Thunderfoot ran to the door, and Lucy was gone. He ran down the driveway and stopped and his hands came up to his face. "Oh, no, oh, no, Lucy," he screamed, and took off toward the road. I dropped what I was doing and ran down to the road and there lying in the middle of the road was Lucy with Thunderfoot kneeling beside her.

The driver of the car was standing there looking helpless. "I'm so sorry," he said, "she ran right out in front of me."

I knelt down and Lucy looked up at me. I couldn't see any damage, except that she had a little blood on her back foot, where it had scraped the roadway. She tried to get up, and I could see that her back legs were not moving, and I knew she was hurt much worse than it looked.

"Stay here and keep her quiet," I told Thunderfoot. "I'm going to call Dr. Pat and get the van."

Thunderfoot shook his head yes and stayed kneeling beside Lucy in the middle of the road. The driver of the car kept a watch for traffic.

I called the vet's office and told them what had happened and that we were on our way, and they told me to back up to the back door of the office and that they would be waiting.

I got a blanket and backed the van out of the driveway and drove down the street and stopped next to where Lucy was laying. Thunderfoot and I gently slid her onto the blanket and lifted her into the back seat and then Thunderfoot climbed in and sat next to her. I closed the door and jumped into the van and took off for the vet's office.

"She doesn't look too hurt," Thunderfoot said. "Do you think she'll be OK?"

"I don't know," I said. "We'll have to wait and see."

We arrived at the vet's office and Dr. Pat came out with a small stretcher and we carefully slid Lucy onto it. By now, her breathing was becoming shallow and she seemed to be semi-conscious.

"She's in shock," Dr. Pat said. "We need to get her stabilized."

We carried her into the operating room and Dr. Pat began working on her. She put an IV in her front leg and began pumping fluid into her, and checking her over for obvious injuries. All the while, Thunderfoot and I stood by, petting her and telling her what a good girl she was.

It took almost a half an hour, but soon Lucy began to look better.

Her breathing was better and her heart rate calmed down, so we moved her over to the x-ray table. We stood by while Dr. Pat took two x-rays and then waited as she went into another room to develop them. She came back a few minutes later and turned on the light in the x-ray viewing cabinet. She slid the x-rays up into the little clips that hold them in place.

"Oh my," she said.

My heart sank. Thunderfoot looked at me, very frightened.

"Her hips are shattered," Dr. Pat said.

"Can she be fixed?" Thunderfoot asked.

"It looks like her large intestine is ruptured, and I can fix that, but her hips are broken so badly, I don't think there is any fix for them," she said.

Thunderfoot and I were stunned.

"I can stabilize her and fix her insides, but there's no way she'll ever walk again," Dr. Pat said.

I didn't want to ask what alternatives there were, because I already knew what had to be done.

"I'm sorry. She's just hurt too badly," she said. "I'll step out and you can think it over and decide what you want to do."

She walked out and closed the door, and Thunderfoot looked at me and his eyes filled with tears, and he grabbed me and we stood there hugging and sobbing uncontrollably for many minutes. Finally, we both were cried out, and we went over to Lucy, who was resting peacefully on the table. We petted her and talked to her, and her tail wagged a bit. She seemed fine, and it was hard to believe that she was so badly hurt inside.

"You know what we have to do," I said.

He nodded and began crying again. I waited a few minutes and then went out and told Dr. Pat that we had decided and were ready.

She came in and got Lucy ready, and Thunderfoot and I both held her and petted her and told her what a good girl she was, and a minute later, our Lucy was gone.

Dr. Pat slipped out of the room and left us alone with Lucy.

After many long minutes, we picked up the stretcher and carried her to the van.

The ride home was torture. Neither one of us said a word; we couldn't.

When we got home, I went to the shed and got a couple of shovels and we walked to the back of the garden, where the other dogs were buried. Bea, Sally and Sophie were all buried there and now we dug a grave for Lucy.

When we were finished, I went in the house and gathered all of her toys up and we carried her over to the garden and put her toys in the blanket with her and wrapped her up and laid her into the grave. Neither of us said a word until we had covered her up.

"That's it," I said. "That's my last dog. I can't do this any more."

We put away the shovels and went into the house. It was four hours since Lucy had been hit and it was long past lunchtime, but neither of us was hungry. We just sat and stared for the rest of the afternoon.

"I guess I better go home," Thunderfoot said finally, several hours later.

"Yeah, I'll see you tomorrow," I said.

"Are you gonna be OK?"

"Yeah, eventually," I said.

He came over and put his arms around me and gave me a hug.

"We couldn't have done anything more. She was just too smart for us."

I shook my head yes. "I don't think I could have gotten through this without you here," I said.

"I'll be here anytime you need me. You know that," he said, and let me go and walked slowly out the door and across the yard toward home.

The house was so quiet. Normally, Lucy would be slobbering all over me to play ball or get her a cookie, but now it was just me, and I didn't like it a bit.

I looked out the window at the patch of fresh earth and felt very alone.

Goodbye, Lucy.

The Big Trip

I woke up the day after Lucy died, much later than usual. First, I was exhausted from the trauma of the day before, and second, Lucy wasn't there to pester me to get up and let her out at dawn, like she usually did.

I went out to the kitchen for breakfast and the paper, and sat there thinking about what I wanted to do that day, and suddenly I realized that I was in a situation that was very unusual for me. I was without a dog to take care of for the first time in almost 25 years, and had not taken a real vacation for almost that long because of the dogs. Oh, I had gone on overnight trips a couple of times, but never felt secure about leaving the dogs in the care of a friend, and never even considered taking them to a place to be boarded for a week with some stranger.

I'm one of those people who think their dogs would wither away and die if they were put into a situation that disrupted their daily routine. Something like a week in a kennel was unthinkable, so consequently, I hadn't taken an extended vacation for a long, long time. I decided that now was the time.

I went to my office and started making calls, and in about an hour, had made arrangements for someone to work at the store, and take care of everything else that needed tending, for the next two weeks.

One of the calls I made was to Thunderfoot's mom, and I asked her if she would mind if he came with me on vacation for a couple of weeks. She was all for it, and since he already spent as much time at my house as hers, she didn't think she'd miss him too much. She was glad he would have the chance to see some new country. I asked her to send him over as soon as he got up.

A while later, he came trotting across the back yard and into the house, stopping at the refrigerator before coming to the living room where I was sitting.

"Well, nice to see you finally got up, and before noon too," I said.

"I didn't have anything else to do, so why exert myself? Besides, I was kinda tired after yesterday."

"I think we should put yesterday behind us," I said, "and con-centrate on planning the first days of our trip."

His head jerked up and he looked at me. "What trip is that?" "The trip you and I are leaving on tomorrow morning," I said. He jumped up and came over to the couch and sat beside me.

"Where are we going?"

"Well, I thought north first, up to northern Wisconsin, and then to Canada, and then across some of the provinces and back into maybe North Dakota and that part of the world and then back home. As far as we can get in a couple of weeks."

His mouth dropped open. "I have to ask mom, but ... "

"I already talked to her, and she said yes. We're leaving tomorrow morning."

"Holy... " He jumped up and started pacing back and forth across the living room, trying to talk but just stuttering. "Canada, and across and Dakota, two weeks. Holy cow."

I just laughed and let him pace for a while. Then I said, "As soon as you get done having your spell, we better get packing."

"Right," he said. "We'll need lots of stuff."

We began making a list of what we wanted to take. By taking the back seats out, my van had plenty of room in the back for a twin mattress, so we planned on putting the mattress from his room back there for a bed. Then we would take some camping gear along and clothes and some fishing gear and a little food. I had planned on camping some nights and staying in motels the rest of the time. I'm not a real hardy camper but didn't mind once in a while as long as the weather was nice and there were shower facilities. However, if I have my preference, I like to camp in motels; it's much easier and much more comfortable.

It took all day, and we managed to get our little camping wagon loaded and ready. I had just changed the oil and serviced the van, so all we needed was a tank of gas and we were ready to roll.

I dropped off the keys to the store with my worker who was going to take care of things for me, and Thunderfoot went home for the evening since his mattress was in the van. The plan was for him to come over at 6 a.m. the next morning.

The night was quiet and much too quiet without Lucy again, and I was glad I was going to get out of the house for a while. I went to sleep without any trouble. In what seemed like just a few minutes, I was startled by Thunderfoot shaking me awake.

"It's almost six and you're still in bed. Holy cow, we're gonna get a late start."

"Relax, we don't have any place to go," I said. "Wherever we are tonight is where we'll be; we don't have a time table and I don't want one. Take it easy. We'll get there when we get there."

"OK, I just want to get out of town before something happens to keep us from going. You know, somebody will call with some emergency and we'll have to stay home."

"We won't answer the phone," I said.

About an hour later, we pulled out of the driveway and drove past his house and honked to his mom, who came out and waved goodbye to us.

We were on our way.

Thunderfoot got the Wisconsin map out and began looking for good stuff to see on the way north. We drove for several hours and then stopped for lunch and a break. After lunch we headed north again and soon were in the "real" north, where there are lots and lots of trees and not so many people. The hills and valleys of home were replaced by slow rolling hills and soon even they became scarce and the landscape became flat. Oaks, maples, and hickory were replaced by pines and birch and poplar.

It was getting dark and I was getting tired of driving when Thunderfoot spotted a campground on the map that was in the Chequamegan National Forest. "Take the forest road 68B and it will take us right to the lake campground," he said.

We finally found 68B and turned onto it. I drove for miles and miles and we found no campground. "Are you sure this is the right road?"

"Well, I think so. It only looks like a little way on the map."

We drove another ten miles and still no campground, so I said, "Let's just stop somewhere here and sleep, and we'll worry about it in the morning."

He was tired, too, so we found a wide spot in the road and pulled to the side and stopped. It was pretty hot and humid in the van, but we were tired enough not to care, and we crawled back into the little bed in the back of the van and went to sleep almost immediately.

It was just getting light when I woke up and the first thing I noticed was the humming sound coming from all around me. At first I couldn't figure out what the noise was, but then I noticed that the van was full of mosquitoes and we were being eaten alive.

I jumped up and began swatting the little bloodsuckers off me and Thunderfoot woke up when he heard me moving around and swatting.

"What the heck are you doing? Holy cow, where did all of these come from?"

We both bailed out of the van and opened the doors and windows to let all of the mosquitoes out. Then I noticed that the window on his side was part way open.

"Did you leave a window open?"

"Yeah, it was kind of hot in there. Not a good idea I guess," he said, scratching mosquito bites.

Indeed, it wasn't a good idea at all.

We turned around and headed out to the main highway, after never having found our first night campground.

When we got up the road a short way, we came to a diner and went in to wash up and have some breakfast. We felt much better after a good face wash and breakfast and brushing our teeth. We still had lots of welts to scratch though.

After gassing up the van, we continued north and soon came over a knoll and there was the north shore of Lake Superior. Thunderfoot had never seen any of the big lakes and was awestruck at the size of the lake.

"It's like an ocean," he said, looking out over the sparkling water that seemed to go forever.

We drove along the lake for several hours and finally got to Superior and had lunch and then crossed into Minnesota.

"I think we'll try to get across the border tonight and stay in Canada," I said.

Thunderfoot was all for that, since he could hardly wait to get to Canada. "Oh man, this is so cool, going to a foreign country."

We got to the border crossing at Pigeon River late that afternoon and the border guard came out to greet us.

"What is the purpose of your visit to Canada?" he said. "Tourism and fishing," I replied.

"Yup, tourism and fishing," Thunderfoot echoed.

"Are you American citizens?"

"Yes."

"And, where do you live in the States?"

"Muscoda, Wisconsin."

"Yup, me, too, Muscoda.

"Oh, do you know the Stading brothers?"

"What?" I said. "The Stading brothers? We hunt turkeys on their farm."

"Oh," said the border guard, "they cross here every fall to go moose hunting and I know them pretty well."

"Well, that kind of took the excitement out of crossing the border," said Thunderfoot. "Here we are, hundreds of miles from home, and somebody knows somebody that we know."

The guard wished us a good trip and off we went down the road.

We were in Canada.

Thunderfoot was looking here and there for something that looked different, but the only thing he could find was the road signs in meters per hour instead of miles per hour.

"I thought it would be a lot different," he said.

"Nope, it's pretty much the same, except they use different money and the metric system," I said.

We stopped at a Provincial Information Booth and went inside for some maps and information on what to see in the area. Behind the counter was a young gal, probably in her early twenties, and pretty as a picture. She was wearing a navy blue uniform of the Provincial Park Service and had blue eyes and blond hair and was a real knockout. Thunderfoot's mouth fell open and he was speechless.

She gave us a lot of information and told us about some scenic things to see and wished us a good trip. All the while Thunderfoot just stood there looking at her with his mouth open like some kind of mental defect.

"Well, you made a good impression on her with all your glib chatter," I said as we got back into the van.

"I never saw such a pretty girl," he said. "I think she likes me, too; she looked right at me and smiled."

Good Lord, the boy was in love and we had just gotten out of the U.S.

We took off down the road and Thunderfoot just sat there shaking his head. I didn't bother to ask; I already knew he was mentally abusing himself for being so dopey acting with the girl.

Later we came to Thunder Bay and found a little motel complex that had individual cabins instead of rooms. I rented a cabin and we drove over to it to unload our clothes and things and got a shower.

After we had cleaned up, we went downtown for some supper and spent the evening walking around the downtown and the harbor looking at the big boats and ships.

It was almost eleven thirty at night, and it was still light out. We were far enough north that we were close to the Land of the

Midnight Sun, where it barely gets dark during the summer.

"I'm going to bed," I said.

"Yeah, me too, but it's hard to sleep when it's so light," he said. About three minutes later I could hear him snoring in his bed across the room.

The next morning, I got up and slipped out to find a grocery store for some breakfast supplies. The cabin had a little kitchen, so I thought a nice homemade breakfast would be a good idea.

When I got back, Thunderfoot was sitting on the porch in his tee shirt and shorts, with his bare feet propped up on the porch railing, reading a Canadian newspaper. "G'day mate," he said with a wide grin.

"That's Australia," I said.

"What ya got in the bag?" he said. "I hope it's vittles."

I went into the cabin and began frying Canadian bacon and eggs and making toast, and Thunderfoot carried a little end table out onto the porch and a couple of chairs, and a few minutes later, we were breakfasting on the veranda.

"Ah, this is the life," he said, leaning back and patting his stomach. "Fresh Canadian air, good food, and all day to do just what you want to do."

We sat for a while and enjoyed the morning and then packed up to start to wherever we were going that day.

He brought the map over to me and pointed to a highway. "If we take this road, we can go and see Kackabecka Falls. The girl at the information place said it's pretty cool."

That sounded good, so off we went to Kackabecka Falls.

We drove about two hours and soon found the road to Kackabecka Falls Park. I was expecting a little waterfall but was amazed as we got close, by the sound of water cascading over a cliff and the amount of mist in the air.

Suddenly we came over a rise in the road and there was Kackabecka Falls. It was a for real waterfall, and quite spectacular. Thunderfoot jumped out of the van as soon as we stopped and ran to the railing. The mist from the falls was boiling up out of the river in great clouds and it didn't take long for our hair and clothes to become damp.

There was a trail that led down to the area above the falls, so we followed it and found that it led right out onto the rocks above where the river plunged over the falls. There were a bunch of teenagers out on the rocks taking pictures, so of course, we had to go out, too. Thunderfoot stood way too close for comfort to the edge and I took his picture. He wanted me to go and stand there, too, but I declined, and had my picture taken at a little safer distance from the edge.

"Wow, this is really cool," he said as we walked back up the path to the van. By now we were both pretty wet, so we got a couple of towels out and dried off our hair and arms and legs.

We took a couple more pictures of the falls and then drove back to the highway.

"Well, Mr. Navigator, where to next?" I said.

Thunderfoot looked at the map, studied it for a while and then decided to keep going west on the road we were on. It would eventually take us across the rest of Ontario and into Manitoba. That sounded good, so off we went.

As we drove, we started seeing Moose Crossing signs along the roadway.

"Look at that, just like our Deer Crossing signs," Thunderfoot said. "I hope we see some moose."

We stopped at a truck stop for lunch and gas, and as I was paying the bill, Thunderfoot asked the guy at the gas station if people saw a lot of moose along this road. The old guy laughed and said that you don't see them very often. If we wanted to see a moose, we better go to the zoo, he told us.

Thunderfoot was a bit disappointed at finding that out, but we paid up and off we went. We hadn't gone five miles when Thunderfoot almost choked on the candy bar he was eating.

"Mmmmoooosh, mooshe, moose!"

I looked where he was pointing and sure enough, there was a moose standing in a little lake, just a few yards off the road. We stopped and watched, and it just kept eating weeds from the lake and didn't run away.

"That's just a baby one," I said. "See how little it is?"

"It's cool. I'm gonna get out and take a picture of it," he said. He grabbed his camera and carefully got out of the van and took a picture. Then he began walking slowly toward the little moose and taking a picture every so often. He got within a few yards of it and it didn't seem to be alarmed a bit.

I opened the window and whispered loudly, "You better hope its mama doesn't see you so close."

He looked back at me with a worried look on his face. Then he began backtracking real fast and by the time he got to the van he was on a dead run.

"Jeez, I never thought about that. I saw a show on TV where a momma moose attacked a guy because he got too close," he panted.

Well, we hadn't gotten attacked, so all was well. The little moose was still standing there as we drove off.

"Those will be some excellent pictures," he said proudly. "We should go back and tell that old guy at the store that he needs to open his eyes a little more often and then he might see a moose or two."

We drove on for a couple of hours and then pulled into a campground that was on a lake and set up our camp. We were a stone's throw from the water, so it wasn't long and Thunderfoot was down at the lake casting while I made some supper. We ate and then just went down to the lake to sit and watch the evening pass.

"Gosh, this is so cool, being here so far from home and in such a cool place," he said.

"This is just what we needed," I said. He nodded in agreement. The next day we passed into Manitoba and continued west. The terrain began to be less hilly and there were more flat stretches of road. We were going along on one of these stretches when we came upon a bridge over a large river, and there were a bunch of cars stopped and people on the bridge looking at something.

"Let's stop and see what they're looking at," Thunderfoot said. As we pulled to the shoulder, we saw a car with Wisconsin plates on it.

"Look, somebody from home," he said.

We walked to the bridge and a lady called to us, "Yoo hoo Wisconsin."

We walked over to her and said hi. "Where are you from?" she asked.

"Muscoda, it's in the southwest part of the state," I answered. "Oh, do you know Leonard Pankin?"

My mouth dropped open. "The sewing machine guy? Sure, I know him."

"Oh, he's my brother-in-law," she said.

Thunderfoot looked at me. "How far do we have to get from home before we don't find people who know somebody we know?"

"I guess farther than this," I said.

We walked to the bridge and saw what they were looking at, which was a river full of logs being floated to the sawmill. We took some pictures and said goodbye to our new friends and took off again.

That evening we stopped in a little town just on the Manitoba border and got a motel room for the night. The campground we were at the evening before didn't have showers, and when we walked into the lake up to our knees to wash up, we found that the water was cold enough that our knees were as far up as we wanted to go. We cleaned up and went out looking for some supper. Down the road there was a little diner and we stopped for the daily special and struck up a conversation with a couple of local guys. Somewhere during the conversation, we got talking about bears. The local guys told us about the town dump where we could see all the bears we wanted, so, of course, we took off at dusk to see some bears.

We took our map, which was drawn on a napkin from the diner, and followed it out of town and into the forest. It wound round and round and it seemed like we were going a lot farther than they had said it would be.

"You don't suppose those guys were fooling us?" Thunderfoot said.

"I don't know. Why would they do that? It's probably not far. If we don't come to it pretty soon, we'll go back and you can look them up and pound knots on their heads."

He smacked his fist into his palm and looked menacing.

Just then we came up over a rise and there was the sign: Town Dump/Beware of Bears.

I looked at Thunderfoot and he grinned.

We parked the van upwind of the pile of garbage and sat back to watch. It didn't take long until a bear ambled up onto the pile and began tearing plastic sacks apart. Then another appeared and then two more.

"Wow, bear city," Thunderfoot whispered.

"I wish we were just a little closer," I said. "A picture is going to look like a pile of garbage with a black spot on it."

We didn't want to start the van and scare the bears, so we had to be content to watch from where we were. Soon, the bears found something that interested all of them on the end of the pile, and they all began moving away toward one area, where they began tearing sacks apart.

"Geez, now we can't hardly see them," Thunderfoot said. "I'm gonna sneak around the back and see if I can get close enough to take a picture."

"Oh, I don't think that's a good idea. What if they decide they don't like you poking around their supper?"

"I'm fast as a gazelle," he said, as he slipped out the door and began sneaking up toward the bears.

He kept the garbage pile between him and the bears and pretty soon he was real close to them. He stepped out from behind the pile and snapped a picture and all the bears stopped eating and looked at him. He had a big grin on his face when he turned to me to give me a thumbs up sign, but then saw how far he was from the van and how close he was to the bears and began to look worried.

He took a couple of steps backward and one of the bears stood up on its hind legs. When the bear stood up, Thunderfoot did an about face and took off running toward the van as fast as his legs would carry him. He had a look on his face that would have been worth a thousand dollars if there had been time to take his picture. The closer he got to the van, the faster he ran. He grabbed the door handle and jumped inside and landed right on top of me.

"Holy cow, he was after me, I can't believe I made it," he panted. I was laughing like crazy. "He who? There's nothing behind you." He looked around and the bears were all contentedly tearing sacks apart and eating.

"That one stood up and charged," he said.

"No," I said, laughing so hard I could hardly talk. "He stood up and when you turned and ran, he went back to his own business. I think he was just seeing what was making the flash."

"Well, why didn't you tell me that? I almost blew a lung out running back here."

"Sorry, oh fleet-of-foot-one. I thought you were just practicing your blinding, gazelle-like speed," I laughed.

"Let's go back to our motel. I've had enough bears for one night."

The next day we entered Saskatchewan and began seeing fields and fields of sunflowers. Sometimes there would be sunflowers for as far as you could see.

"I never thought there were so many sunflowers in the whole world," Thunderfoot said.

Saskatchewan is as flat as a table and the farmers there take advantage of it. The fields were enormous and other than that, the drive was pretty monotonous. We drove and planned how far we should go west before we started south and then back toward home. Finally we decided to go into North Dakota and see the Badlands and then on south from there.

We crossed the border into North Dakota and found a park to camp in for the night. That night Thunderfoot read about the Badlands and how they were formed. We couldn't wait to see them the next day.

After breakfast, we started south and came to the first part of the Badlands. It was pretty amazing. As far as you could see, there was nothing but Badlands, desolate, rock, sand, and cactus. By noon, several hundred miles later, we were still looking at the same type of terrain. By late afternoon, we were getting pretty tired of the Badlands. Finally, Thunderfoot announced that we were not far from South Dakota. When we entered South Dakota, the Badlands kept right with us, since they go from North Dakota through much of South Dakota, too.

Our destination was Custer State Park, which was in the Badlands, of course. But the park was in an area that wasn't so desolate, and had a real nice campground, with showers, so we set up camp.

That evening, we talked with some other campers who had taken a hiking trail out into the Badlands and said it was a lot of fun. It seemed like a good idea, so we borrowed their map and decided to take a hike the next morning.

We got to the parking area for the trail, and followed the markers to the first natural formation and from there to the next and so on. It was hot and sunny, so we were both wearing shorts and tennis shoes and tee shirts, and I had a canteen on my belt. The trail went up some pretty intimidating hills, and many times, Thunderfoot had to crawl up a ledge and then give me his hand to get me up over the top. We saw some mule deer and took some pictures of some really interesting rock formations.

The hike took almost three hours, so when we got back, we were famished and headed to the park headquarters, where there was a lunch counter. As we drove down the road I spotted a dead snake in the road. I slowed down and could see that it was a rattlesnake.

"Wow, look at that, a dead rattler," I said.

"Let's get out and look," Thunderfoot said.

I didn't even slow down. I knew better than to get him near a snake, when he knew how deathly afraid of them I was. I knew that some way, the snake would end up draped over my head or something to that nature, so I had no intention of giving him the chance to get near it.

As we pulled up to the restaurant, a park ranger was just coming out.

"Hi," I said. "Did you see that rattlesnake that's laying up the road?"

"Oh, another one?" he said. "We get them here in the campground all the time. They're not as much a problem here as they are out on the hiking trails. A lot of these people go out there without snake boots and a snakebite kit and they're the ones we have to look out for. Have a nice day."

I suddenly lost my appetite. We had just finished the hiking trail without boots, snakebite kit, or even the knowledge that we should be careful. And, the comment of snakes around the campground all the time made me feel like some other place down the road might be more to my liking.

Thunderfoot grinned. "In the campground all the time?"

"Do you know how far it would be to walk home from here?" I said.

He just grinned and put his arm on my shoulder. "Don't worry, let's go eat."

Now I'd have to sleep with one eye open.

The next morning, Thunderfoot was browsing through the park brochures and suddenly looked up with an excited look on his face. "Did you know they have buffalos here?"

"No, I didn't."

"It says that there are over a thousand wild buffalo roaming freely through the park. Let's go see them."

That sounded like a good way to spend the morning, so we

loaded up and went buffalo looking. Of course we had no idea of where the buffalo were, so we stopped at the Ranger Station to ask.

"Well, they're out on the prairie someplace," the ranger said. "You have to drive the roads and watch for them."

That seemed simple enough. After all how hard could it be to see a critter as big as a VW Beetle? Well, we spent the morning driving and saw nothing but prairie and more prairie.

"Do you know what the father buffalo said to his son?" Thunderfoot asked as we drove along.

As much as I hated to, I answered that I didn't know.

"Bison," he said, and broke into fits of laughter. "Get it, bison, bye son?"

We continued on our quest and he would burst out laughing every so often, "Bison, jeez, that's a good one."

After lunch, Thunderfoot got the park map out and we began looking at more remote places. He spotted a road that cut right across the middle of the park and went through some wild looking country.

"Let's go here and take this little road," he said.

"Are you sure that's a road?" I asked.

"It's on the map, it must be."

So we found the road, and it was much less of a road than we expected. In fact it was just a sand rut that looked pretty neglected.

"The road less traveled," Thunderfoot said. "Robert Frost."

I was impressed with his knowledge of Robert Frost, but not impressed with the road.

"I don't know if we should be on this road."

"Oh, come on, I'll bet the buffalo are just up the way here."

So, off we went on the road less traveled, and that proved to be the understatement of the day. We were on prairie and it was pretty good going for most of the way, and then we started up into the hills. The road was more like a logging road, made for trucks and four-wheel drive vehicles than a minivan. Soon we

43

were well up into the hills and the road became more like a track than an actual logging road, with rocks and gullies and all kinds of nasty obstacles.

"This is going to wreck the van," I said.

"It'll probably get better up farther," he said unconvincingly.

All of a sudden, he grabbed my arm and yelled stop. I looked at where he was looking, and right out the window on his side of the van were three baby bobcats, sitting in a tree.

"Holy cow, look at them," he whispered.

"Stay still, I'm going to get out on my side and take their picture," I said.

I quietly opened the door and carefully slipped up over the side of the van and snapped a picture of the little cats. They looked at me, wondering what the heck I was doing. I took a second picture and then heard a really nasty, Yeooow!, right behind me. I turned slowly, and there on the bank about six feet from me was the mama cat, in a crouch, with her ears laid back, looking real unfriendly.

I froze for an instant, and then very slowly slid into the seat of the van and closed the door. The mama cat stayed right where she was, so I put the van in gear and slowly moved from between her and her babies.

"Holy cow, she was mad at you," Thunderfoot said, as we looked back down the hill toward the cat, who was now by the tree where her babies were sitting.

"I thought I was a goner," I said.

"Maybe we better get out of this place, it might be dangerous."

"Oh yeah, you think?"

Well, the road went higher and higher on the hill and soon we were snaking up a track that was solid dirt and rock on my side and a one hundred foot drop, almost straight down, on Thunderfoot's side. Every once in a while, we had to stop and he would have to get out and roll a big rock or lift a branch or limb out of the way. My hands were beginning to cramp up from holding the wheel so tight. Thunderfoot was sitting in the seat right next to me, not wanting to get so close to the sheer drop on his side.

Finally, we got to the top and the road improved a little. We continued out the ridge and suddenly we were on a blacktop road again.

Thunderfoot looked back as we passed a sign that was at the end of the track we had just come from. "Uh oh," he said. "Road closed to public. Park vehicles only."

"Oops," I said. "Maybe we better not take any more of those little roads."

By now the day was almost shot, and we still hadn't seen any buffalo. Thunderfoot studied the map and suggested we ask around the campground and see if anyone had seen some, so we visited some of our neighbors and found a couple who had seen a lot of them, just a couple of miles from the campground.

"Tomorrow, we'll score," said Thunderfoot.

The next morning, we took off for the area that we had been told about and started out on a decent road that led up into the northern part of the park. We were going along, looking hard for buffalo when we came up over a little knoll and suddenly, right in front of us, there were about a thousand buffalo.

"Wow, Buffalo City," Thunderfoot said.

We stopped the van and just sat there as the buffalo worked their way toward us. They were walking down the valley and covered it from side to side. Soon, there were buffalo all around the van, some of them as tall as it was.

We were actually looking up at some of the big bulls, as they ambled past us, belching and farting.

"Whew, they make an awful stink," Thunderfoot said, as one of the bulls let some gas go right at his window.

"Yeah, they're almost as bad as you," I laughed.

"Funny," he said, and then broke into an out of tune rendition of Home on the Range. "Oh, give me a home, where the buffalo roam."

"Quiet," I said, "you'll stampede them."

We sat there for over a half hour until the whole herd had passed us by.

"Well, we saw some buffalo," I said.

"No fooling, mega buffalo," he said.

Since our buffalo mission was completed, we decided to leave Custer and go to Mt. Rushmore. It was a place I'd always wanted to see and as long as we were this dose, I thought we better do it.

We got into the Black Hills late that evening and stopped at a motel for the night. We walked into the office and an old fellow came to the desk to register us.

"Oh, from Wisconsin," he said, "Whereabouts in Wisconsin?" "Southwest part," I said. "A little town called Muscoda."

"Oh yeah, I know where Muscoda is. I'm from Fennimore originally."

Our mouths dropped open. Fennimore is about eighteen miles from Muscoda.

We talked with him for a while and then went to our room.

"I'm not believing that we keep bumping into people from home like that," Thunderfoot said.

It was pretty uncanny.

The next morning we took off through the Black Hills for Mt. Rushmore. The Black Hills are more like mountains than hills and in many places we drove through tunnels that were one way only. If you were already in the tunnel, a car on the other end had to wait, but if you both entered at once, one had to back up. It was pretty interesting. We wound through the narrow roads, and suddenly Thunderfoot said, "Wow, look at that."

I looked up the road, and there was Mt. Rushmore. We were still miles from it, but it was awesome already. We drove up to the viewing area and parked and then walked up onto the viewing deck. There was a recording playing about the building of the monument and in the background America the Beautiful was playing. We stood there looking up for a long while, and I looked over at Thunderfoot and he had a tear in the corner of his eye.

"Pretty awesome place," I said. He nodded.

We stood there a long time and then went into the snack shop and got some souvenirs and hiked back to the van.

"Gosh, I never thought I'd see something like that, or most of the stuff I've seen the past few days, and I guess it kind of got to me," he said.

"Hey, there's nothing wrong with getting emotional about something patriotic like Mt. Rushmore. You'd have to be pretty callous not to be proud to be an American when you're standing there looking up at it," I said.

"Well," I said, "I've got one more thing I want to see while we're here in South Dakota, and I don't know if you're gonna like it or not."

"What is it?" he said.

"There's a place called Spearfish, and it is known world wide for its Passion Play."

"You mean like in the Bible?" he asked.

"Yeah, they have an outdoor theater and the play is outside with cows and ducks and all kinds of people, just like in the old days. I've read about it and I think it's worth going to see it."

"Hey, you haven't taken me anyplace that wasn't fun yet, except maybe up that mountain on those back roads, so let's go for it."

We got the map out and found our way to Spearfish that afternoon. We went to the site of the play and bought our tickets for the performance that evening, and then got a motel and some food.

That evening we joined hundreds of other spectators at the outdoor set, and dozens of townspeople who were extras in the play and watched with awe as the story of the crucifixion took place before our eyes. The set was about two city blocks long and in the end, the man playing Jesus was led down the street to a hill and nailed to the cross, and then hoisted up on top of the hill. By then it was dark, and stage lightning and thunder made the scene so real that Thunderfoot and I both had goose bumps.

After the play was over, we walked down the street to our motel.

"Wow, I won't ever think of Easter the same again," he said.

It was truly an inspiring evening, even for two guys who would rather play hooky from church to go fishing on most Sundays.

The next morning, we decided to begin heading east and working our way back toward home. We had been on the road for almost two weeks and it was time to get back to the real world. We chose a route that took us through some country that we hadn't seen yet, and spent the next two days traveling leisurely toward home.

We were driving along, and the radio was beginning to fade, when Thunderfoot absentmindedly punched the button for our favorite station at home, and it came in.

"Well," he said, "you can tell we're home. The radio buttons work again."

We pulled into town and I told him we had to make one stop before we got to his house. I pulled into the gas station and told him to run in and get a newspaper.

He came back to the car with the paper opened and folded to the want ad section, Pets, Dogs and Cats.

"This what you're looking for?" he said, grinning.

"You read my mind."

"Look at the third one down."

I read the ad: Golden Retriever puppies, 4 males, 5 females, ready to go now. The phone number was one for a town just a few miles away.

"I'll call as soon as I get home. You spend the evening with your mom so she can get used to you again, and tomorrow we'll go puppy shopping."

He was all grins, from ear to ear.

We got to his house and he unloaded all of his gear. His mom was happy to see us back in one piece and took his laundry off to begin washing it.

He walked back to the van with me and when we got to the door, he grabbed me and hugged me. "I don't know how to thank you for the trip. It's something I'll never forget for my whole life."

"It wouldn't have been half as much fun without you to share it with," I said.

"What time should I be over tomorrow?"

"Whenever you get up will be fine," I said.

He grinned, punched me in the shoulder, and walked off to his house.

That pretty much said it all.

Thanks, Thunderfoot

Katy

I was just finishing my breakfast when Thunderfoot came bounding into the kitchen.

"Did you call about the puppies?" he asked.

"Yup, they've got four girls left. I told them we'd be up this morning to look at them."

"Oh boy, oh boy," he said, as he grabbed a bowl from the cupboard and poured himself some cereal.

He wolfed the cereal down and we put things away and took off for the farm where our next little friend waited for us. As we pulled into the driveway and our mouths dropped open. There were about a dozen golden retrievers galloping around the place and another five or six in a pen, plus a bunch of puppies that were tumbling around in a fenced-in part of the yard.

"Holy cow, these people like goldens," Thunderfoot said.

We got out and were surrounded by big friendly slobbering golden retrievers, all trying to get as much attention as they could from these strangers. We walked up toward the house, followed by our new friends, and the lady in charge came out.

"You the guys looking for a puppy?" she asked.

"That's us," Thunderfoot answered. "Looks like you like golden retrievers pretty good."

She laughed and explained to us that the six dogs in the pens were their males and all of the loose ones were females of various ages that they had as either pets or used for breeding purposes to raise litters.

We walked to a shaded part of the yard where the puppies were fenced in and climbed over the low fenced-in enclosure. The puppies were all excited to see us and began vying for our attention.

I told the lady that we wanted a female, so she picked up the males and held them in her arms, amid much protesting. We got down on the grass with the girls and began looking them over. One was from a litter that was born two weeks ahead of the others. The other three were sisters. We watched them and began picking them up and playing with them. The three sisters were pretty feisty and wild, but the older pup was really laid back and real snuggly. Thunderfoot picked her up and she nestled right down in the crook of his arm and began going to sleep.

He looked at me with a smile. "A little angel," he said.

The lady walked over and said, "That one is the last one from the other litter, and I want to tell you why."

She took the puppy from Thunderfoot and laid her on her back.

She had a little hernia on her belly where the umbilical cord had been.

"I've had this before, and they aren't any problem," she said.

"Most times they grow shut on their own, but sometimes they need a little surgery to close them. The other families were afraid of having problems, so no one took this puppy, but I'll guarantee her and if she needs surgery, I'll pay for half of it."

I took the pup in my arms and she was so sweet and gentle acting that I decided right then and there that I wanted her. I didn't care about the hernia and I guess I felt a little sorry for her for being the last of the litter.

Just then one of the lady's daughters came out of the house and the lady told her to go and get the mother of the puppy and bring her out so we could meet her.

The daughter came out with an older dog, and as soon as we saw her, Thunderfoot and I looked at each other, wide eyed. She was an exact copy of my old dog Bea, same color, same head shape, same white on her face from old age, and same mannerisms.

The old dog came up and we petted her and talked to her, and soon, she was leaning up against my leg, just like old Bea did many years ago.

"Well, that settles it," I said. "This is the one."

I paid the lady and got the papers for the puppy, while Thunderfoot held her in his arms and nuzzled her.

We got into the truck and took off, and within a mile, the puppy was sleeping in the crook of his arm.

"Gosh, she's a sweetie," he whispered.

When we got home, we put the puppy in the yard and let her run around and look over her new home. After a while, she became tired and needed a nap, so we went into the house and Thunderfoot sat in the rocker and rocked her to sleep.

"What are we gonna call her?" he asked.

I hadn't decided on a name yet, so we both thought for a while trying to find a good name for her.

"It can't be something goofy like Queenie, or Lady. It's got to be a good name for a girl. Something short and tough," he said.

I tried to think of a tough sounding girl's name but couldn't come up with any. Suddenly I thought of a tough woman from a play I once saw.

"How about Kate?" I said. "Like in The Taming of the Shrew." She was a tough gal.

"Kate, Katy. Yeah, that sounds good," he said.

He rocked the puppy and whispered her name in her ear. "Hi, Katy." I got out the registration papers, began filling them out and filled in the name: Ka Ka Ka Katy.

"What's all the Ka's for?"

"There's an old song that I used listen to at my grandma's house," I said. "It went, Ka Ka Ka Katy, beautiful Katy, you're the only ga ga ga girl that I adore, and when the ma ma moon shines, over the cow shed, I'll be waiting at the ki ki ki kitchen door."

"Ok, just don't sing that around any other people," he said, shaking his head like I had lost my mind.

That night, Thunderfoot decided to stay over and sleep in his room, so Katy would have a place to sleep that would be warm and so she wouldn't be lonesome for the other puppies.

They went to bed, and a while later, I peeked in to see him

laying on his side with Katy snuggled up against his chest, her head laying on his arm, sleeping like an angel. They were two pretty satisfied youngsters.

The next morning, Thunderfoot hustled Katy outside to go potty and she did an admirable job. Then we had breakfast and decided to take her for a little fishing trip down to the river bottoms sloughs.

We loaded the john boat into the back of the truck and threw in some rods and reels and a few baits, and took off for our favorite lake.

When we got there, Katy was fascinated with all the new things to look at and chew on and she had a great time exploring while we launched the boat and transferred the gear. She wandered off through the tall grass and we had a hard time finding her until we saw her little blonde tail sticking up out of the grass a short way away.

Thunderfoot picked her up and put her in the middle of the boat, and he went to the front end, and we began paddling out into the lake. Katy could just barely see over the side of the boat, so we didn't have to worry about her falling in, and we began casting plugs in and around the lily pads trying to catch a bass or northern.

It didn't take Katy long to figure out how to climb up on the middle seat, so she could see better, and soon she was scampering back and forth across the seat, looking at all the wonderful new things. We drifted into the lily pads and she quickly was reaching over the side of the boat, trying to touch one of the big flat leaved pads.

"Look at her," Thunderfoot said. "She thinks she can walk on the lily pads."

He had just finished the sentence when Katy stepped out over the side of the boat onto a lily pad, and disappeared with a little splash under the water.

"Oh my gosh," Thunderfoot gasped and threw his pole into the bottom of the boat and jumped to the middle seat. He looked over the side and then stuck his arm down into the water and came up with what looked like a blond drowned rat.

Katy didn't seem a bit fazed by her dunking. She shook a little and climbed up onto the front seat where Thunderfoot had been.

"She's a brave little thing. She was on the bottom, and just kind of walking around," he said. "I don't think she had any idea what was going on."

It was funny, but we decided to keep a better eye on her for the rest of the fishing trip.

He sat back down in his seat, and soon Katy climbed up in his lap and curled up for a nap.

"Try not to make a lot of noise. Kate's tired," he whispered.

We fished for a while and then went home. Thunderfoot held Katy in his lap, so she could look out the window while we drove.

"You know," I said, "you're gonna spoil her. Pretty soon she'll be a big dog and she'll think she has to be in your lap all the time."

"I could think of worse things," he said, grinning.

That evening, he hem-hawed around for quite a while, and finally I asked him if he wanted to stay again.

"Maybe just one more night, so Katy will feel secure," he said. She was one lucky dog. He was one happy boy.

Welcome home Katy.

Thanks, Thunderfoot.

The Grass Is Always Greener

The water level in the river was at an all time low and consequently, our favorite duck pond was almost dry. Thunderfoot and 1 had been scouting a couple of weeks before the season and had found that the little lake we hunted on was now a mud hole with a tiny puddle of water right in the middle that was hardly big enough to hold even a few ducks. All of the other ponds in the river bottoms were in the same shape, and the numbers of ducks were just as dismal as the water levels.

"There aren't any ducks around and I don't blame them for not stopping by here," 1 said. "There's hardly enough water here for them to find a place to land."

"I know, but what are we gonna do for opening day?" Thunderfoot asked.

"You know, I used to hunt up on the Mill Pond bottoms, and they aren't affected by the river level, because they're fed by the Mill Creek. It's almost always the same level, so there should be good water there."

We would have preferred to hunt our regular ponds, but we had no choice, so off we went to scout the Mill Pond bottoms. Sure enough, there was water, and lots of ducks. We walked to the high bank of the creek and sat on a log and watched until dusk as dozens of flocks of ducks came from the nearby fields and streams. The sky was glowing orange with a slate blue border creeping in as the flights of ducks settled quietly onto the pond for the night.

"This is where all of our ducks are," Thunderfoot said, smiling, as the light faded to dusk.

"Well, now we know where to go on opening day."

We prepared to hunt unfamiliar territory on the first day of the season, so instead of having a canoe, decoys, blind, and all the comforts of our regular spot, we had to rough it with a portable blind and a couple of folding stools. We each took two decoys, and with them added to our guns, ammo and other gear, we were pretty well loaded down as we trekked off toward the marsh.

The Mill Pond was formed many years before, when a dam was built at the end of the valley and a hydroelectric generator was installed, providing the area with electricity. The dam had served the area for many years, until the appetite for electricity outgrew the capacity of the generator. Now, it was used occasionally to generate extra electricity in peak usage times, but it was not economically feasible to keep it going all the time. The pond that was formed when the project was begun was still a great place for fishing and hunting for waterfowl.

It was fed by a creek that was a trout stream much farther upstream. It meandered for many miles through two counties before it emptied into the pond. The creek ran through a pasture and was bordered by a high bank on each side that was good solid ground and easy walking. As you got closer to the pond, the hard bank turned into a marsh and walking was much harder if not impossible.

"We have to decide which side of the pond we want to hunt on," I said. "We'll have to cross the creek here where it's running across the pasture or otherwise we'll be in too much mud to get to one side or the other."

"Which side do you think?" he said. "Either is all right with me."

"OK, let's go on the other side," he said.

We walked to the creek and began following it toward the pond.

A short way from where we joined it, the creek turned to the right, and there was a tree laying across it.

"This is the bridge," I said.

Thunderfoot looked at me. "Did you cut this tree across the creek?"

"No, a friend of mine did, a long time ago. Go ahead, it's safe." He stepped out onto the tree and began tight rope walking to the other side. It was a snap for him, and he stepped off onto the far bank in a few seconds.

"Your turn."

I stepped onto the tree trunk and since I was a lot heavier than Thunderfoot, it began to swing and sway. I inched my way forward and looked down at the swift water running under me. It was about five feet deep, and probably ice cold, since it was the end of a trout stream. I worked my way along and almost went over the side a couple of times, but managed to get to the other side, much to Thunderfoot's chagrin.

"You hoped I'd fall in, didn't you?" I asked.

"Of course not, then you would have whined all day about how cold and wet you were. Let's get to the duck pond."

We took off toward the pond, found a good-looking spot to set up our little blind and deployed our gear. We each took our two decoys and waded out into the pond a short way and set them out.

The mud was sucking at our boots as we waded back.

"Boy, this stuff's really sticky," Thunderfoot said.

"Yeah, it's a good thing we have our chest waders, and not our hip boots. This stuff would pull your boots right off."

We settled in to wait for noon which was the opening of the season, and right on schedule a few minutes after noon, a little flock of ducks came flying down the pond, and flew along the shoreline on the other side and kept on going. Soon, another flock came by and they too went along the other shore.

"Jeez, what's wrong with some coming over here," Thunderfoot said. A while later a flock of ducks came from the other way, and they too skirted the other side of the pond.

"Well, this is just about enough to make me a tad bit mad," he said.

"Be patient, they'll come on this side, just wait and see."

Famous last words. We sat and watched ducks fly along the other side of the pond for the next two hours and not a duck came by on our side.

"What are we doing wrong?" he asked.

"I don't know, maybe they just like that side better." "Let's pack up and go over there," he said.

"Oh, man, we have to go all the way back up to the creek and cross and then all the way back, it will take an hour and a half. We've only got a couple of hours of hunting left anyway. I don't think it's worth it."

"Let's just wade across. It's only a foot deep all the way," he said. "Oh, I don't know. What about the mud?"

"How bad can it be? If it gets too bad, we can turn around and wade back."

Well, that seemed to be the best plan, so I rolled up the blind, Thunderfoot folded up the stools and we each carried our guns out to the decoys. We each picked up the lead weights of the two decoys we had placed, rinsed the mud off them, and stuck the weights into our back pockets. The decoys swam along behind us like a couple of trained ducks.

"Come along, Daisy and Donald," Thunderfoot chuckled as we waded out across the pond.

It was about a hundred yards across to the other side, and all was going well, until we got to the middle. The mud was only about a foot deep, until we came to the old creek channel and then we stepped into the channel and the mud became deeper real quick. In about two steps, I was up to my waist and Thunderfoot was up to the middle of his belly.

"Uh oh, I think we're in trouble," he said. "I don't think, I know!" I said.

I tried to back up, but I was stuck and sinking. I began wallowing around, like a beached hippo and soon was in mud up to about the middle of my belly, too. With the foot of water on top of the mud, I was at the maximum depth that my waders would allow before I got wet.

Thunderfoot was struggling trying to get free and suddenly managed to pull himself back up onto the shallower mud.

"I'm out,"he panted.

"I'm happy for you. I'm stuck for good here," I said.

Other than the fact that I was holding my gun over my head to keep it dry, I wasn't in any pain or discomfort. I did, of course, feel like one of the stupidest people probably in the entire state at the moment.

"Go back and get rid of your gun and the other stuff, and then come back and get mine, and maybe I can get out if I'm not holding all this stuff," I said.

He nodded and waded back to the shore with his two ducklings swimming along behind him. Soon, he returned and took my gun and the blind and my ducklings back to the shore with the rest of the gear.

I tried to get loose, but couldn't budge. I had no leverage and there was just no way that I could get out.

"Find a log or something that I can use to push on to try to push up out of this stuff," I yelled over to him.

He took off for the woods.

I stood there with my fingers laced together and placed on top of my head. I couldn't put my arms down because if I did, they'd get wet. As I stood there, a bullhead swam up to me and acted like it was trying to figure out what the big thing standing in the middle of the pond was, and probably wondering if it was edible.

"Hurry up!" I shouted. "The bullheads are starting to think about feeding on my carcass."

Soon, Thunderfoot came panting down the bank with a long log dragging behind him, and then he waded into the pond and brought the log out to me.

"Here, try this," he said, sliding the log through the water to me. I pushed the log in front of me and had to put my arms down into the water to push down on it, and began trying to pry myself from the muck. It wasn't working, so Thunderfoot grabbed down into the water around my waist and began lifting as hard as he could. Between the two of us, I moved a few inches. We tried again, and this time I moved a little more. Again, and again we lifted and pulled and pried, and finally, I came loose from the mud.

We were both panting and sweating when I finally got my feet free, and just laid there in the water for a few minutes catching our breath. I was so exhausted, that I couldn't get to my feet, and crawled the fifty yards back to the bank. When I got there, I just collapsed onto the dry ground.

"I thought I was a goner," I said.

"Wow, I don't think anyone has ever been stuck so bad as that," Thunderfoot said, gasping for breath.

By now, it was almost quitting time, and it really didn't matter.

We both were completely exhausted and wet and covered with mud from head to toe, inside and outside our waders. Both of us had mud all over our faces and Thunderfoot's hat was even covered in it. We tried to wipe as much mud off as we could, so we could pick up our guns, then loaded up our gear and started back to the truck.

When we got to the pasture and the bridge, we stopped and looked back toward the pond. The water was like chocolate milk from all the mud we had stirred up, and just as we started to turn away, a flock of mallards landed right in the spot we had put our blind originally.

"Well, that just does it," he said. "I don't think I like this new duck spot very much."

He walked across the log and stopped on the other side.

I started across, and the log began to wobble and, of course, to complete a perfect day, I fell in, right in the deepest part of the creek. The water was just as cold as I thought it would be, and after I got to my feet and found my gun on the bottom, I handed it up to Thunderfoot who was standing on the bank looking concerned.

"Here, take this and shoot me," I said as I handed the gun to him. He broke out laughing and held a branch out for me to hang onto while I climbed out of the creek. I laid on my back and

Thunderfoot held my legs up as high as he could get them so some of the water drained out of my waders.

The cold water was running out of the waders and soaking into my back. "Well, I guess that pretty much ends a perfect day," I said as I struggled to my feet. "Yup," he said, grinning. "I think tomorrow we'll try fishing or squirrel hunting, or maybe yard work, anything but duck hunting here again."

"Yard work?"

"Sorry, my mind must have been damaged by all the mud." Thanks, Thunderfoot.

The Great Goose Hunt

The fall goose hunting season was upon us, and Thunderfoot and I were getting ready for a trip to the Horicon Marsh. I had just purchased some new goose decoys and we were getting them ready for the trip.

"Wow, these are really cool," Thunderfoot said as he slid the head and neck into the shell body of one of the geese.

"Yeah, with those two dozen full body shells and fifty silhouettes, we should be in good shape."

He opened the box with the silhouette decoys in it and took one out. "Jeez, they look like a road killed goose," he said, examining the flat piece of rubber.

The silhouettes were shaped like the outline of a goose as seen looking from above, with a little paint on the sides to simulate the gray color and a curving piece of material on one end representing the head and neck.

The idea was to place the silhouettes in among the full bodied decoys and make it look like a larger flock of geese to any flock that was passing by that might be looking for company. The silhouettes were about one third the cost of the regular ones, so economy was a major factor in my choosing them.

"We'll have seventy-five birds out, so that should be plenty to attract some real ones," I said. Thunderfoot agreed.

We packed up our gear, which included the decoys, a piece of camouflage material for a blind, lunch, stools, guns, and shells and decided to go to bed early so we could get an early start in the morning.

What seemed like only a couple of hours later, we were driving through the darkness toward the Horicon Marsh. I had called an acquaintance that had a farm outside the intensive zone of the marsh and asked him if we could hunt in one of his fields that day, and he had given us permission. When you hunt outside the intensive zone, you hunt in an area where you are not required to be in a blind. Inside the intensive zone, you must hunt from a blind that is rented out by the landowner. Not that renting a blind is any problem, but we wanted to use decoys and they weren't very effective so close to the marsh. The geese usually wanted to land in the fields outside the marsh area to feed, and that is where we planned on hunting.

We got to the farm while it was still dark and decided on a field that was mostly alfalfa with some picked corn rows still standing in it. We erected our blind just inside the rows of corn and then began placing our decoys in little family groups in the field. This took quite a while and by the time we were done, the sky was turning dark blue. The sounds of honking geese began coming from the vicinity of the marsh, which was a couple of miles away.

"We better get hid," Thunderfoot said, and we sprinted to the blind and got settled.

Soon, flocks of geese began appearing in the sky from the marsh and some drifted toward us. They looked like shoe laces drifting on the wind as they flew through the gray morning sky.

"Here comes some," Thunderfoot said.

The geese came over us and looked at our decoys but kept going across the road and circled once and then began to drop into a plowed field.

"Well, that's nice," Thunderfoot said.

In a few minutes another flock came our way, and they circled our decoys once and on their second trip around, they set their wings and glided into the plowed field across the road with their cousins.

"Uh oh," I said. "This doesn't look good. Pretty soon there'll be more real geese over there than we have decoys and we'll be out of luck."

Sure enough, the next two small flocks landed in the plowed field and then the rest of the morning, we watched as hundreds, no, probably a thousand or more geese landed just out of our reach. There we sat with our measly little flock and us sitting in our blind, feeling pretty glum.

"There's no way we can sneak up on them, and if we spook them, they'll all just go someplace else," Thunderfoot said.

I just shook my head. "Let's go ask the farmer if we can hunt there this afternoon, and then go spook them and set up and hope some of them will come back."

That suited Thunderfoot, so we drove over to the farm and the farmer was OK with our plan. We went back to our field and packed all of our gear up, including all the decoys and moved camp to the plowed field. As we drove up to the edge of the field, the thousand or so geese got up amid much honking and confusion, and began flying away. The noise was deafening, and the sky was full of geese but in less than a minute, things quieted down and we watched the geese heading off toward the marsh for a mid-day siesta.

"They should come back since we didn't shoot at them," I said. "At least, I hope so."

We made two trips each and managed to get all the gear out into the field. Our problem was that there was no place to set the blind up. The field was an old cornfield that had been picked, and then chisel plowed, so there wasn't anyplace that the blind wouldn't look out of place. The geese would see it and know it meant danger and would probably avoid us. There were lots of corn stalks and stubble in the field, which was why the geese were there in the first place.

"Why don't we gather up some of these corn stalks and make a place to lie down, and then cover up with the stalks, and when the geese come, we'll sit up and shoot them?" Thunderfoot said.

It sounded about as good a plan as we could come up with, so we deployed our decoys and got our little beds ready in the middle of them.

There weren't any geese to be seen anywhere, so we went

back to the truck and had lunch and took it easy for an hour. Then we began seeing small flocks of geese drifting back out from the marsh to feed for the afternoon.

"Time to get back to the field," I said, and we headed back and laid down in our cornstalk beds and covered ourselves up. We were both wearing waterproof camouflage coats and pants and had hunting boots on our feet, so we were pretty well camouflaged when we added a few cornstalks. We had also painted our faces with camouflage make-up, to keep our white faces from showing up and scaring the geese. All in all, we felt pretty secure there, waiting for the geese to begin showing up.

We laid there about a half hour when we saw a little flock of geese coming our way. "Lay still, they're coming," I said.

The geese circled us once and then set their wings and began settling into the field. "Now!" I said, and Thunderfoot and I sat up and began shooting at the descending geese. We both emptied our guns and the geese flew away.

"Wow, it's kind of hard shooting like this," he said.

"No kidding," I said. "It's hard to turn to shoot to the side. Oh well, if all of those geese come back that were here this morning, we'll do lots of shooting and figure out how to do it."

We laid back down and waited for more geese. A few minutes later, I heard the sound of thunder, a long way off in the west. "Sounds like a storm is coming."

Thunderfoot raised up and looked to the west. "It's pretty black, but it's a long way away."

We waited and soon the thunder came again, and it was louder and closer. I looked over my shoulder, and the storm had moved a lot closer and it was getting black and ugly looking, real fast.

"That storm is going to be here in a few minutes. Maybe we should head back to the truck."

"Are you gonna melt? We're dressed in waterproof clothes. What can a little rain do to us?" he said.

Against my better judgment, I decided that we probably

would be OK.

"Besides, if we get up and move, you know some geese will land right here where we're laying," he said. He was probably right about that, too.

So we stayed.

The rain started as a sprinkle a few minutes later. A big drop splattered onto the ground, here and there. It sprinkled for a minute or two and then the light sprinkle became a steady shower. A minute later it began to rain hard, then it turned to a downpour, then a cloudburst, and then an all out monsoon. It was raining so hard that I could barely see Thunderfoot only ten feet from me. He had pulled the hood of his coat up over his face and all I could see was steam coming up from the collar of the coat. The nice dry field turned to a black gooey mess, and soon little rivulets of muddy water began running down between where the rows of corn had stood. One of those little rivulets began running right up the back of my jacket.

"Oh, this is real nice," I said.

"Quit complaining. This can't last long, as hard as it's raining." I could barely hear him over the noise of the rain splattering on my coat and into the corn stalks.

It rained as hard as I've ever seen it rain for the next half hour, and we were still laying face up in the middle of the field. I wondered what the farmer, nice and warm and dry in his house, was thinking about the two idiots laying in his cornfield.

"OK, maybe you're right, this isn't gonna quit," Thunderfoot said finally. "Besides, I haven't seen a goose in the air for a long time."

"Geese have more sense than to fly in this weather," I said.

We both sat up and sloughed to our feet. The field was pure mud, sticky and black and deep enough that we sunk up to mid-calf when we began picking up the decoys.

"This is about enough to make me give up hunting for geese," Thunderfoot said as his feet went out from under him when he bent to pick up a silhouette.

It took us about an hour to make about four trips each to the truck to get all the gear out of the mud. By the time we were done, we both were covered with the black stuff from head to toe, and were sweating up a storm inside our heavy clothing.

Just about the time we finished, the rain let up and the sun began to show beneath the clouds in the west.

"Isn't that lovely," Thunderfoot said, as he pulled his muddy boots off and threw them into the back of the truck. His socks, that had been white earlier, were now hanging off the end of his feet and were completely black.

We took off our outer clothes and boots and socks and ended up wearing soaked tee shirts and our underwear as we drove out of the farmyard toward home. Everything we had was covered with mud and laying in the back of the truck. I turned on the heater to warm us up and soon the cab was warm and toasty, making us feel a little better.

"You know, I think maybe geese are a bit too difficult for us.

Maybe we better stick to something easier to hunt, like clay pigeons," Thunderfoot said.

I looked over at him, and he grinned at me through a mud covered face.

"I just hope we get home without any trouble, seeing as how we're in our underwear," I said.

"We'll be fine. If you want, I can drive."

I declined. "I guess we probably better go through the drive-through for some lunch. We probably would create a bit of an uproar if we walked into a cafe like this," he said, laughing.

"I don't know which would scare them worse, our muddy faces or our lack of clothing," I said.

"Let's not find out."

Thanks, Thunderfoot.

They Shoot Horses Don't They?

"Why don't we go up to my grandpa's and do some rabbit hunting tomorrow?" Thunderfoot asked.

"Yeah, I guess we can do that," I replied. "We usually have pretty good luck up there, and there isn't much else that we have to do. Let's do it."

The next morning, we drove up to his grandpa's farm and stopped by the house to visit with his grandparents for a while. Of course, like any grandma, we had to have some fresh cinnamon rolls and hot chocolate before we went to the woods to hunt. With our bellies full, we promised we would stop back after we had hunted, and began walking back toward the woods.

Grandpa's land had a huge ditch that had been filled with trees and brush over the years as land was cleared, and the ditch was a great place to hunt rabbits. It was way back on the backside of the farm and we had to walk back across several pastures to get to it. As we came up to the fence that enclosed the pasture, I noticed a horse down near the other end.

"When did your grandpa get that horse?" I said.

"Oh, a while ago," Thunderfoot said. "He got him from a neighbor who didn't want him anymore."

I watched the horse, and as we approached the fence, he came to attention and his ears pricked up while he watched us. Then he began walking our way, looking kind of menacing.

"He looks mean," I said.

"Oh, cripes, he's not mean. He's just curious."

I wasn't so sure. The horse came closer but then stopped and watched us from a fair distance.

"Come on, we've got to cross this pasture to get to the rabbit place," he said.

"Maybe we should hunt someplace else. That horse looks

like he doesn't want us in his pasture."

"Are you scared of a horse?"

"I don't like horses," I answered. "When I was just a kid like you, we had a family reunion at one of my uncle's farm, and after we ate, all of us kids were going to ride the horse. Well, the other kids got on and the horse went around the barn and back and they got off and the next one got on. When it was my turn, the horse got behind the barn and then stopped. So, I kicked him in the belly like I was told to do, and he laid down and rolled on his back. He almost crushed me. I think he was trying to kill me."

Thunderfoot was standing there with his mouth agape and then burst out laughing. "What a sissy. Tried to crush you."

"Yeah, well a few years later, some of my friends and I went to one of the guy's farms to ride their horses one day, and we all got on and rode up to the top of the hill, and then my horse decided to go back to the barn and took off like a bat out of hell and ran under an apple tree and almost took my head off," I said. "That was the last time I got on a horse."

"Yeah, there's a horse conspiracy out there and they're planning on assassinating you," he chuckled.

"Laugh all you want. That horse doesn't like me," I said, indicating the horse standing at the other end of the pasture.

"Watch," he said. "I'll go across and you'll see that he isn't mean." He climbed up and over the barbed wire fence and started walking across the pasture. It was about a hundred yards across, and the horse watched him but didn't move. He got to the other side and turned around and spread his hands and shrugged his shoulders. "See, no mad horse."

As much as I hated to, I slid my gun under the fence and climbed up and over. Once I was on the other side, the horse began watching me and his ears came forward, like he was listening for me to say something wrong so he could charge. I began walking toward the other side and he took a few steps toward me. I stopped and the horse stopped.

"Come on, just keep walking and he'll leave you alone,"

Thunderfoot said from the safety of the other side of the fence.

I began walking again and the horse began walking toward me. I was getting pretty nervous now, and didn't know whether to stop or keep going. I was coming to the middle of the field and had to decide soon. I looked at the horse and now his ears were flattened back and he really looked mad. I began walking faster and the horse began trotting toward me.

"Uh, maybe you better get moving," Thunderfoot said. "He looks like he may come after you."

Oh, great, here I was at the point of no return, and I had an angry horse coming at me at a much faster rate than I could run. But, heedless of the fact that I was much slower than my pursuer, I took off at a dead run for the safety of the fence. The horse began to trot and then to gallop after me.

"Hurry up, he's gaining on you!" Thunderfoot shouted.

I was going as fast as I could go but the horse was getting closer and closer. "Shoot him, shoot him!" I yelled at Thunderfoot.

Now I only had about ten feet to go, and the horse was right behind me with his teeth bared and he was snapping his jaws at me, trying to bite me. I got to the fence and my right foot hit the middle wire while I hurled my body over the top wire in one motion, and I landed on my back on the other side. My gun went flying through the air and landed in the brush.

The horse came to the wire and stood there, staring at me.

"See, I told you he was mean. Horses don't like me. I told you."

I was stammering like a fool.

Thunderfoot was bent over double with laughter. "Jeez, you vaulted the fence. I didn't think you could do that in a hundred years. Where did you get that burst of speed? Shoot him! Shoot him!" More stupid laughter.

When death at the hooves of a horse stares at you, even a full figured guy can move pretty fast.

I was still laying on the ground panting as the horse trotted off and stood in the middle of the field, like he was telling me that he'd be waiting for me if I wanted to take another try at it.

I got to my feet, picked up my gun and walked over to the fence.

The horse stiffened up, thinking that I may be coming back over for another confrontation.

"That's the meanest horse I've ever seen," I said. "No wonder the neighbor didn't want it."

Thunderfoot was still laughing as we walked back to the rabbit ditch. We hunted for a couple of hours and had lots of shooting but connected on very few bunnies.

"Well, grandma wants us to stop for something to eat on the way back," he said, "and I'm getting pretty faminished."

"We're going to have to go around the horse this time," I said. "I'm not good for two record sprints and high jumps in one day."

We hiked up to the end of the valley and then climbed up the hill and around the pasture. We put our hunting gear in the truck and walked up to the house and were greeted with some wonderful smells coming from the kitchen.

"Any luck?" grandpa said.

"Not much with the bunnies," Thunderfoot said, "but, a new world record was set for fifty yard dash and high jump."

Grandpa looked at me, not getting the joke.

"The horse chased me and your grandson thought it was hilarious," I said.

"Oh, yeah, he's a bit spirited, but I don't think he'd hurt you."

"Who, the horse or the grandson?"

Thanks, Thunderfoot.

Kirby

Thunderfoot had come over about lunch time and was sitting complaining about not being able to go fishing because of the minus 20 degree temperatures outside. It was mid-January and one of the coldest days of the year. I believed that his mom had suggested that he come over to see what I was up to, because he had just about driven her crazy with his pacing around the house.

"I can't understand why all of these cold days have to come on the weekend when I don't have to go to school!" he lamented.

"Yeah, that's a real tragedy," I said, mockingly.

"No, really, we should be out doing something and here we sit," he whined.

I wasn't going to let him talk me into anything that would require me to go out in the subzero temperatures and driving wind, so I just stuck my nose into a book and ignored him.

He watched a couple of fishing shows on TV and then began to pace, trying to think of something to do. As he walked past the living room window, he stopped and looked out.

"Hey, look, there's a dog out there."

"So what, there are lots of dogs around here," I said.

"Yeah, but look at this poor guy; he looks like he's starving to death."

I got up and walked over to the window. There was a stray dog watering my flagpole, and he was indeed skinny. In fact, as I looked closer, I could see all of his ribs and his backbone sticking up through his skin. He looked to be part golden retriever and part collie, but he had been on his own for a long time. His tail was covered with burrs, and he had lots of dirt and grime covering his coat. We watched as he sniffed around and then began sniffing his way across the yard toward the neighbors.

Thunderfoot looked at me. "We should help him; he's gonna freeze to death if he doesn't get some food and some place to sleep where it's warm."

As much as I agreed with him, I didn't need another dog to look after, but I couldn't turn my back on him. It was supposed to be in the minus 30s that night, and as skinny and poor looking as this poor fella was, I doubted if he would survive.

"Let's go see if he'll come to us," I said.

We pulled on our boots and coats and hats and walked out into the yard. We began looking for the dog, but he was gone.

"There he is," Thunderfoot said, pointing across the road to the neighbor's yard.

We walked over and found the dog had walked through a gate in the backyard and was inside a little pen that the neighbor had to keep her kids from straying all over the neighborhood. The dog was standing in the other end of the pen.

I walked in and closed the door. "You stay here and if he turns out to be mean, let me out quick," I said to Thunderfoot.

I walked toward the dog and he began to shiver and whine and cower. I squatted down and talked real low and mellow to him, but he wouldn't come to me. He was afraid of me.

"Run over home and get some of that sliced ham that's in the fridge," I said to Thunderfoot. He hooked the gate and sprinted across the street and returned in a couple of minutes. He handed me the ham, and I walked back toward the dog.

I took a piece of ham and tossed it to him. He sniffed it and gobbled it up like it was his first meal in a long time. I talked to him a bit more and he shuffled toward me a bit. I tossed him another piece of ham, but this time I tossed it half way between us. He snuck forward and picked it up, and stayed there. I took a couple of steps toward him and held out my hand with a piece of ham in it. He stretched out his neck and took it from me. The next piece was hardly out of my pocket when he greedily snapped it up.

We were buddies now.

I petted him and fed him the rest of the ham. His tail was wagging so fiercely that his whole body moved back and forth. "He's a real friendly guy," I said.

"Here, I brought Katy's slip collar and leash. See what he'll do if you put it on him," Thunderfoot said.

I slipped the collar over the dog's head and he fell into step right beside me. "He's been on a leash before," I said, as I led the dog over to Thunderfoot. He was on his knees and petting the dog, and they were fast becoming buddies.

"Let's take him home and we'll feed and water him and put him in Katy's kennel. Then I'll call the radio station and sheriff's department and see if anyone's looking for him. We can fix him up a nice warm bed in the kennel for the night, and then we'll see tomorrow if anyone claims him or not."

Thunderfoot thought that it was a good idea, and we took the dog home and gave him a huge bowl of dry dog food with a full can of canned food on top of it. He eyes almost popped out when he saw it and he wolfed it down in no time. Then he had a good drink and immediately crawled into the bed in the kennel and went to sleep. The poor guy was exhausted.

That evening, I took him another big bowl of food and some more water and he woke up just long enough to eat again and then went right back to sleep.

"He's been out, trying to survive for a long time and he's pretty tired," Thunderfoot said, as he looked in on the dog. "What are we going to do if nobody claims him?"

"Let's wait and see," I said.

By the next day, we had no information on the dog and nobody called despite several mentions on the radio station of a found dog, so we needed to make a decision as to what to do with our new friend.

"Let's see what Katy thinks of him," I said. "If she likes him, maybe I'll just keep him, but if she doesn't like him, I'll have to find a home for him. I'm not going to turn him out again." Thunderfoot grinned from ear to ear.

We brought the dog into the workshop and I went into the house to get Katy. Both of the dogs were real excited to see each other, and they went into a frenzy of sniffing and posturing, and seemed to get along. We let them be together for a while and just sat and watched. Soon, they were both satisfied that they were friends and laid down side by side to take a nap.

"Well, the princess seems to like him," Thunderfoot said. "Yeah, she seems to like him just fine," I agreed.

The next battle was going to be a bath and cleaning of our new friend. He was filthy and his tail was stiff with burrs, to the point that I didn't think we could even brush them out. We took the brush and began brushing him and finally got out the scissors and began cutting clumps of hair from his tail. When we finished, his tail looked kind of ragged, but it was free of burrs. Once we had him de-burred, we decided to try to give him a bath.

Katy was real interested in what we were doing until we began running water in the bath tub, and then she took off for the living room, not being fond of baths. The new dog was glad for all the attention and didn't know what was happening until we lifted him into the tub and the warm water. He wasn't exactly thrilled at the idea of a bath but didn't fight it, and soon we had him covered in suds and were scrubbing the grime from him. Once we got him wet we could see just how skinny he was. The poor devil was just a skeleton with skin on it. We washed and rinsed him and then toweled him off and turned him loose. He galloped into the living room and played with Katy for a minute, and then took a tour of the house and came back to the living room. He did a couple of circles on the living room floor and flopped down and stretched out and said, "Hmmmmmmm." He was home.

"Looks like he likes it here," Thunderfoot said, smiling.

We watched the two dogs sleeping side by side on the floor and I began to assess what the new guy was. He looked exactly like a golden retriever from the neck to the butt. His head was narrower, like a collie, and he had a white stripe in the middle of his forehead. His tail was more like a collie also, standing up more than a golden's. The rest of him was golden retriever.

"If we keep him, we'll have to think of a name," I said.

"How about Skunk?" Thunderfoot said.

"Skunk?"

"Yeah, he's got that stripe on his head like a skunk."

"No. We need something that goes with Katy.
Katy and ..... "

He was deep in thought. "Katy and... How about Kirby?"

"Kirby," I said. "Yeah, I like that."

Just then Kirby looked up at me. "How do you like that name?"

I asked. Kirby thumped his tail in agreement and went back to sleep.

I waited a week just to be sure nobody would come to claim him and then made an appointment with the vet to get Kirby checked over. He seemed to be fine and got his full dose of vaccinations and de-wormed, just in case he was missing anything from wherever he lived before.

He and Katy became great friends and have gotten along great ever since. Thunderfoot has taken a shine to him since he was the one that found him in the yard.

A few weeks later, we were sitting and watching the two dogs frolicking in the snow and Thunderfoot looked at me and said. "I wonder where Kirby would be right now if we hadn't gone after him?"

"He'd probably be dead," I said. "He wouldn't have made it much longer without food and shelter."

"We did good, huh?" he said, grinning.

"Yeah, we did good."

"Whoever abandoned him must not have taken much interest in him or they would have seen what a nice guy he is," he said, as Kirby came running toward us looking for a little petting. He grabbed Kirby and wrestled him into the snow and soon Katy joined the fun. I watched as the three of them rolled and played in the snow.

"Their loss, our gain," I said.

Thanks, Thunderfoot.

Take Me Out to the Ball Game

"Take a look at what's on my desk," I said to Thunderfoot as he walked into the house after a spring day at school.

"It better be good," he said. "I've just been imprisoned in school on a day that would have been perfect for fishing."

He walked into my office and suddenly I heard him say. "No way, box seats behind the home plate."

He came running back into the living room holding four tickets to a doubleheader at County Stadium for the following Saturday. "Where did you get these?" he asked.

"One of the companies that I buy merchandise from had a drawing and I won. I don't suppose you'd like to go with me?"

"Suppose, you better suppose I will," he said, jumping up and down. "Why don't you ask a couple of your buddies to come, too," I said. "Who should I ask?"

"I don't care. Whoever you want."

He thought a while and then decided on Scott and Trent. They were both kids that came hunting and fishing with us often and I liked both of them, so I said that they were fine with me and off he went to tell them the news.

Saturday came and we got the group together at about 7 a.m. so we could get a good start on the three-hour trip. Of course I figured at least an hour to stop for breakfast and another hour or so for pit stops, and that would put us at the stadium at about noon, which was plenty early for the first game of the doubleheader which started at one o'clock.

We had hardly gone a mile from town when I could hear the two in the back seat whispering something to Thunderfoot. "Just wait a few minutes, I'm sure he's planned for it," he said.

"Planned for what?" I asked.

"Well, Scott is kind of faminished, and he was wondering if we were gonna stop for breakfast soon?"

"We just left town," I said. "Scott, can you last a while if I stop and get some donuts?"

Scott thought that a few donuts would keep him alive for a while, so I stopped at a convenience store and got a half dozen donuts and some cartons of milk to hold them over until we could get to where I was planning to stop for breakfast.

On we went, and soon we were about half way to Milwaukee and I took an exit to a little shopping area that had a breakfast buffet restaurant. "OK guys, this is breakfast."

They were all sacked out and began stretching and yawning and one by one came to life and shuffled into the restaurant.

As we walked through the door, they all looked wide-eyed.

There, laid out in front of them, was every kind of conceivable food that could be eaten for breakfast in the entire country. There were eggs, pancakes, waffles, sausages, bacon, ham, grits, fruit, rolls, cereal, and a few things that I wasn't too sure of what they actually were.

"Anyone who leaves hungry has no one to blame but themselves," I said as they attacked the buffet.

We spent about an hour in the restaurant and the boys sampled practically everything on the menu. They were all sitting back in the booth groaning and moaning about how stuffed they were, as I got up to pay the check. Soon, I was driving on toward the stadium and they were sleeping again.

An hour later, we were coming into Milwaukee and they woke up and began playing some game about license plates that I didn't get the gist of, and it wasn't long until we took the exit to the stadium. We parked and the boys piled out and began excitedly hurrying toward the gate marked on the tickets. I had to hustle to keep up, and when we got to the gate, I gave each of them a ticket and we went inside.

The stadium was filling up, and we got to our seats, which were the best I had ever had. We were right behind home plate and about ten rows up from the field.

"These are awesome seats," Thunderfoot exclaimed, and the other two chimed in with a couple of more "awesomes."

There was a lot of hustle and bustle, and before long the vendors started hawking their overpriced snacks and souvenirs. The boys each had to buy a baseball cap, and soon they were digging into peanuts and popcorn and big glasses of pop.

"How can you guys eat already?" I said.

"We're just lucky." Thunderfoot grinned as he popped a salted in the shell peanut into his mouth. "We're young; we burn up food like a furnace."

A little later, they sang the Star Spangled Banner and the game was on. The boys cheered and booed and were having a great time. About halfway through the fifth inning, Thunderfoot announced that he had to go up and get a Polish sausage.

"The Polish sausage guy hasn't come by here for three innings," he said. "I'm gonna go up and get one. Anybody else want one?"

By then I was beginning to get a bit hungry, so I told him to get me one, too. "No problem," he said and off he went up the steps.

By the seventh inning, he wasn't back yet, and I was beginning to get a little worried. I was getting more worried when game number one ended, and he still wasn't back.

"When the second game starts, all the people will go back to their seats, and I'll go up and see if I can find him by the Polish sausage stand," Scott said.

We waited for the crowd to get back to their seats and the second game was underway. Scott went up the steps and was gone for about fifteen minutes when he returned without Thunderfoot. "I can't see him anywhere," he said. "I looked all over the place."

I was getting pretty worried but didn't know what to do about it. I thought about going up and seeing if they could page him over the PA system but didn't know if that was possible. He had to be someplace in the stadium, but where?

The fourth inning was just over, and I was now beginning to panic. Scott and Trent both assured me that Thunderfoot could take care of himself and not to worry, but I could tell that they, too, were beginning to wonder what had happened to him.

I decided that if he wasn't back by the end of the fifth inning, I was going to see what I could do about having him paged when, all of a sudden, there he was, walking down the aisle to our seats with a big grin on his face.

"Where have you been?" I asked.

"What, why?"

"You left two hours ago for a Polish sausage. Where did you go to get it, Poland?"

"Oh, well, I kinda got turned around a bit, and took a wrong turn," he said nonchalantly.

"So, where were you all that time?"

"Well, when I came back out from all the tunnels, see that scoreboard out there in center field? Well, I was right there."

"Center field?"

"Yup, I could see you guys. I waved but nobody waved back."

"You've got a real sense of direction."

"Yup, that's why I'm such a good guide," he said, grinning.

"Weren't you scared?"

"Why should I be scared? I wasn't lost, just in the wrong part of the stadium. I met a lot of nice people that I visited with. No problem."

"Well," I said, "if you need to go for anything else, take one of these guys with you so you don't get lost. By the way, where's my Polish sausage?"

"Oh, I ate that in center field. I thought it would be cold by the time I got back here. I can go for another for you."

"No thanks. You just stay here where I can keep an eye on you." Look of indignation, then a big grin.

Thanks, Thunderfoot.

 Fly In

Thunderfoot and I were just finishing the dishes when the phone rang. Since I was up to my elbows in soap suds, he answered the phone.

"Oh, hi Lump, yeah, he's here. He's washing the dishes; I'll get him." He held the phone out to me as I dried my hands off

I took the phone and it was Rick, one of my fishing buddies, who was nicknamed Lumpy. We talked a bit and I found that he was looking for two people to go to Canada on a fly-in fishing trip with him and his son the following month.

"Yeah, uh huh, six nights, yeah, oh, that's not bad, uh huh, OK, yeah. Oh yeah, I think I can find a partner," I said, looking at Thunderfoot questioningly. "OK, let's figure on it, the 16th, OK, yeah. I'll call you next week and we can get together and do some planning."

I hung up the phone and went back to the kitchen sink. "Well, what did Lump want?"

"Who? Oh, Lumpy, I forgot you call him that. Oh, he had a fishing trip proposition for me."

Thunderfoot was just about to explode. "OK, what trip did he have to ask you about?"

I acted like I didn't hear him. It was kind of fun to make him sweat, since he always had such great sport making fun of me when he got the chance.

Finally, he came to the sink and took the dishrag from my hand.

"What trip!"

"A fly-in trip to Canada," I said.

His mouth dropped open. "Fly-in, like with a plane?"

"No, like we'll flap our arms real fast. Of course with a plane," I said.

"I hope you were talking about me when you said you had a

partner," he said.

"Well, actually, I guess, well, yeah, who else would I take?" I said. He let out a whoop and began pacing back and forth across the floor. "When are we going?"

"The third week of June. We drive to a little town in Ontario and then take the plane to Marshall Lake and they leave us there for six days and then come back and pick us up."

"That's only a few weeks away; I gotta go pack," he said and started for the door.

"Whoa, we have lots of time to pack. We're going up to Lumpy's this weekend and have a meeting to make a list of gear and food. We have a weight limit, so we have to be careful on what we take."

Saturday afternoon we drove to my friend's house, which was a few miles away, and met up with him and his son Chris. Chris was a couple of years older than Thunderfoot, but they had known each other for many years from fishing and hunting trips they had taken together with us.

We grilled out and then sat down to make a list of items for the trip. We figured out the food needed for each meal, with a meal of fish each day, and then made a list of clothes and fishing equipment for each of us to take.

The cabin came with a boat, motor and gas, for every two fishermen and we had to furnish our fishing gear and food, plus our clothing and a few extra items for good measure. We each had a sixty pound limit on our gear, so we had to pack light.

Thunderfoot was beside himself, worrying about having enough stuff along. He reveled in lots of gear and if it were up to him, he'd take everything he owned.

During the next few weeks we managed to collect everything that was on our lists, and it all got deposited on my front porch. Finally the big day came, and we loaded up and took off for the North Country. Thunderfoot and Chris were so excited that they were babbling like a couple of geese in the back seat as we left town. Twelve hours later, they were sacked out as we pulled into the parking lot of the outfitter that was going to fly us into the lake.

"Wake up, you two sleeping beauties," I said. "We're here." They woke up slowly and finally realized where they were and bounded out of the van and took off for the dock and the floatplane.

"Whoa, you guys, come back here and carry something down there with you," I said, and they each came back and picked up some of the gear.

We met the outfitter, and he introduced us to our pilot, who looked to be just a kid, too. He looked like he was maybe 21, if that, and had shaggy blond hair and an easy attitude. It didn't take him long to start goofing around with the kids, and Lumpy and I looked at each other with a misgiving look.

"How old do you think he is?" I asked.

"I don't know, but if I was a bartender, I'd check him for an ID," he said.

Well, obviously, he knew how to fly the plane or the outfitter wouldn't have hired him. At least we hoped so.

We packed the plane and climbed inside. It was pretty tight, but we were ready and no matter how tight, we were on our way.

The pilot untied the ropes that held the plane, stepped onto the float and climbed in and started the engine. "One of you can come sit up here, eh," he said, looking at me. I climbed up through the little opening in the fuselage and sat in the co-pilot seat. "Buckle up, eh."

He revved the engine up, and we began taxiing down the lake. It was a little choppy on the water and the ride was pretty bumpy. We went a long way down the lake, and then he pushed his feet on some pedals and we turned around and were looking back at where we had come from.

"OK then, here we go," he said, and he pushed in the throttle and off we went down the lake. It was noisy and really bumpy and we kept going and going and going, toward some orange milk jugs that were anchored down the lake a short way. As we began to pick up speed, we lifted off the water a little and then banged down again, only to lift again. The milk jugs were getting closer and closer, and I was beginning to think we weren't going to leave the lake before we got to them, when suddenly, we lifted up and cruised right up over the end of the lake.

I looked over my shoulder, and Thunderfoot's face was white.

He grinned and blew out his breath, like he had been holding it for a long time.

Once we were up, it was nice, and we could see down into the trees and swamps below. I leaned over to the pilot and asked him if he ever saw bears or moose or any other wildlife, and he shook his head yes.

On we flew, and everyone was getting pretty comfortable when suddenly the plane dropped like a rock over onto its left side and fell toward the woods below.

"A couple of moose, eh." The pilot pointed and grinned. I looked around in the cockpit for my breakfast, because I was sure it had slipped out when we dropped so fast. The rest of the group was hanging on with white knuckles in the back.

"Jeez, you don't have to show us any more wildlife if that's OK with you," I shouted.

The pilot smiled and took us back up to regular flying altitude. On we went for another twenty minutes until suddenly he put the plane over on its side again and began dropping onto a fairly large lake. "This is it," he said, motioning toward the lake with his head.

We dropped like a headshot duck and leveled off just as we got to the water, and then made a nice landing about a football field away from the dock. The pilot taxied up to the dock and shut down the engine and jumped out and tied up the plane.

"Here we are, eh."

Thunderfoot looked a little green around the gills as he climbed out of the back of the plane. "Was that fun or what?" he said, clutching his stomach.

When everyone was out on the dock, we began unloading all the gear. Soon we were unloaded, and we walked up to the cabin. The pilot showed us how to turn on the gas tanks that were outside behind the building and light the gas stove and gas refrigerator inside. He got a couple of outboard motors out of a little shed and showed us where the gas and oars and other gear were. Then he took us down a path that led back into the woods to the privy.

"So, when you get some fish, clean them and then take the guts out in the boat and dump them in the lake," he said.

"Why not bury them?" Thunderfoot asked.

"The bears will come and dig them up," he said. "The last guys here had a bear right up by the cabin, eh."

Thunderfoot shook his head yes, his mouth hanging open.

"If something happens that you need help, lay a white tee shirt on the dock, and someone will come and help you. I'll fly by in a couple days and check on you, and any other plane that sees a white shirt on the dock will stop. So don't dry your laundry on the dock, eh?"

We thanked him and soon he was taking off for home, leaving us in the middle of nowhere with tee shirt communications.

Thunderfoot watched the plane as it disappeared over the trees.

"How far are we from other people, do you think?"

"Oh, it's a long way to a town, probably a hundred miles or so, but there could be some other fishermen on another lake near here."

He nodded and picked up some of the gear and walked up the dock to the cabin.

We all pitched in and soon we had everything that needed to be inside the cabin carried up. We went inside and found that it was pretty primitive. There were two sets of cots stacked up on top of each other like bunk beds and a stove that was built out of a 55-gallon barrel in the middle of the room for heat. Then there was a gas range and a gas refrigerator and a kitchen table and half a dozen chairs, two of which matched. There were some open cupboards on the wall and a sink that had no plumbing attached to it. Underneath the sink was a bucket that caught the water, which was then hauled outside and dumped. The water for washing and drinking came from the lake.

"It looks like we have roommates," Thunderfoot said, looking at the mattress.

Obviously, there were several mice that lived in the cabin when it wasn't occupied by people because there were mouse pellets all over the place.

"Well, let's carry the mattresses outside and shake them off and then we can start cleaning up the place before we bring our stuff in," I said.

We all pitched in and soon had the cabin ship-shape.

"We've got plenty of time to go fishing, don't we?" Thunderfoot asked.

"Yeah, I guess. It probably doesn't get dark till 10 or 11 o'clock up here, so I guess we can go and try to catch some fish for supper."

Off we went, to the dock. We chose a couple of boats from the pile stacked on the dock and put two motors on them and put a gas tank, life jackets and oars in each one. Then we loaded our tackle boxes and poles and shoved off.

Since it was our first time on the lake, we stayed together, making each of us feel a little safer. I had a map of the lake provided by the outfitter, and we took off for a place where a small stream ran in. When we got there, we found a little rapids where the stream entered the lake and began casting into the pool below the rapids. It didn't take but a minute for Thunderfoot to rear back on his rod and boat a nice walleye. He held it up, grinning from ear to ear.

"Look at that beauty," he said.

Just then Lumpy and Chris both set their hooks into identical fish and a second later I felt a tick on my line and soon was boating another identical walleye.

"Jeez, they're all twins," Thunderfoot said.

We fished for another hour and had more than enough fish for supper, so we motored back to the dock and tied up the boats. There was a fish-cleaning bench on the shore by the dock and the boys ran ahead and got their fillet knives and a pail for fillets and met us on their way back as Lumpy and I went to the cabin to begin preparing the rest of the supper. Soon, Chris came up to the cabin with the fillets and asked, "Should we take the guts out in the boat?" I looked at Lumpy, and he shrugged like he didn't see anything wrong with the two boys going out alone.

"Yeah, but don't goof around. That water's really cold and if you fall in, you'll freeze up."

We watched out the front window as they jumped into the boat and took off to dump the guts. They looked like Tom and Huck, only dressed a little warmer. Thunderfoot was driving the boat and they went about a half mile from shore and then stopped and dumped the fish guts. Then, of course, instead of turning around and coming back, they had to do a few circles and jump their wakes before they returned. We watched them in the diminishing light, two kids, having the time of their lives.

That evening, we ate fresh walleye fillets, fried potatoes and beans, and if I had ever had a meal that was better, I couldn't remember it.

"Holy cow, I'm gonna explode," Thunderfoot said, patting his belly. We heated some water for dishes and before Lumpy and I had them done, both of the boys were dozing in their chairs.

It was getting chilly, so I went outside and carried in an arm full of firewood that the last group of fishermen had left for us. I filled the barrel stove up and soon the fire was crackling and popping. We all got ready and climbed into our sleeping bags and were asleep in no time. The last thing I remembered was that the stove was so hot that it was glowing red and it lit the cabin with an eerie glow.

Blam! Blam! Blam!

I woke with a start. Blam! I couldn't figure out at first where I was and finally I realized that I was in the cabin when, Blam!, the sound came again. I looked up from the warmth of my sleeping bag and could see Thunderfoot in his underwear and tee shirt, barefoot, with a frying pan held over his head. There was some light coming in through the windows from the stars and moon. Blam! He hit something on the kitchen counter.

"What in the Sam Hill are you doing?" I said.

"Those mice are all over the place. They were eating our popcorn and I heard them, so I'm smacking them when they come back for more. Shhhh, here comes one." Blam!

By now everyone was awake and watching the show. Thunderfoot would stand real still, and soon a mouse would sneak out onto the counter toward the bag of unpopped popcorn. He would let them get out in the open and then slam them with the pan, and lift the lifeless carcass up by the tail and drop it into the stove.

"How many have you got so far?" Chris said.

"I think that makes 18 or 19," Thunderfoot said. "I kinda lost count."

You could see him grinning in the low light, as he turned to look at us. "I'll quit when I get an even two dozen."

The action slowed up a while later. Either he had killed all the mice, or they were getting wise to him and staying out of sight.

"Well, that'll be enough for tonight," he said, and climbed back into his sleeping bag. "Night all."

The next morning, it was freezing in the cabin. The stove was out and so I hurriedly got into my clothes and went out to get some kindling and wood to get things warmed up. It didn't take long for the stove to heat up, and I began making breakfast, which aroused the rest of the crew.

"Hmmmm, I smell food," Thunderfoot said from down inside his sleeping bag.

"I thought you'd never be able to eat again," I said.

"Actually, all that mouse slamming made me pretty hungry," he said, as his head poked up from the sleeping bag with a big grin. "What a mouse killer I am, huh?"

"I found a whole bunch of traps in the drawer over there," I said.

"Let's set some of them with some peanut butter and maybe we can get rid of the rest of them."

He jumped up and dressed and began preparing the trap line, while I finished getting breakfast ready.

After breakfast, we hauled up some water from the lake and cleaned up the dishes. Then we heated up some more for washing, and in an hour or so, we were at the dock ready to go fishing for the day. We had made up a box with a couple of frying pans and a kettle and some cooking oil and plates and utensils for a shore lunch. The night before I had boiled some potatoes which I put in the refrigerator overnight, and they were in the box, too.

"Each boat saves six fish for lunch," I said as we took off "And we'll meet on this rock at about noon," I said, pointing to a spot on the map.

Off we went in different directions to explore the lake. It wasn't that we didn't want to fish with Chris and Lumpy, but this way we had a better chance of finding some good spots to fish by searching more of the lake.

Thunderfoot and I headed up to the end of the lake that was shallow. We wanted to find some places to fish for northerns. Now, in Canada, the locals think that a northern is a junk fish and hate them. Where we come from, we love to fish for them. They're good fighters, and just about always willing to bite, and good eating if you take them home. We began to see more and more weeds and soon could see that we were coming into a bay that was filled with a huge weed bed, probably the home of lots of northerns. We shut off the motor and began casting spoons into the weed pockets and in a short time were battling a northern each. Once we found the spoon that they liked best, we got a fish on almost every cast. We were having a great time as we drifted deeper and deeper into the bay.

Suddenly, Thunderfoot whispered, "Look, there's a moose."

I looked the way he was looking and, sure enough, there was a huge bull moose standing in the water about two hundred yards away from us.

The moose was standing knee deep in the water and didn't seem to be bothered by us. He stood there looking at us, and then suddenly stuck his head into the water and a while later came up with a mouthful of aquatic weeds that he proceeded to munch on. Soon he went down again and picked up another mouthful of weeds. He was huge, with broad antlers and looked like a big black Buick. His antlers had weeds and lily pads hanging from them.

"Let's try to work our way over closer, and I'll get some pictures," Thunderfoot whispered.

I put the oars into the oarlocks quietly and began rowing slowly toward the moose. I kept the front of the boat toward the moose so Thunderfoot would have a clear view for his pictures. We kept going closer and closer, and Thunderfoot was kneeling on the front seat taking a picture every so often. The moose didn't seem to mind a bit.

We were only about twenty yards away, and I stopped rowing, thinking that it was about as close as we should get.

"Go closer," Thunderfoot urged.

Against my better judgment, I pushed on the oars a few more times and we slid closer yet. Now we were only about ten yards away, and the moose had his head under water. When he came up, he looked at us and he didn't look friendly. He let out a bellow and shook his head, causing water and plants to fly through the air.

Suddenly, he began walking our way.

"Go back, quick," Thunderfoot said, looking over his shoulder at me.

I reached back and pulled the cord on the motor and it

didn't take. I pulled out the choke and pulled the cord again, and this time it took but I still had it choked, so it sputtered. I pushed the choke in and revved the handle and it roared to life. I reached around the side and slid the gear shift lever into reverse and when I looked around again, the moose was only a few feet from the boat and was coming on a dead run. The water was flying from his hooves as he rushed toward the boat.

"Go back, go back, fast!" Thunderfoot said. He was still kneeling on the front seat of the boat.

I gunned the motor and we began moving backwards, but not fast enough to get ahead of the moose.

Thunderfoot was now leaning backwards away from the moose, who looked like he was ten feet tall. "Go fast, go fast!"

The weeds were fouling the prop, and I couldn't get the boat to move any faster without turning it around, and I thought the moose would surely catch up to us if I tried to turn it.

Thunderfoot now crawled down off the seat backwards and was on his hands and knees, crawling backwards toward the back of the boat. The moose's head was towering over the front seat. He let out an enraged bellow as he bumped the front of the boat with his hooves.

"We gotta go fast, we gotta go now!" he said as he tumbled over backwards and landed at my feet.

Then, just as suddenly as he charged us, the moose stopped and stood there shaking his head at us as we motored backward through the weeds. We were about thirty feet away when I thought it was safe to turn the boat around. As soon as we got turned around, we made tracks for a safer distance. Once we were about a hundred yards away, I stopped the boat.

Thunderfoot was sitting on the floor of the boat at my feet. He looked up over his shoulder at me. "Holy cow, I almost peed myself." I began laughing. He just sat there with his mouth hanging open. "I thought we were goners," he said. "Did you do that on purpose?" "No way, the weeds were getting stuck in the prop. These boats aren't made to go backwards. That's why they have a point on the front."

"Wow, I didn't know those things could go so fast and were that big. That thing was twenty feet tall."

"Well, probably more like eight or nine feet tall," I said.

"You weren't looking up at him from where I was sitting," he said.

Just then I noticed that he had bits of weed from the bull's antlers hanging from his hair.

"Maybe that's enough weed bed fishing for a while. What do you say we go and catch some walleyes for lunch?" I said.

"Yeah, someplace away from the weed beds would be fine with me." We stopped at a little island and began catching walleyes off a reef that stuck out into the water. In a short time, we had our share of "lunch fish" and headed up the lake to the meeting place with Lumpy and Chris. They were already there and had a fire going.

"How was your morning?" Lumpy asked.

"Oh, just ducky," Thunderfoot exclaimed. "My illustrious partner here tried to get me trampled by a huge enraged moose."

Lumpy looked at me questioningly.

"We got a little too close to a moose and he didn't like us, but I wasn't the one who kept saying 'get a little closer' if I remember right," I said, looking accusingly at Thunderfoot.

"I was looking through the viewfinder of the camera and he looked pretty small until he charged and then I looked at him for real and he was mega big," he said.

That got a good laugh from our friends, but Thunderfoot still kept accusing me of some kind of plot to get him murdered by a moose.

We had a fabulous lunch. Actually, it was the exact same thing we had last evening for dinner, and then all laid back on the rock for a siesta in the mid-day sun. About an hour later, Thunderfoot woke up and began waking everybody so we could go and do some fishing during the afternoon.

We spent the rest of the day on the water and that evening,

the boys cut some firewood while Lumpy and I prepared supper. We were just finishing up when the boys came in with an armload each of firewood, and dropped it on the floor near the stove. It was beginning to cool off, so we lit a fire and ate supper as the cabin began to warm up and feel real cozy.

After supper we had a rousing game of Monopoly and it was getting to be bedtime when Thunderfoot and Chris decided to go out and bring in some more firewood. They were barely out the door when they came crashing back in screaming like banshees.

"There's a skunk right outside the door!" Thunderfoot yelled as he nearly tore the screen door off the hinges.

We snuck over to the door and sure enough, there was a big skunk scratching through some of our garbage that we had bagged up to put in the garbage can.

We closed the door and decided to get along with what firewood we had for now.

That night it began to blow and rain, and by morning, it was really cold inside the cabin. The skunk was gone and we carried in some firewood, but it was sopping wet, and wouldn't burn. We finally decided to pour a little gas on some kindling and got that going and that dried out the wood enough to get it going, too, and soon had the cabin toasty warm again.

We had breakfast and tidied up the place a bit but took our time because the weather looked pretty threatening. In another half hour, it began raining really hard and the wind whipped up and the lake began to look less and less inviting. Soon big waves were crashing in on the dock, so we all donned our rain gear and went down to lash the boats down and take everything that we wanted to keep dry up to the cabin. When we got back inside the nice warm cabin, we all decided that we could stand a day inside instead of out on the angry lake.

"Let's play some cards," Thunderfoot suggested. "Chris and I will take on you two old guys, twenty-five cents a game and ten cents a bump." I looked at Lumpy, and he smiled and nodded yes. He and I had been partners many times in Euchre games, and were pretty good partners.

We cut cards to see who would deal and soon the game was going along at a good pace. Lumpy and I took the lead, but then Thunderfoot got a lone hand, which scored four points and he and Chris moved ahead of us. Soon, he got another loner and the game was over. "It looks like you experts owe us fifty-five cents," he said smugly.

Lumpy and I paid up and then I said, "How about fifty cents a game and a quarter a bump?" The boys grinned and agreed.

We began pretty even and soon Thunderfoot got another lone hand and the boys took a lead. The Chris got a loner two hands later and we were behind by eight points. I tried .to push a poor hand and we got bumped, and the next hand Lumpy got us into trouble with a shaky hand also and we got another bump. It was Thunderfoot's deal and he managed to dump the cards on the floor for the fourth or fifth time while he shuffled, and when the cards were dealt, he had another lone hand. Wham, we were beaten again, and this time it cost us a dollar each.

"Care to try to get your money back?" Thunderfoot asked, grinning like the cat that had just eaten the canary.

"OK, wise guy, buck a game and fifty cents a bump?" I said.

"You're on."

Well, it wasn't pretty. Lumpy and I got bumped the first two times we tried to make trump, Thunderfoot dealt himself two loners and Chris got one loner, and soon we were at the point where we were almost beaten again. We were playing a hand that I had made trump, and I took a trick and led an ace. Thunderfoot trumped it and that beat us. As we threw the cards in, I noticed that Thunderfoot was trying to slide his last card under the rest of the cards lying on the table. I grabbed his hand and took the card from him. He was holding the suit that he had trumped. "You little cheater, you reneged."

"What? Was that suit played?" He was trying hard to look innocent.

"You know darn well it was played, you cheater."

94

It was Thunderfoot's deal and he dumped the cards onto the floor again.

"For someone with such good luck, you sure can't shuffle the cards worth a darn," I said. But, suddenly, I got a thought. Every time he got the cards, he managed to drop them on the floor, and every time he did that, he got a lone hand. I watched as he picked up the cards and put them into a pile, with his hands under the table, and then shuffled. But his shuffle was not exactly a shuffle. It was more like just a shuffle of the top few cards. He dealt the cards out and naturally turned over an ace. I had nothing, so I passed. Chris passed, and Lumpy passed. Thunderfoot picked up the ace and passed the rest of the cards over to Chris. "I'll play it alone," he announced.

I looked at Lumpy and he realized the same thing just as I had.

Thunderfoot was stacking the deck and getting lone hands almost every time he dealt. "You little cheater!" I said.

Thunderfoot looked at me with that choirboy look of innocence.

"What are you talking about?" You could almost see the halo above his head.

"I'm talking about you getting a lone hand every time you deal," I said.

"I'm just lucky," he said, keeping up the innocent act.

"Yeah, well, let's see your cards," I said, grabbing the cards from his hand. He had the four highest cards and an ace. He looked over at me indignantly. "That's it, I quit. If you're gonna look at my cards, I don't want to play any more." He tried hard to make Lumpy and I believe that he was just lucky, but we weren't buying it. That was the end of our card game.

Later, we decided to play Monopoly, and Lumpy and I didn't fare any better. Chris and Thunderfoot ganged up on us and soon they both had properties with lots of houses and hotels, and Lumpy and I had mismatched pieces of property that were worthless. We were both being whittled down dollar by dollar, when I landed on one of Thunderfoot's green properties with three houses on it. "That will be $950," he said.

It was about enough to break me, but I began counting money and after I had mortgaged almost everything, I came up with the money. A couple of turns later, Chris landed on the same property, and Thunderfoot said to him, "That's $600."

"Whoa, wait a minute. How come I paid $950 and Chris only has to pay $600?"

Thunderfoot looked puzzled, then scratched his head, and you could tell he was cooking up some story in his head. "Oh, my gosh, I must have read the wrong line on this card. I thought I had four houses on it but only had three. I guess I owe you a refund of $250."

He counted out the money and I took it, smiling to myself that I had caught him cheating again. I picked up the dice, and then it hit me. The little rat owed me $350, not $250!

"That's it, I quit, you little cheater," I said.

Thunderfoot put on his most innocent face but he knew we were onto him, so that was the end of our game day in the cabin. It had cost Lumpy and me a little cash but in the long run it had passed the time, and even though we were playing with a couple of cheaters, we did have fun. We ate supper, sat and talked a while and went to bed, glad to get the rainy day over with.

The next morning it was sunny and beautiful, and we all went out and had a great day of fishing. Thunderfoot and I caught dozens of northerns while fishing with spoons along a string of islands and then we all met for shore lunch.

That afternoon we went to an area that was supposed to have lake trout and fished for them without much success.

On the way back to camp, Thunderfoot and I came around an island and got a glimpse of a black bear running from the shoreline just ahead of us. We stopped on the lake by where we had seen the bear but couldn't find him, so we went on home. "I wonder if that's the bear that came into the camp when the last guys were here?" Thunderfoot asked.

That night, I woke up with Nature calling me in a most urgent manner. Now, the privy was behind the cabin, about fifty yards back into the woods. There was a little path through the trees back to it. It was built of logs and not exactly the place you wanted to go to in the middle of the night. Why they had chosen to build it so far away from the cabin escaped me, but I supposed the obvious aromatic scents that wafted from it were less noticeable if it was farther away. That did me no good in the middle of the night. As hard as I tried, I couldn't go back to sleep and the longer I waited, the more urgent I needed to get up and get going.

Finally, I couldn't wait any longer and got up and slipped on my sweatpants and a jacket and some shoes over my bare feet. There was still a glow of light from the stove, and I looked on top of the refrigerator for the flashlight that was suppose to be sitting there. We had designated one flashlight as the privy light, and it was supposed to be there at all times, just for this kind of emergency, but it was gone. I searched and searched but couldn't find it and the longer I searched, the more urgent my need to go became. There was no more waiting, so I decided to go without it.

I walked out of the cabin and it was dark. It was as dark as I have ever seen it. No stars, no streetlights, no moon, just complete darkness. There was a breeze blowing through the tops of the trees making a spooky howling sound. I stood on the porch for a couple of seconds to let my eyes adjust, but still couldn't make out anything that looked like a path. I started toward where I thought the path was, and began walking slowly, with my hand out in front of me trying to feel my way back to the privy. This was insanity! Not only could I not find my way back there, but if I did, the odds of me finding my way back to the cabin were slim. And then I remembered the bear. We had seen that bear just down the lake from the cabin earlier in the evening. Suppose he had come up to check out our garbage. I imagined my hand out in front of me, coming in contact with a wet, cold nose, and then feeling up higher to a hairy forehead, and the bear opening his mouth and snapping my hand off, and I became utterly terrified.

I couldn't take another step. The hair on the back of my neck was standing straight up, but I couldn't go back until I did my job, so civility be damned, I dropped my sweatpants and let her go right on the path to the privy. I had a roll of toilet paper with me and hastily finished up and sprinted back to the cabin, knowing that at any second I would hear a roar and a giant bear would spring on me and eat me. By the time I got on the porch, I was shaking like a leaf and could barely open the screen door. Now that I was so close to safety, I became even more terrified as I groped for the handle of the door. I finally found the door handle and flung the door open, jumped inside and slammed the door shut.

Once I made it inside, I felt pretty foolish, but I was still shaking from the cold and the fright. I slipped back into bed and went right to sleep.

"Oh, my gosh! Who did this?" I heard Thunderfoot bellow outside the back door.

I groggily rolled over and lay there, wondering what he was hollering about as he came through the back door.

"Who pooped on the back path?" he asked.

The other two of our party, the innocent ones just looked stupefied, wondering what the heck he was talking about. I tried to look innocent and asked him what he was yelling about.

"Somebody pooped on the path." "Maybe it was a bear," I suggested. "A bear that used Charmin?" Everybody looked at me.

"Where was the flashlight that was supposed to be for the privy?" "Oh, I had that in my bed, in case I needed to go out during the night," Thunderfoot said.

"Well, had the flashlight been where it was supposed to be, there might not be poop on the path," I said.

"Oh, well, in that case, I guess we can forgive you," he said magnanimously.

"In that case, take the shovel out and get rid of it," I said. "And put the flashlight back up on the refrigerator where it's supposed to be."

He didn't argue for a change.

Later that day, we were out fishing, when Thunderfoot took a can of chewing tobacco out of his pocket and tapped it against his hand, and took a pinch of the nasty stuff and put it in his lip, spilling it all over the bottom of the boat.

He put the can away and went on fishing as if this was a normal happening.

I just looked at him and kept looking until he said, "What?" "What did you just do? Did you put some chew in your mouth?" "Yeah, Chris gave it to me. He chews, you know."

No, I didn't know.

"Just because Chris chews doesn't mean you're going to," I said.

"Do you suppose your mom would appreciate seeing you with a big wad of that stuff in your face?"

He just looked at me and shrugged.

By now he had had the stuff in his mouth for about five minutes, and I could see he was swallowing the juice, so I thought I'd give him a little more time and see what happened.

He sat in the front of the boat and began to look a little pale.

Soon, he kind of laid his head back on the edge of the boat and slid down on the seat, so he could partially lie down.

"What's the matter, big shot?"

"I'm feeling a little dizzy, kinda woozy in my stomach," he mumbled.

He kept getting paler and paler, and suddenly, he threw his fishing pole into the bottom of the boat and hung his head over the side and "fed the ducks."

"Oh, I think I'm gonna die," he murmured.

"Good, I hope you feel terrible. Remember that the next time you think about putting that junk in your mouth," I said, without any pity.

He laid there for quite a while and finally felt well enough to fish again. That evening, I saw him go over to Chris and give him back the can of snuff. I think he learned his lesson.

We spent our last day on the lake and that evening after supper, Thunderfoot was suddenly missing, so I walked out on the porch to look for him. I could see him down on the dock by the starlight and walked down and sat by him on the bench.

"What a week," I said.

"Gosh, I can't believe we've been here a week already. What a great time this has been. I can't believe I'm in a place like this. I never thought I'd do something like this in my whole life," he said. We sat silently for a while, listening to the sounds of the water lapping at the sides of the boats.

"Just look at all those stars," he said. "Pretty awesome," I said.

"They look clearer and closer than they do at home," he said. "The air is clearer, and there isn't any other light to hide them up here."

Just then the Northern Lights began dancing across the north horizon. We watched as they climbed into the sky and began swirling and sparkling and making vivid patterns in the night sky. Bright shafts of gold and red climbed and then fell back, like waves on a pond.

He put his arm on my shoulder. "You know how much I appreciate you bringing me on this trip, and all the other trips and other stuff that you do for me. I don't know how to thank you enough," he said.

"You just did. Nothing else required," I said as I gave him a squeeze around the shoulders.

Soon Lumpy and Chris came down to the boat dock and joined us. The four of us sat and watched Mother Nature's light show. It was the perfect ending to a perfect week.

Thanks, Thunderfoot.

State Fair Fun

"Our State Fair is a great State Fair, don't miss it, don't even be late." Thunderfoot was singing as he came across the backyard toward me. I was on my hands and knees pulling weeds from the garden.

"My, gosh, what did you do with the money?" I asked.

"What money?"

"The money your mom gave you for singing lessons," I said.

"Oh, real funny, I'll have you know that I'm an excellent singer," he said indignantly.

Actually he wasn't half bad, but I always took the opportunity to poke a little fun at him whenever I could. I was usually way behind in the practical joke category because he was always on the lookout for a way to make fun of me.

"Have you ever gone to the State Fair?" he asked.

"Yeah, a long time ago. Why?"

"Oh, I just thought it might be a fun thing to do, and it's starting this weekend, you know."

I hadn't been to the State Fair for many years, and actually it did seem like it would be a good time, so I agreed that we should go. We made plans to go on the following Saturday. Thunderfoot asked if he could take his pal Dillon along and I said that was OK.

Saturday morning, we left early since it was almost a three-hour drive to the fairgrounds. We didn't go far until we had to stop for a breakfast break, and as soon as we were back on the road, the two boys both snuggled down in their seats and napped until we were at the fairgrounds parking lot. We parked and went to the entrance and got our tickets and began looking at all the fun stuff that the fair had to offer.

We had to go to the rides first, and I mostly watched as the boys climbed onto the rides and flew through the air on various contraptions that went round and round and up and down. I was content to watch from the sidelines on most of the rides, but the boys got me to get onto a few, most of which were not exactly my type of entertainment.

After a couple of hours, we had to stop for lunch and had brats, corn on the cob and cream puffs for dessert. The boys were ready for some timeout, so we decided to go through the exhibits in the barns and see some of the animals and things that the fair was really about.

First we went into the sheep barn and looked at the many kinds of sheep and lambs that were all finely groomed and being shown. Then we went to the pig barn, but didn't linger too long there because of the aromatic nature of the place. Next came the rabbits and other pet-type critters, including the fancy poultry exhibits.

As we were walking down the aisles, Thunderfoot and Dillon stopped at a cage that held some fancy chickens, and Thunderfoot lifted up the little door and stuck his hand into the cage and took an egg that one of the hens had laid that day.

"What are you doing?" I asked.

"What, nothing."

"What are you going to do with that egg?"

"Egg, what egg?" he said, giving me his most innocent look.

"The egg you took from that cage."

"Oh, that egg. I'm just gonna take it and find someplace to put it." I looked at him with a disapproving look, but he ignored me and kept walking away, so I just gave up and joined him and Dillon as they left the building.

"Let's see the cows next," he said, as he led the way into the dairy barn exhibit.

As we walked in, we came 'to the bulls first, and they were truly impressive. I had never seen a bovine of any nature that was as huge as some of the big bulls that were tethered to the stalls. Some of them were so huge that they were standing halfway out into the walkway and we had to get uncomfortably close to the rear ends of them to get by.

Thunderfoot and Dillon were goofing around and making wisecracks about the bull's anatomy and I gave them a disapproving look. I tried to hurry them past that part of the barn before they made one of the huge animals mad.

We started down the next aisle, and soon the two boys were making eyes at a young girl who was brushing one of the cows. She was a young farm girl with blond hair and was as cute as they come. She apparently was spending a lot of time in the barn because there was a lawn chair and a trunk with lots of clothes and things in it. Her blond hair was tied up in a ponytail, and she smiled at the boys as they came by. Thunderfoot was making eyes at her, flashing his baby blues, trying to impress her. She was trying to act unimpressed, but you could see that she was enjoying the show, too.

As they walked by, Thunderfoot slipped the egg that he had pilfered earlier from his pocket and showed it to her and then slipped it into the pocket of Dillon's shorts when he wasn't looking.

The cow that the girl was brushing, raised her tail just then and began peeing into the gutter of the barn. The cow's tail had been carefully shaved and just a little powder puff of hair was left on the very tip. As she let go her stream, the powder puff was just at the right angle and got soaked with the pee. Just then, Thunderfoot smacked Dillon in the pocket where the egg was and took off running down the aisle, laughing like a fool, thinking he had impressed the girl by breaking the egg in Dillon's pocket.

He had only taken about half a step when the cow raised her tail and began to whip it up over her back to swat a fly. The tail flew into the path of Thunderfoot who was running past her backside, trying to get away from Dillon. The little muff of hair on the end of the dripping cow's tail hit him in the open mouth at about mid-swing, and made a kind of "Splooosh" sound as it hit. He stopped, dead in his tracks, as the cow pee splattered allover his face and shirt, and over his shoulder onto Dillon, who was chasing him.

There he stood for a second or two, like in stop motion, with his hands spread out to the sides like he had been crucified. Then he turned around, cow pee dripping from his mouth and nose.

"Oh, my God, I got hit by cow pee!" he stammered.

Dillon fell over backwards onto the floor and doubled up with laughter. The cute little girl fell back onto a couple of hay bales laughing, and fortunately, there was a lawn chair right behind me. I sat down in it, laughing until I thought I'd have a coronary.

Poor Thunderfoot just stood there, dripping.

Pretty soon, everyone in the barn was laughing and pointing at the boy covered with fresh cow pee. Thunderfoot just stood there with his arms out to the side, waiting for somebody to come to his rescue.

Finally, an older man, possibly the girl's father, came over and pointed Thunderfoot to a water hose on the floor. He walked stiff legged over to it and the man hosed him off.

Thunderfoot's mouth was still wide open and the man squirted water into it to rinse out the cow pee. Dillon went over and washed off the over-splash that had hit him and turned his pocket inside out and rinsed out the egg that had started the whole episode.

Thunderfoot came back and I was still having a hard time catching my breath. 1 had tears running down my face and was panting from laughing so hard.

"I suppose you think this is funny," he said.

"I think this is hilarious," I said, starting to laugh again.

"Let's go. I've seen enough cows for a long time," he said and stomped out of the barn.

Dillon and I followed him outside. "Well, anyone want anything to drink or eat?" I asked.

Thunderfoot glared at me. Dillon said, "Yeah, I'm a little thirsty. I think I could drink something. How about you?" he said, looking at Thunderfoot.

"Oh, you two are a real riot. Just a laugh a minute," he

said. "Let's go to the tee shirt stand, and I'll buy you a new shirt."

He perked up at that. "So, you do feel sorry for me?"

"No, I just don't want you sitting in my car with that cow pee shirt all the way home."

"Gee thanks, you're such a swell pal," he said, trying to pout. Then he began to grin. "I guess it was pretty funny, probably. But I don't think I made a very good impression on that cute little blonde girl."

Probably not, but I'll bet she'll never forget him.

Thanks, Thunderfoot.

Fore No More

"Are you sure you know what you're doing?" I asked.

Thunderfoot just looked at me with one of his exasperated looks.

"Of course, I know what I'm doing," he said.

"Well, I better be able to watch my TV when we're done, and it better be the same as before," I said.

He had taken the cable and wires off the back of my new TV and was attaching some kind of electronic game to it so we could play with his new game machine. I hadn't been in favor of the idea in the first place, and now that I could see what he was doing with all the wires and gadgets that he was attaching, it made me pretty nervous.

Finally, he had everything working to his satisfaction and told me to sit on the couch, so he could show me how to play.

"You see, this thing is the joystick. It controls right, left, up, down, and this thing makes the guy jump. Now, you start here, and see, he jumps and now you go right ... "

I watched as some little cartoon character climbed over blocks and obstructions in some kind of race to someplace important. It seemed easy enough, so I took the joystick and began maneuvering the thing that made the little man jump and run, and apparently I did something wrong, because the machine went, woo, woo, woo, and my turn was over.

Thunderfoot took the joystick and began running and jumping and seemed to be having a great time for the next ten minutes or so, until he finally had racked up several hundred thousand points to my couple of dozen, and the machine went woo, woo, woo, and he handed the joystick back to me.

"Your turn."

I moved the little man over one block and began to go over another, when the machine went woo, woo, woo, and I was again

106

finished with my turn.

"Too bad, gotta move faster," he said, maneuvering the little man through the maze of obstructions. Fifteen minutes later, I was reading a magazine, when he finished his turn and handed me the joystick.

"You gotta pay attention. You'll never learn this if you don't watch," he said.

"I'll never learn if I get to play for ten seconds and then have to watch you for half an hour. Isn't there some game that we can play that I get to play for a while, too?"

"This is the easiest one," he said, shrugging his shoulders.
"Well, this is lots of fun," I said, unenthusiastically.

I took my turn, which lasted about a full minute and then gave the joystick back to him and went into the kitchen to fix us a snack. When I came back he was still playing, so I went back to my magazine.

"I guess you don't wanna play?"

"Is it that obvious?"

"OK, what should we do then?"

I couldn't think of anything right off the bat, so he began taking the game apart and restoring my TV: When we turned it back on, miraculously it worked and just happened to be tuned to a channel that had a golf game on.

"I used to play that silly game," I said.

"No foolin'? I didn't know that. Why did you quit?"

"Well, I wasn't very good at it, and it's a frustrating game," I said.

"I've always wanted to try it," he said.

"I've still got my clubs somewhere here," I said.

"No kidding. Let's get them out and see them."

We went out to the garage and dug the clubs out of an old cabinet.

They were dusty and dirty but still in good condition, considering that I hadn't played with them for almost twenty years.

Thunderfoot took an iron out and began chopping holes in my backyard, trying to hit a ball across the street.

"Take it easy on the grass," I said.

"Let's go play," he said, shaking his head yes.

I wasn't too enthused about the idea, but I guessed that he probably would never let up on me about it, so I agreed. We dusted off the dubs and drove about 15 miles to a public golf course.

I showed him how to grip the dub and how to tee it up and then drove my first ball straight into the rough on the right side of the fairway.

"Good shot," he said, enthusiastically. "That's down there a long ways."

He teed up a ball, lined up his shot and made a perfect drive straight down the middle of the fairway half way to the green.

"Are you sure you never played this before?"

"Nope, just watched it on TV a couple of times."

We played to the green and I three putted for a double bogey while Thunderfoot took a par.

"That's good, huh, a par?"

"Yes, that's good."

The next couple of holes were the same. He played like Tiger Woods and I played like, well, like me.

"This is fun. How come you quit playing?" he asked.

"Well, I played in high school, and then in college I had a friend who was on the golf team and he taught me a lot of good stuff, and I got pretty good at it. Then I began to get worse. I don't know what happened, but my game got worse and worse, so I decided to quit rather than play like crap."

He shook his head like a psychiatrist. "Uh huh, uh huh."

On we went and a few holes later, I was playing my ball to the green, which was just about 40 yards ahead. The only problem was that there were two big pine trees right in line with it, so rather than chip around them, I decided to make a high shot over them, so my ball would land right on the middle of the green.

I lined it up and made sure to get under the ball, gave it a mighty whack, and it went up and up and hit the left pine tree dead center. It hit about five feet down from the top, made a "whop" sound and bounced back right over my head and landed on the fairway behind me.

I could hear Thunderfoot chuckling behind me, but I kept my cool and walked back ten yards to the ball and lined it up again. I aimed, swung, and up the ball went, up and up, and "whop" hit the same tree in almost exactly the same spot, then bounced back about ten yards over my head and behind me.

"Mfffff, mffff," came the muffled chuckles from behind me.

I looked at the ball, looked at the club and looked to the right of the fairway at the cornfield that bordered the golf course. I wound up and threw the club as hard as I could into the cornfield.

"Mffff, mfff..."

"Bring the rest of the clubs when you get done, I'll see you at the car," I said and walked calmly off the course.

A while later, Thunderfoot came walking up to the car carrying the golf clubs and my nine iron.

"I went out in the corn and found your club," he said, not looking at me.

"Oh yippy. How nice," I said.

He turned away, and I could see him shaking from laughter. When I began to see how foolish I looked, I said, "Go ahead and laugh, I'm not mad at you."

He cracked up and laughed till tears came out of his eyes. "I don't think I've ever seen you so mad," he said. "There was smoke coming out of your ears almost."

We loaded up and drove home. When we got to his house, I pulled in to let him off. "Just take those clubs home with you."

"What? You want me to take them?"

"Yup, take them and play with them or take them and throw them in the river. I don't care. Just never let me see them again."

He looked pretty pleased but stopped just short of the house. "I hope you're not mad at me," he said.

"Nope, I'm not mad at you, but from now on, we'll stick to something that I'm good at, like fishing."

He opened his mouth and started to say something about him being a better fisherman, too, but thought better of it and went into the house. Some days it's better to just shut up and let well enough alone.

Thanks, Thunderfoot.

The Big One Didn't Get Away

The official end of summer was upon us, and Thunderfoot and I decided that we should go fishing for northerns one last time. It was Labor Day weekend, and it was blistering hot, threatening to storm, just the way we liked it for fishing for big, toothy northern pike. For some reason, northerns always were hungry or maybe angry, on those hot humid days, so we thought it was a good idea to take advantage of the weather and spend the day fishing before hunting season started and our minds strayed to other endeavors.

"This is way better than going to some softball tournament and wasting the whole day doing nothing," Thunderfoot said as we slid the canoe into the lake.

Normally, we used the little flat bottom johnboat, but this lake didn't have a good place to put a boat in. It was a long carry through the woods to get to the water, so we had decided to use the canoe that we used for duck hunting. The johnboat was too heavy for such a long carry but was more comfortable to fish from. The other thing was that the johnboat was longer and roomier and much more stable when fishing, but we really wanted to fish this particular lake, so the canoe had to suffice.

"Get up in the front," I said, "and I'll push off."

Thunderfoot stepped lightly to the front of the canoe and sat down, and I pushed it off the bank and climbed into the back seat. We wobbled and tilted like crazy until we got our "sea legs" and began paddling toward the first weed bed that looked like it might have a few northerns hiding in it. Thunderfoot laid his paddle down and began getting his rod ready before we were near the weeds, and as soon as we were in range, he rifled his bait across the lake and into the weed cover. He had hardly begun to retrieve his lure when the water exploded and a nice northern grabbed his bait and headed back into the deep weeds.

"Yahoo! First fish of the day," he yelled.

He fought the fish and I moved the canoe into the weeds to help him get closer to it, and he finally brought a nice northern to the surface along with about ten pounds of weeds. He reached over the side and lifted the fish out of the water, removed his lure, and turned to see that I was appropriately impressed, then released the fish back into the lake.

"The old Pike Killer does it again," he said, admiring his lure. "Oh, that's the Pike Killer this week," I said.

"Yup, this one's been my favorite for quite a while."

We moved back out of the weeds and began working through the rest of the weed bed, and soon I was fighting a bass and Thunderfoot caught another northern.

This particular lake was about a mile long and only about a hundred yards wide, so we usually worked our way to the end of the lake on one side and then planned on working back on the other side.

The sun was becoming almost unbearable, so we tried to stay in the shade of some of the tall trees on shore. A short time later, Thunderfoot got his Pike Killer in a tree as he cast, and the lure was hanging down in the water with the line up over the branch, about six feet off the water.

"I'm gonna just reel it up as close as I can, and then just flip it over the branch," he said.

He began reeling up the slack line and the lure was dipping back and forth on top of the water, when a nice bass came up and inhaled it.

"Whoa, holy cow! I got a fish on!" he shouted.

He was fighting the fish back and forth under the branch that his line was dangling from. Finally he pulled the fish from the water and lifted it up in the air.

"Paddle over there so I can get that fish off," he said, grinning.

I paddled over to the fish and he reeled up his line as we went to keep the fish in the air. When we got there, he reached out and took hold of the fish and unhooked it and let it go back into the lake. Then he reeled his lure up to the branch and flipped it over and into the boat.

"The master at work," he said, grinning from ear to ear. "Paddle me back to a respectable casting distance, would you?"

"Why, yes, of course, Bwana."

Big grin.

We got to the end of the lake and paddled across to the other side to begin our trip back. There was a good-looking spot back under some overhanging branches coming up just ahead.

"Watch me side arm one into that hot spot," he said, swinging his rod to the side, so his lure would go under the branches.

Just as he swung, I bent over to pick up my tackle box, and as he swung the rod forward to cast, his Pike Killer hit me in the top of the head and imbedded itself there. Smack!

"Yeeeeouch, don't pull, don't pull!" I screamed.

He was sitting with a stupid look on his face, trying to figure out where his lure had gone. He turned toward me and his mouth dropped open.

"Goooh, yikes, I think you got your head in my way."

He began to reel up the tangled line, and the lure began to pull and twist in my scalp.

"Stop, stop, don't pull! It's in there tight," I said.

He quit immediately and laid the rod in the bottom of the boat carefully.

"Let me come back there and see how bad it is," he said and began crawling back toward me.

"Take it easy, don't tip this thing over. I don't want to be on the bottom of the lake with a rod and reel attached to my head," I said.

He got back to me and I tipped my head forward, so he could see the lure.

"Oooh, uh, I think it's pretty far in," he said.

"Oh, great. Well, let's paddle over to the bank and see if we can get it out," I said, thinking that it would be better on dry land than in the unstable canoe.

We paddled over to the bank, and Thunderfoot got out to guide the canoe alongside the bank so he could take a clipper and cut the line, freeing me from the rod and reel. I climbed out and sat in the grass. Immediately, the air was full of mosquitoes. They came up out of the grass in clouds, and soon we were covered with the blood thirsty little monsters, adding to my misery considerably.

"See if you can pull it out with the pliers," I said.

"Are you sure? You really want me to pull on it?" he said, brushing mosquitoes away.

"Well, try it, and we'll see if I'm brave enough."

He took out his needle nose pliers and parted the hair so he could see the hooks.

"One isn't in very far, but the other one, oh man, it's in a long way." "How far, past the barb?"

"Yup."

Oh, great, that wasn't the news I wanted to hear. "Well, see what you can do."

He took a deep breath, and I could feel him gripping the hook and then he pulled quickly and let out a sigh.

"One is out."

"Try the other one," I said.

I could feel him gripping the other hook, and it hurt like the devil. I held my breath, and he took a deep breath and suddenly, he plopped down in the grass, his face deathly white and with a confused look on it.

"Are you OK?"

"Whew, I got kind of woozy, I guess," he said.

"Try it again."

He gripped the hook again and the same thing happened. He sat down and got real pale and pasty looking.

"I don't think I can do it. It's in a long way and when I grab it with the pliers, the skin kind of puckers up and wow, it's really gross."

Well, now what to do. I knew I couldn't get the hook out by myself, and we were almost a mile from the truck on a Monday of a holiday weekend.

"Let's paddle back and see if we can go and get some help," I said. We climbed back into the canoe and paddled back to the end of the lake where the truck was waiting. We carried the canoe and gear up to the truck and drove back to town. By now, the top of my head was kind of numb feeling, so I was doing OK. Poor Thunderfoot didn't dare look at my head, or he began to feel faint.

I didn't know of anything else to do, so I drove to the hospital and went to the emergency room.

As we walked in, an older lady came to the reception desk. "How may we help you?" she said.

"I need to get a fish hook taken out," I replied.

"OK, we'll need you to fill out these forms," she said. "Where is the hook?"

I bent my head down so she could see.

"Oh, my God, forget the forms, come this way right away," she said.

That made me feel real confident.

I went down the hall to the examining room and sat on a bed until the doctor came in.

"So, a little fishing accident," he said, surveying my head. "Nice job," he said, looking toward Thunderfoot, who looked down but had to grin.

He cleaned off the area with something that stung like crazy and then said the dreaded "this might pinch a little" as he stuck a needle into the top of my head. Pinch, my butt; it hurt like heck.

Thunderfoot couldn't keep a straight face as I grimaced in pain. The doctor waited a few minutes and visited with us about how our day had been prior to the hook being imbedded in my skull. Then he took a pliers and I could feel him doing something up on top of my head. Thunderfoot looked away. In a couple of seconds, the Pike Killer was back in its owner's hands.

Thunderfoot took the lure and looked pretty upset when he saw the doctor had cut the barb off the hook that had been in my head.

"Jeez, you ruined the hook," he said. "Oh, sorry, that's OK," he said, smiling.

The doctor bandaged up the top of my head and we went out to the desk, completed the forms and I paid the lady for the services.

"Well," I said. "That was an expensive fishing day."

"I suppose you know I'm sorry," he said.

"Well, I didn't think you did it on purpose."

He patted me on the back. "Of course, my Pike Killer is ruined."

"I'll give you a new hook, and it'll be as good as new."

"Cool, you know, we still have half of the lake to fish, and it won't be dark for quite a while," he said.

"OK, let's go, but I want to stop home first and get my old football helmet and safety glasses."

"Oh, real funny."

I wasn't trying to be funny.

Thanks, Thunderfoot.

Surely There Will Be Better Days

The ducks had abandoned us for the past two weeks at our regular hunting place. We had our blind and all our gear on our favorite pond in the marsh, but for some reason, the ducks had stopped coming there.

"I think we scared them all, and they're too smart to come back near us," Thunderfoot said.

I wasn't so sure and didn't know what the reason was, but I did know that we weren't getting any action, so we needed to try a new plan.

"There have been a lot of ducks flying into the Goose Pond," he suggested.

"Yeah, so what? How do you suppose we're going to get to the Goose Pond?"

"We'll wade and push a canoe over there, and hunt from the canoe," he said, like it was as obvious as the nose on my face.

Now the Goose Pond was about a half mile from our duck pond, and the only way to get to it was across the swamp. It was smack dab in the middle of the marsh and was surrounded by water, tall grass and floating bogs. Of course, that was why the ducks had decided to make it their home.

"Oh, I don't know about that. It's got to be half a mile, and there isn't much dry ground between here and there. That would be an awful lot of work."

Just then we saw a nice flock of mallards flying along the river and watched them turn and circle the Goose Pond once and then set in.

Thunderfoot looked at me and nodded his head. "See, what did I tell you? We'll get lots of action there. Are you ready to go?"

I wasn't ready, but I knew that every time a duck even flew close to the pond, I'd get an earful of "I told you so," so I gave in. We tossed a couple of decoys into the canoe and the water jug, and told Katy to get in, then paddled the canoe to the end of our pond. When we got to dry ground at the end of the pond, we began carrying the canoe across it until we got back to mud and muck. Then we slid the canoe through the grass and pushed and pulled it toward Goose Pond. Katy walked along for part of the way, but then the muck got too deep, so she had to ride in the canoe, making it even harder to push.

When we had gone about a third of the way, I called for a rest break. I was sweating like a camel driver in the Sahara and puffing and gasping for breath, waiting for the "Big One" to take me from this incredible situation that I had agreed to. Thunderfoot, of course, was barely breathing hard and chomping at the bit to get going.

"If we take breaks all day, we won't get there before dark."

"If I drop dead, you'll have to push the canoe by yourself."

We began again and pushed for another hundred yards or so before I had to stop again. This went on for almost an hour, and finally we made it to the pond.

Goose Pond was only about twenty yards across and almost a perfect circle. It was surrounded by tall cattails and in the center of the pond was a huge beaver lodge. Of course, all of the ducks that had been on the pond were now gone, scared away by the noise of a canoe being pushed through the marsh and an old man gasping and wheezing, trying not to drop dead.

The pond was deep, so we had to get into the canoe. We paddled to the center and put out the decoys, and then we slid back into the cattails and maneuvered the canoe sideways, so we could both shoot without shooting over each other's head.

I was drenched in sweat and began to get cold as I sat there.

Thunderfoot and Katy were both real comfortable, since they hadn't worked up a sweat between them.

We had been sitting there for about fifteen minutes when we spotted a pair of ducks coming our way.

"Here comes a pair," I whispered, and Thunderfoot nodded.

I turned toward my right a bit, so I could get a better shooting angle, and just as I did, the front of my right thigh clamped tight with a huge cramp. I gasped a quiet "Arrrrgh" and tried to straighten my leg out when suddenly the left one cramped up in the same place.

I let out a bellow, tried to get my legs straightened out, and began thrashing around in agony.

Thunderfoot looked back over his shoulder with panic on his face. He was gripping the sides of the canoe, which was swaying side to side, as I fought the cramps and tried to get into some position that would allow me to work them out of my legs.

"Jeez, be careful, you'll tip us over," he shouted.

Just then my left calf cramped, and I let out another agonized bellow. Now I had three cramps at once, and I was rolling around in the bottom of the canoe like one of those big Nile crocodiles that you see that crazy guy from Australia trying to slip a noose around his snout. Once the noose is on, the croc goes into a series of "death spins" and writhes around thrashing and wrecking everything in sight, which is just what I was doing now. Katy moved to the front of the canoe, where Thunderfoot was hanging on for dear life, when my right calf cramped.

"AAAAArrrrrrgh!" I screamed.

Now Thunderfoot was becoming alarmed. "Are you fooling with me? Hey, what's wrong? Are you dying?"

"Cramps," I managed to say through clenched teeth.

I was doing my best to get my legs straightened out, but it wasn't working very well. Finally my right front thigh loosened up and then I got my right calf to stop cramping. I was able to lay on my side and eventually got both of the other cramps to stop.

When the cramps finally quit, I was panting like a dog and pretty well spent.

"Are you OK?" Thunderfoot asked, genuinely concerned.

"Well, so far. If I can sit back up without cramping again, I'll be alright," I said.

Cautiously, I slid back toward my seat and carefully lifted myself up onto it. Very carefully, I slid my legs back under me, expecting at any moment for them to seize up again. No cramps.

"Wow, I hope that's the end of that," I said.

"Me, too. You almost tipped us over," Thunderfoot said. "Thanks for your concern for my welfare," I said sarcastically.

"I was concerned, but what could I do? Shhhh, here comes some ducks."

We crouched down and the ducks came sailing into the pond.

Thunderfoot shot and missed. I didn't shoot because it would have required me to twist too far to the left, and I didn't want to take a chance on another cramp from that position.

We did some shooting and got a couple of ducks as the day wore on, but soon we began to notice that there were many ducks landing in the woods about fifty yards from where we were sitting.

"Is there a pond back in there?" Thunderfoot asked.

"Must be. Those ducks wouldn't go in there if there wasn't water." "Let's sneak over there and see," he said, shaking his head yes.

I was pretty well rested now and had dried off, so what the heck, I might as well get all sweated up again, so I agreed.

We backed the canoe out of the reeds and paddled as close to the woods as we could get before we had to abandon the canoe and go on foot. Fortunately, we found a good trail that the beaver who lived in the Goose Pond had made, dragging brush and small trees to and from the pond, so it was pretty easy walking.

I had Katy with me and told her to heel, and Thunderfoot was behind us. As we got close to the pond, Katy began to get excited and got ahead of us.

"Kate, heel." She stopped and waited for us.

Off we went another ten feet, and she snuck ahead again. "Kate, heel."

She waited and in another ten feet she was sneaking ahead again. I grabbed her tail and took off my cap and popped her on the butt with it.

"Heel!"

She looked up at me and sat down on the trail.

"Come on, Kate. Let's go," I said and started down the trail. Katy stayed sitting. Thunderfoot passed her and she still sat there, looking peeved at me.

"Katy, come."

She laid down.

I looked at Thunderfoot, and he was doing his best not to laugh. "I think she's mad at you for hitting her with your hat," he said. "Let's go on to the pond. When she hears us shoot, she'll come running."

We snuck up to the pond. Thunderfoot went to the right and I went to the left. & we cleared the cattails, about twenty-five ducks took to the air. I lost my balance trying to turn to shoot and before I could get my feet out of the sticky muck, I tipped over and fell down. Thunderfoot began shooting and managed to bring down one duck.

"Nice shooting," he said, laughing as I got up covered with sticky black swamp mud.

"Kate, come here!" I shouted. No Katy.

"She's still sitting there," Thunderfoot said.

The duck wasn't far from me, so I decided I could get it myself. I took a couple of steps and soon realized that the pond was deeper than my hip boots. Now I was at the very top of the boots so I stood on tiptoes and as I tried to turn around, I sunk in just enough that both boots filled with water.

"Now you might as well go get it," Thunderfoot said, snickering like a fool.

He was right, so I waded in up to my belly and got his duck. When I got back to dry ground, Katy got up and started down the path toward the canoe.

"Best we don't hit her with a cap again," Thunderfoot said.

"No kidding."

We hiked back to the canoe and then decided it was time to start back to our regular hunting pond. It didn't take quite as long going back because we had made a pretty good trail through the swamp on our way over. We finally got back and put the canoe away in its little hiding place and started back up the trail to the truck.

Thunderfoot was hiking merrily along with his duck, and I was plodding along looking pretty sad. I was limping on both legs, cut and bleeding from hundreds of grass cuts from the saw grass I had sloughed through, wet from the top of my head to the middle of my body, and from there down, covered with mud. My boots were making a slurping sound as I walked with them still full of water.

Thunderfoot got ahead of me and then stopped to wait where the bank rose up to the truck.

"Didn't have a real good day, did you?"

"Not the best," I said. "At least I came out alive. I thought I was going to have a heart attack when I got the cramps."

Thunderfoot began to snicker. "I'm sorry. It was pretty funny with you wallowing around in the canoe like a head shot cow."

I had to grin a bit, too.

"Just think how mad the rescue squad guys would have been if you had died out there. They would have had a heck of a time dragging your body out," he said.

That was a cheery thought.

We got to the truck and I went to the driver's side door to get my gun case.

"Uh, maybe you better ride in the back and let me drive home.

With all that mud on you, you'll stink up the truck real bad."

The perfect end to a perfect day. A ride home in the back of your own truck with a wet dog as a companion.

Thanks, Thunderfoot.

We've Had Better Ideas

After the debacle of pushing the canoe across the marsh the previous weekend, I was not exactly looking forward to any more expeditions to the duck swamp the following Saturday morning. Thunderfoot was heading across the backyard with his camouflage duck hunting clothes on, and I knew he would be pestering me to go duck hunting. The problem was that the duck population was almost non-existent at this particular time.

We had had a dry fall, and many of the good potholes in the marsh were dried up, or what little water there was was just a puddle in the middle of what used to be a nice sized lake. There were a few that were tended by beaver that had remained pretty full, but most of those were almost inaccessible. I was still sore from the previous weekend and wanted nothing to do with any more long hauls across the marsh.

"So, what ya doin' today?" Thunderfoot said, as he opened the refrigerator and began rummaging.

"Not pushing the canoe across any swamp."

"Oh, come on, don't be such a baby. That wasn't so bad."

"My legs are still sore from all the cramps, and my arms are just healing up from all the cuts from the saw grass. No more of that for me."

"I've got a better idea," he said, grinning and shaking his head up and down like one of those little plastic baseball player souvenirs you buy at the ballpark.

"Oh Lord, what now?"

"Let's take the canoe and go out by the bridge by the old Lockhard farm and put it in and cruise down the creek to Blue River. It's only about two or three miles, and we can take turns sitting in the front. We should be able to jump-shoot some ducks that are sitting in the creek. I figure that since the marsh is so low, a lot of the ducks will be using the creeks." His head was really going up and down now.

"How are we going to get back?" I asked.

"My mom will come and pick us up a couple of hours after we go, and she can take us back to the truck and then we can go back and get the canoe."

Well, it didn't sound like too bad of an idea at that. An hour or two paddling the canoe downstream on the creek wouldn't be so bad. He probably was right; there would be ducks sitting on it because of the low water conditions in the river bottoms.

"OK, that sounds pretty good. Let's try it."

He let out a whoop and grabbed the phone to call his mom.

"What time should I tell her to come and get us?"

"Well, let's see. It's almost ten now. An hour to get everything loaded and ten minutes to drive to the bridge, and what, two hours to paddle three miles? Tell her to pick us up at around 2:30. That will give us some extra time so we don't have to hurry."

He thought that was fine and called his mom and asked her if that would be OK with her. She agreed to meet us at the highway bridge just outside of Blue River, a small town just west of us, at 2:30 that afternoon.

We loaded the canoe and a couple of seat cushions, two paddles, our guns and a couple of boxes of shells. We debated whether or not to wear our hip boots. Since we would have the canoe to pick up any ducks we might get, we might not need them. After thinking about it, we decided that we might need to get out of the canoe to stretch and to switch places from front to back when it was time for one or the other to assume the gunning duties. So we decided to wear our hip boots after all.

It was a beautiful fall morning, so I decided just to wear a short sleeve shirt and a vest to hold my shells instead of my heavy canvas hunting jacket. Thunderfoot already had his heavy coat on, so he decided to use it rather than run home for his vest.

We had a hard time convincing Katy that she couldn't go. The creek was pretty deep in some places and was the lower end of a trout stream, which had very cold water. I didn't want a dog getting excited and tipping us over into that cold water. Besides, we would be able to pick up any ducks ourselves, so she had to stay home and rest for the day.

It only took a few minutes to drive to the creek and park by the bridge. The creek was about 12 to 15 feet wide with high muddy banks and it wound through some woods along a hillside for a couple of miles. Then it took a turn to the north and went under the highway bridge where we would be picked up, and from there it emptied into the river. The water was pretty fast and real cold, and we wobbled a little as we took off from the bank. After a few hundred feet, we got our "sea legs" and the canoe settled down. We began to paddle leisurely along a pasture where a dozen cows stared at us, probably wondering what kind of strange critter we were. Thunderfoot was in the front of the canoe with his gun loaded, and it was propped up in the bow of the boat between his feet. My gun was uncased and unloaded and laying in the bottom of the canoe.

The idea was that we would paddle silently, with the back person doing most of the paddling and steering, while the front person would be ready to shoot at any ducks we might surprise. If we got a duck or two, we'd pull up someplace and switch places, letting the back person move to the gunning position. That way we wouldn't be shooting over each other's heads. I felt much better doing it this way, because as much as I trusted my little buddy, I didn't like the idea of him following a flying duck through the air and forgetting my head was just a few feet below the muzzle of his gun.

We had paddled about three hundred yards when the stream turned and headed into the woods. About fifty yards into the woods, the stream turned sharply to the right and on the corner was a big logjam.

"Whoa, we can't go over that," Thunderfoot said.

I back paddled the canoe so we wouldn't get swept into the jam.

"We'll have to pull out and carry it around."

I maneuvered us to the bank, and Thunderfoot stepped out onto a log and held the canoe steady while I stood up. I stepped out onto the mud and sank up to the middle of my thigh. Now I had one foot buried deep in the mud and the other up in the canoe.

"Hold this canoe steady. I'm stuck." I struggled to get my dry foot out of the canoe and tried to get it to solid ground but only managed to get it a bit higher than my stuck one. Now I had both legs mired in the sticky goo.

Thunderfoot was snickering as I pulled first one then the other leg up and slopped my way up to dry ground. The bank was real steep, so I had to hang onto a small tree to keep myself from flopping back into the stream.

"Can you lift your end up?" Thunderfoot asked.

"Yeah, I think so." I lifted the end of the canoe up onto the bank and as soon as I let go of the tree, I slid into the mud again. Thunderfoot walked the log over to the bank and put his end of the canoe up on the bank.

Meanwhile I was pulling myself out of the mud again and as soon as I was out, I climbed up onto the bank.

We picked up the canoe and carried it around the logjam and down a less steep bank and put it back into the stream.

Thunderfoot climbed in and then I got in. We began our journey again. We went about fifty yards, and the stream turned again and there was another logjam.

We paddled into the bank again, but this time it wasn't so steep, and we managed to get the canoe out, up over the bank and back in without me getting any muddier. We continued down the stream and this time we went almost a hundred yards before we found a big tree that had tipped over in a storm and fallen across the stream.

"Should we try to go under it?" Thunderfoot asked.

"No way. We'll get part way under and get stuck and then we'll really be in a mess. Let's portage again," I said.

We slid the canoe in next to the tree, and Thunderfoot stepped out onto the trunk while I waited for him to slide us closer to the bank. Then I carefully stepped up onto the trunk and we tight roped the canoe across the tree trunk to the bank. We carried it to the other side and set it down in the grass.

"Before we put this back in, I want to walk ahead a little way and see if there are more obstructions," I said.

I walked down to the next corner and it was free of any brush, but there were six wood ducks sitting in the corner who flew away as I walked up.

"Oh, that was good. Why don't you just go ahead and chase all the ducks away and then I won't have to shoot," Thunderfoot said.

We got back into the canoe and paddled for about six or seven minutes until we got to the next brush pile. This time it was really steep so I maneuvered the front of the canoe to the bank and Thunderfoot stepped up onto the bank from the seat of the canoe. Then I tried to walk to the front of the canoe while he held onto the bow while laying on the bank. I got almost to the front before I tipped and had to step out into the water. It was about six inches deeper than the top of my hip boot, and cold, real cold. Now I was standing in the water with my right leg hanging over the side of the canoe. Of course my left foot was stuck in the bottom, so the only solution was to step into the water with my right boot, which instantly filled with the ice water, too.

I pulled and tugged and made my way up onto the mud and then crawled up over the bank to dry ground. Thunderfoot pulled the canoe up and over the bank while I laid on my back and held my legs up in the air, so the water could run out of my boots. At least, the water cleaned the gooey mud off the outside of the boots.

I could hear Thunderfoot snickering as he dragged the canoe around the brush and slid it back into the stream.

I sat there, feeling kind of sorry that I had ever started this journey and glanced at my watch.

"Jeez, it's almost 1:30 already," I said.

"Holy cow, you can still see the bridge where we put the canoe into the creek," he said, looking back toward the hill.

I looked, and we had probably only come a couple of hundred yards as the crow flies but had probably gone a mile by creek.

"If the rest of the stream is like this, we'll never make it by 2:30," I said.

"Best we get going."

We paddled another seventy-five yards and turned the corner to our next obstruction. By now, it was no surprise. We got out and slid the canoe up the bank and then climbed up ourselves. There was a lot of brush along this stretch of stream, and as we began carrying the canoe through it, we realized it was prickly ash. Thunderfoot, of course, had on a canvas coat, and I was bare armed. We had to carry the canoe through the torturous stuff for about twenty yards before we could get back into the stream, and by the time we got back into the canoe, I was bleeding profusely from about fifty gouges in my arms and face.

We had just gotten into the canoe and began downstream when a small flock of mallards rose up out of the tall grass ahead of us, and, of course, Thunderfoot was paddling instead of shooting, so they flew off without even a shot being fired.

The next three hours were a nightmare of mud, logs, nettles, prickly ash, sweat, and an occasional duck that went on its way unbothered. I lost count of how many times we dragged the canoe up and down the bank, but it was beginning to get dusk when we saw something moving through the brush along the creek ahead of us. Soon we saw that it was Thunderfoot's mother walking along the creek looking for us.

"I thought you two goofs had drowned yourselves," she said. "We couldn't be so lucky," I said.

"Well, it's about a half mile to the car," she said.

"Hey mom, how many brush piles between here and the

car?"

Thunderfoot asked.

"None that I saw. Why, are there some upstream?"

He looked over his shoulder at me and we both began laughing like fools. His mom shook her head and began walking back toward the car. I was as tired as I had ever been, covered with mud and sweat and dried blood and hadn't fired a shot all day. Thunderfoot was still dry but pretty pooped, too, and he still had all of his shells.

"Well, this was a good idea, huh?" he said over his shoulder. He turned and gave me a big grin.

"It won't rank as one of our best, but who knows, we'll probably come up with something just as stupid one of these days."

He got a silly look on his face and said, "Let's race home." "Take Your Mark, Get Set, Go!" We began paddling like we were in the Olympics and quickly passed his mom, throwing a big wake up along the creek bank and laughing like a couple of maniacs.

I bet she wondered about us sometimes.

Thanks, Thunderfoot.

A Friend In Need

Thunderfoot and I were really glad to see deer hunting season arrive. We had been on some pretty fruitless duck hunting excursions during the past fall. Hopefully the deer season would provide us with a little more hunting action, instead of all the hunting we had done previously without much luck.

We had scouted the farm where we would be hunting and had chosen our stands the previous Saturday. I would be sitting at the corner of the fence where two neighboring lands joined our hunting farm and watching a huge field. Below me, there was a logging road that wound up the hill, and I could watch the ridge above the road and the top of the field, which was wide open but would require a long shot.

Thunderfoot was below me, where a patch of woods extended up into the field. He would be sitting right on the corner of the patch of woods where many deer trails came together. When deer came into the field, most of them went toward the patch of woods so they could get back into cover faster rather than cross the open field. That was where I wanted Thunderfoot to sit, so he could have a good chance at a deer and wouldn't have to make such a long shot. It also gave me a good view of him, so I could keep an eye on him.

The night before season, he came over and stayed in the spare bedroom where he slept before most major hunting or fishing trips. We had supper and then tried to watch a movie but kept losing interest and began telling deer stories. He was talking about the huge deer that he had seen the previous season that had "been behind some does" so as not to afford him a good shot. I kept accusing him of having "buck fever," and we were arguing about that for most of the evening. Finally, I thought I was sufficiently tired to go to sleep, so we went to bed.

It seemed like just minutes had passed when the alarm went off, and I looked at the clock, which read, 4:30 a.m. I laid there a minute and then sat up on the side of the bed. As I sat there, I imagined that I could smell toast and bacon, and suddenly realized that I actually could smell toast and bacon. I got up and went to the kitchen, and there was Thunderfoot making breakfast.

"I was awake, so I thought I'd get us a good breakfast," he said, as he broke eggs into the frying pan.

"Who are you?" I said. "What did you do to the grumpy kid that usually sleeps here?"

"Oh, ha, very funny," he said. "I'm always ready to go when it comes to hunting or fishing."

I sat down and he put a plate of bacon and eggs in front of me and we had our breakfast. Afterward, we cleaned up the kitchen quickly and loaded our lunch into our backpacks. We had made the lunch the previous evening, and it was an integral part of any outdoor trip that we took.

I always felt that a backpack full of lunch was essential to keep the hunter content and made it easier to sit longer. This was especially important during deer season. If you sat still longer, the odds were that a deer would walk by you eventually. Those that could sit would see deer. Those who lost patience and began to walk around would spook the deer. Of course, we needed some of those less patient hunters in the area to make the deer come past us, too.

We each had a backpack and each had a thermos of hot chocolate.

Thunderfoot had packed four sandwiches for himself and made three for me. Plus, we each had a sack full of chocolate chip cookies, a bag of salted in the shell peanuts, and the most important item of all, some Kit Kat candy bars. The first year I ever shot a deer, I was eating a Kit Kat as the deer came to me, so I decided that Kit Kat was my lucky charm and always made sure

I had some with me on every deer hunt. Of course, my lucky hat may have had something to do with it, too, so I made sure both were packed and ready to go. I had bought a new hat that same year and, like many hunters, felt I would be jinxed if I didn't have my lucky hat along, so I was still wearing the old dilapidated thing, despite all the nasty names Thunderfoot had called my precious headwear.

We loaded up the gear and drove through the darkness to the farm. We parked at the old buildings and gathered up our gear and began hiking up the hill. Of course, Thunderfoot was going like it was a cross-country race, and soon I began to huff and puff, trying to keep up with him.

"Hold it," I gasped. "I've got to slow down or you'll be dragging me back to the truck like a dead deer."

He turned around and I could see the grin on his face in the low light from the stars. "Sorry, I was in a hurry to get to my stand," he said. "I guess we've got time. It's over an hour till we can shoot."

I removed my outer jacket to keep from getting all sweaty, and we began hiking again and made several more stops on our way to the top. When we got to the top of the road, we stopped and looked out over the field.

"Well," I said, "I'll talk to you later. Good luck."

He punched me in the arm, "You too," he said and walked along the top of the woods to his stand. I walked up the hill farther to my corner and sat down. We each had a folding chair with us, so with our comfortable chair, lunch, hand and foot warmers, and lucky candy bars, we were ready for a day in the outdoors.

I arranged my food and gear and loaded my gun and stood it against the fence. It was about twenty degrees out, so my breath was scope. He followed them and must have been imagining he was goose hunting. I noticed movement out of the corner of my eye, and coming across the field, directly above Thunderfoot, were three deer. One was a buck and the other two were does.

They were walking along, going straight at him. By now, the geese were right overhead, and one of the does actually looked up at them. Thunderfoot was still watching the geese through his scope, and the deer were walking closer and closer to him.

I couldn't do anything but watch. It wouldn't do any good for me to shoot at them and I didn't want to anyway, since they were going to him. So I just lowered my gun and watched the fun.

The deer were about thirty yards from Thunderfoot when he lowered the gun and laid it in his lap. He stretched his neck from side to side and looked up the hill. You could see him stiffen up as he saw the deer standing there looking at him. The deer, of course, saw him move, too, and were alert and ready to bolt back up the hill. Both hunter and hunted faced each other for several seconds, and then Thunderfoot tried to slowly raise his gun. That movement was all it took for the deer to decide the game was over, and they turned and bounded up over the top of the hill as Thunderfoot struggled to get them in his sights.

As he lowered his gun, I could see him shaking his head. Then, he stopped and looked slowly my way. I was sitting there laughing, and you could see the look on his face. He shook his head from side to side, as if to say, "I'll never hear the end of this." Score two for the deer.

He looked at his watch and then stood up and began hiking up the hill to me. 1 couldn't suppress the grin on my face as he got to my stand.

"I can't believe you let those deer walk up to me while I was watching those geese," he said.

"What? How does this suddenly become my fault?" I said, laughing.

"Why didn't you get my attention and warn me?" "What was 1 supposed to do? Fire a warning shot?"

"I just can't believe it," he said. Then he sat down on the ground and began rummaging through my lunch sack.

"What are you looking for?"

"Something to eat. Mine is all gone."

"Maybe if you did something besides eating and bird watching, you might actually get a deer."

Killer look.

We sat there a while and he tried to make me promise that I'd never tell anybody about the incident, and finally he went back to his stand. My lunch was now all gone anyway, so there wasn't any reason for him to stay.

We sat there until the last hour of the day and never saw another deer. I whistled to him as the time ran out, and we both folded up our stools and leaned them against a tree. We would leave them there because we would be back tomorrow, and there wasn't any reason to carry them back and forth up and down the hill.

We began walking down the hill, talking in hushed tones, and as we got to the bottom, I laid my gun and backpack on the ground by the gate and began to climb over. I put my left foot on the second wire up from the bottom and swung my right leg over the top wire. I put my right foot on the third wire up and as I put my weight on it, the wire came loose from the post and I fell over the fence with my left leg still on the other side. A barb from the top wire had dug into my crotch and ripped into my pants and leg and firmly impaled me on the top wire.

Instantly, I was hanging upside down from the top wire, with a sharp spike of metal imbedded in my leg.

"Yeeeeow!" I screamed. "Help me, I'm hooked."

I was looking upside down at Thunderfoot who was laughing so hard he could hardly stand up. He was trying to help me upright from the wrong side of the fence.

"Climb over and help me," I said.

He went to the other end, hopped over the fence like a gazelle and came over to where I was hanging. By now, I had managed to get hold of the fence post and had partly righted myself.

"We gotta get you off that top wire," he said.

He examined my leg where the barb was imbedded. "Oh,

yuck, it's stuck right into your leg."

"Can you get it out?"

"It's right next to your, uh, you know, not a place I want to be messing with."

Now was not the time to be worrying about anything like that.

"Forget that. I don't care where it is. Get me off it and hurry up; the blood is rushing to my head."

Perhaps his fear of my wrath was greater than his fear of getting too close to another guy's crotch area, because he grabbed hold of my leg and lifted as much as he could and then took his other hand and manipulated the barb out of my leg and torn pants. When he got me loose, I flopped to the ground like a darted elephant.

"Holy cow, that is a nasty hole in your, well, you know."

"What do you mean?" I asked, not knowing exactly where the hole was but knowing it made my whole crotch hurt.

"Well, it's kind of in that little area that is kind of right below everything. Actually you're pretty lucky it wasn't a little farther in front. You would have had to wait for the EMTs to help you if it was there," he said, grinning.

I got up and had to walk like a bowlegged cowboy. Thunderfoot gathered up all the gear and loaded it up. I let him drive home because it hurt like heck to move my legs, so I just sat quietly in the passenger side.

When we got home, I took my clothes off and tried to examine the damage with a mirror. I couldn't get a good look at the puncture but washed the area as best I could.

"I need you to help me," I said from the bathroom. No answer.

"Hey, come here."

He came to the door, but didn't open it. "What?"

"Come in here and put some iodine on this for me. I can't see it and it needs some kind of disinfectant so I won't get an infection."

"Put iodine on where?" "On the cut, where else?"

"No way, I got as close to that as I ever want to get, back at the farm." "Well, then I guess we'll have to forget hunting tomorrow so I can make a doctor's appointment to get it done."

The door opened. "Give me the iodine."

I was watching him in the mirror as he tried to dab the iodine on without looking.

"You're gonna have to watch where you are putting it," I said.

"Come on, it's just a butt. Don't be such a sissy."

"Yeah, but you're not looking at it from the angle I'm looking at it." Finally he got some iodine on the wound, and I got dressed and we sat down to have something to eat.

We were eating quietly when he began laughing. "That was a real smooth move on that fence."

I moved a little on my chair and my crotch gave me a little stab of pain. "I'm glad you liked it," I said. "Tomorrow I'm going to open the gate and go through."

He laughed again and we ate in silence for a while.

"Sorry about the crotch thing. It's a guy thing, you know."

"Yeah, I understand. But thanks for helping me," I said.

"No problem."

"You know," I said, "I'd do the same for you anytime." He turned pale. "Jeez, I hope you never have to."

Thanks, Thunderfoot.

Over the River and Through the Woods

We were experiencing one of the snowiest winters we had seen for many years. Thunderfoot and I had just finished clearing out my driveway and had come into the house for something to eat.

"Jeez, snow shoveling makes me hungry," he said, opening the refrigerator and snooping around inside.

I moved him out of the way and began getting the ingredients out for a couple of omelets while he went into the living room and turned on the TV I whipped up a couple of ham and cheese omelets and a pile of toast and called him to eat. I didn't have to call twice, as he came on the run.

"Boy, that smells good," he said, smearing jam onto a piece of toast and plowing into his eggs. "Hey, I was watching a show about fishing crappies at night through the ice."

"Oh, yeah," I said, "I've done that, up to the park. They have a lot of crappies, and a guy I used to work with had a shanty up there. We used to go up after work and fish them. It was fun, and we did pretty well."

"How about Gutwielers?" he asked. "What about it?"

"It's full of crappies, and I bet we could go down there tonight and set up the tent and catch some."

"I've never seen anybody fish at night on any of these lakes."

"That doesn't mean it can't be done. Come on, let's have a little adventure," he said, grinning and nodding yes.

We decided to give it a try, so we went to the hardware store and got some mantles for the lantern and filled it and the heater with fuel. Then we got some minnows and, of course, prepared a snack to take along. Thunderfoot never went anywhere without a snack.

We waited for the afternoon to pass, and I took a nap while Thunderfoot watched fishing shows and ate me out of house and home.

We loaded up the ice shanty and the rest of the gear and started for the river bottoms just as the sun was going down. By the time we got everything loaded onto the shanty, it was dark, and we began pulling it down the path to the lake. The path was made by people walking in the snow. We were pulling a shanty that was four feet wide and six feet long, and it was piled with about a hundred pounds of gear. There hadn't been many people on the lake that day, and with the snow from the previous night, it was tough going.

I was in front pulling and Thunderfoot was in back pushing. "Are you pushing or just hanging on?" I panted.

"I'm pushing. Try pulling a bit more and talking a bit less," he retorted.

The snow was almost up to my waist in places and it was like pulling a refrigerator that was tipped over on its side. I was struggling and sweating, and we were only a few feet from the bank.

"There's no way we're going to get this thing out to the lake," I said as I stopped to catch my breath.

"Oh, come on. We're almost there."

"We aren't even half way."

"Let's take the gear off and just pull the shanty, and then come back and get the gear."

I knew that he was determined to get to the lake and do some fishing, so I agreed, and we pulled the empty shanty off into the darkness. As we got to the lake, we tried to get our bearings so we could set the tent up in the right area, where we hoped the crappies would be.

We finally decided on the spot and popped the tent up, and then waded back through the snow to the rest of the gear. By the time we got back, I was sweating up a storm and just about done in.

First we had to shovel off a space on the ice for the shanty to sit, and then we drilled four holes in a line that would accommodate the cutout section of the floor of the shanty, and slid it over the holes. Thunderfoot kicked snow up against the outside edge of the shanty to make a seal and we crawled inside. I carried my bucket in first and positioned it on the far side, and then Thunderfoot came in and sat on the other side by the door. He brought the lantern in, and I was trying to get situated when he struck a match to light it.

"Be sure you have it pumped up and the little pumper-thing locked," I said.

"Yeah, yeah, I know how to do this. Do you think this is my first time?"

I could hear him pumping and things clanking as he struck a match and held it up to the lantern. As the flame entered the little hole in the bottom of the chamber where the mantles were, there came a huge "Whoooof" sound, and the lantern exploded into a huge ball of flame.

Thunderfoot dropped it on the bottom of the shanty floor and dove out through the door. I was on the wrong side of the shanty and the blazing lantern was between me and the door, really shooting flames up into the air. I managed to get my heavy mittens out of my bucket and grabbed the thing with mittens on my hands and tossed it out through the open door into the snow.

There was a "Shhhhhhhhhhh" sound as the lantern sunk into the snow and went out.

"Jeez, what are you trying to do, cremate me?" I shouted.

I could hear him at the door. "Maybe you better light that lantern after all. I think there's something wrong with it." I could see his grin in the starlight.

"No kidding. I think I'll light it outside this time," I said.

I picked up the lantern and found that he had forgotten to turn the little valve that lets air into the mixture and that was what caused the flare-up. I lit the lantern and got it adjusted so it was working perfectly and then took it into the shanty and sat down.

"Whew, that was pretty exciting," he said, grinning.

"Yeah, real exciting, especially from the inside of the shanty.

Thanks for your concern for my well-being. I see you abandoned me like a rat leaving a sinking ship."

He looked at me and shrugged.

We got our fishing gear out and cleaned the ice chips out of the holes, baited up and lowered a baited hook into each of our four holes. Thunderfoot's bobber had hardly hit the water when it went down and he grabbed the pole and lifted a nice crappie out of the cold water.

"See, I told you it would work. Look at this beauty."

Things were looking up. I watched my bobbers expectantly for a bite, and he re-baited his and put it back into the ice hole. We picked each pole up and jigged it every so often to entice a fish into biting, but got no more bites.

A half hour passed and not another bite. Then an hour had passed. "That was kind of a short feeding period," I said.

"Either that or a small school of crappies," he said, laughing.

I sat there and shook my head. "I have to admit, I thought we'd get some fish, but one is just an insult."

We ate our snacks and decided to call it a night. Thunderfoot had put his crappie in the minnow bucket so it was full of life, and he put it back down the hole. "Go tell all your buddies how well you were treated," he said to the fish as it swam down the hole.

By now the moon had come up and it was pretty well lit outside, so we could turn out the lantern and work by moonlight. We decided it wasn't worth the effort to try to take everything in one trip, so we carried the gear back first, and then came back for the shanty. I got rid of my heavy coat on the first trip, so it was a little easier the second time back to the truck.

We pulled the shanty up over the high bank and to the truck and slid it inside the box. I was puffing a little, and we just stood there catching our breath when a coyote howled a few hundred yards away in the river bottoms.

"Wow, that was cool," Thunderfoot said quietly. "Yeah, it was."

"You know, I saw a show on TV the other day about calling in coyotes at night," he said.

"Well, that sounds like fun. I'll lend you my coyote calls, and you can try it and tell me about it afterward."

"Oh,funny."

Thanks, Thunderfoot.

911 Here We Come

It was a Sunday afternoon in late February, and Thunderfoot and I were driving home from a day of ice fishing. It hadn't been a particularly productive day, and we only had a few fish to show for the effort. But, as usual, we weren't feeling too bad about it because it had been a glorious day to be out in the fresh air. It had gotten into the upper 40's during the early part of the afternoon and the sun beat down on us as we enjoyed the nice weather and visiting with the other fishermen who were on the lake with us.

We were driving along and Thunderfoot was babbling about the ice going out soon and how we needed to be getting the boat ready for early walleye fishing when he suddenly yelled for me to stop the truck. I slammed on the brakes, not knowing what he was yelling about, and he rolled down the window on his side and pointed to the creek below us in the pasture.

"Look, there's a deer in the water down in the creek."

I looked and, sure enough, there was a doe swimming down the creek. I shut the motor off and we watched as the deer got close to the bank and tried to get up on the ice that was along the edges of the creek. The water had been higher earlier, and the ice had frozen on the creek when it was higher. Now, the water had fallen, and the ice was at a downward angle from the top of the creek bank to the water. The deer couldn't get a grip on the slippery ice and fell back into the water. She swam down the creek a short way and tried again, only to fall back into the water again.

"She can't get out," Thunderfoot said, looking at me for some kind of solution.

"I wonder how she managed to get in there in the first place," I said. "It doesn't matter how she got in, she can't get out now. What are we gonna do?"

"What can we do? She won't come to us."

"We can't just sit here and watch her drown. Let's go see what we can do to help her," he said and opened his door and started walking down the road bank toward the creek.

I didn't want to see the deer drown either, but I had no idea how we could save her, so I got out and followed him toward the creek. What else could I do?

When we got close to the creek, the deer panicked and started to struggle up the ice, only to fall in and go clear under the water. When she came up, she struggled up onto the ice again and slid back again.

"We've got to get back from here, or she'll exhaust herself and drown for sure," I said.

We walked away from the creek, and the deer continued swimming downstream and kept trying to find a place to get out.

"What are we gonna do?" Thunderfoot said.

"We have to stop and think about it and try to plan some way to help her. She won't know that we're trying to help her, so she'll panic when we go near her."

Thunderfoot was looking downstream and suddenly looked at me. "Look down there, the bank is pretty low there. If we could get down there ahead of her and break up some of that ice there where it's low, she could get up on the ground."

It did look like a good place to try, so we hustled away from sight of the deer who was paddling along slowly, looking for an exit from the water. We ran down the creek about an eighth of a mile ahead of her and walked down to the creek to the place where the bank was only a foot or so above the water level. I found an old fence post, and we began chopping the ice out of the way and soon made a nice little ramp for the deer to climb out of the water.

"That's good, and here she comes," Thunderfoot said as he looked up the creek.

The deer was on the other side, seeing us on the bank below her, and we backed up so she could climb out. By the time she saw the opening in the ice, she was too far past it and on the wrong side of the creek, so on she went, down the creek. She was beginning to tire out and you could see that she was struggling for breath.

"Oh, no, she missed it! We gotta go farther down and find another spot like this," Thunderfoot said as he began running ahead of me.

I picked up the old fence post and tried to keep up as best I could.

We got ahead of the deer again and found another spot like the last one, and again chopped ice until we had a good ramp open for her.

Just below us there was a tree hanging across the creek, and Thunderfoot looked at it and then at me.

"Let's go across on that tree and then the deer will see us on that side of the creek and come to this side and find her ramp."

"Cross on that tree?"

He didn't even wait for me and jumped up on the trunk and scampered across like a squirrel. I stepped up on the trunk and began walking across as fast as I dared.

"Hurry up, she's not far away."

I moved as fast as a guy my age could and finally got to the point where there was ground below me and jumped down. The deer was just above us and began to swim across to the other side to avoid us. She was almost past the opening in the ice, when she noticed it and swam with all her might to get to it.

"Oh, no, she's gonna miss it again," Thunderfoot whispered. The deer struggled against the current and got her front two feet up onto the bare ground and hung on. She rested a minute and then made a jump and jumped up onto the bare ground and up on the creek bank.

"All right!" Thunderfoot whooped.

The deer stood there panting heavily and shaking like she was very cold, but she was safe and would warm up as she began to dry off. She took a few steps and stopped and looked back at us, and then hopped across the pasture and into the woods.

Thunderfoot slapped me on the back. "We did good."

"Yeah," I said, "we sure did."

"Well, now all we have to do is get back on the other side of the creek and hike a couple of miles back to the truck," he said.

I looked back up the creek and sure enough, we were almost two miles from the truck. "Jeez, it didn't seem like that far when we were coming down here."

He stepped up onto the trunk of the tree and walked across like one of the Wallendas from the circus.

"Are you coming?" he said as he got to the other side.

"You know, I made it across just barely the last time, and this has turned out to be a good day all around, so I think I'll walk back up on this side and then walk to the bridge and back up to the road from there. I'd hate to spoil such a nice day by falling in the creek."

"Yeah, that's probably a good idea, or I'd have to make a ramp for you to haul you out, too."

It would probably take a crane.

Thanks, Thunderfoot.

Say Meow

Thunderfoot had a couple of days off from school because of teacher conferences, so he was at the shop with me, helping me get the spring turkey hunting merchandise out and priced. I was working on the clothing and he was arranging the calls and accessories when the delivery man came in with a package for me.

We chatted a bit and he fed the dogs a cookie each, and then he told me of a strange encounter he had just that morning.

"I was coming down the road out by Castle Rock when I saw something walking up out of the ditch on the right. I slowed down, thinking it was probably a deer or dog, and as I got right up to it, it stepped into the road. It was a cougar," he said.

When Thunderfoot heard that, he dropped what he was doing and came over by us. "A cougar?"

"Yup, a full grown cougar."

"You're sure it wasn't just a big cat? You know, there are some big barn cats around." I said.

"This wasn't a barn cat. It was probably four to five feet from nose to butt and then had a three foot tail behind that," he said. "It was a cougar, no doubt."

Thunderfoot was dumbfounded. "There aren't cougars in Wisconsin."

"Well, then this critter was doing a good cougar impression," the delivery man said.

"You know," I said, "I heard of a county cop who has seen a cougar on his property, and I think he lives right in that area."

"You guys are foolin' with me," Thunderfoot said.

"No fooling, I saw it," the driver said as he started for the door. Thunderfoot was shaken.

"So what?" I said. "If there's a cougar, it's not going to hurt us any."

"Yeah, but they're like lions. They could eat people."

"I'm sure we're not in any danger from a cougar, if it exists."

We went back to our work and nothing more was said about the incident. About two weeks later, a man came in to look at pistols, I showed him what I had in stock and he decided on one that he wanted to buy.

"I have my service revolver, but I want to have a back up gun, and this will do fine," he said.

"You're a cop?"

"Yes, I'm on the county sheriff's department," he said, and laid down his driver's license for identification for the paperwork for the pistol. "Are you the deputy that I heard about that has seen a cougar on his farm?" I asked as I saw the name on the license.

"Yeah, that's me. I've seen him three times."

"So it is real," I said.

"Oh, yeah. I was in the barn about three weeks ago, and he walked right through the barnyard not fifteen feet from me. He's real alright."

I told him about the delivery man, and he told me that the place he had described when he saw the cat was just over the ridge from his farm.

"It's wild country up in there," he said. "There are some big rocky areas that are real steep and deep valleys that are almost inaccessible, so there are lots of places for him to hide. Plus, lots of deer, rabbits, squirrels and raccoon probably make it pretty easy for him to eat, so he's probably pretty content."

I was impressed with this new account of the cat. Now I really began to believe in it and couldn't wait to tell Thunderfoot about my new information.

That day after school, he came into the store to see what was going on, and I told him about my visit from the county cop.

"Oh sure, you're just trying to spook me," he said.

"No fooling. He's coming back on Saturday to pick up the gun, after the waiting period. You can ask him yourself."

147

Saturday came and Thunderfoot was there, waiting for the man to come in and get the gun. When he arrived, I asked him to tell Thunderfoot what he had told me. By the time he was done with the story, Thunderfoot was standing, listening with his mouth hanging open like a simpleton.

"See, I told you," I said.

He seemed to be more upset about the cat than necessary, so I asked him what was wrong.

"Have you ever looked at a map of that area? If you go across the hills instead of by road, that place is probably only a half mile from where we turkey hunt," he said, grabbing a county map and opening it. "See here, there is where we hunt, and here is the road where the guy saw the cougar. Notice how short the distance is from here to here?"

"So what? That cougar isn't going to bother us."

"Oh, that's easy for a big guy like you to say, but I'm just the right size for a good snack."

I began laughing, thinking he was making a joke, but he was dead serious. I had never seen him get so shook up over something like this, so I dropped the subject.

A couple of weeks went by, and our turkey season was on us. We were hunting in the same place we had hunted for years, and we knew the terrain and where the turkeys lived, so our scouting was minimal. We made our plans for where we would hunt opening morning and left that morning in the darkness for the turkey woods.

It took us about twenty minutes to get up into the woods and to get situated by two large oak trees. It was still dark, and the turkeys hadn't gobbled yet, so we sat in the dark about ten feet away from each other and waited for dawn to come. I was getting pretty drowsy and my eyes were getting heavy when I heard a sound behind me like something had fallen from a tree or someone had taken a step and stepped on a twig. I came fully awake now and listened carefully. The sound came again. It sounded like a real soft step on leaves and grass.

I looked over at Thunderfoot but couldn't see him. He was sitting on the backside of a big oak tree, and I could just make out his fanny pack sticking out alongside the tree.

There was another step, this time much closer. I tried to think what could be making such a noise. There were no cattle in the woods. Squirrels were still in bed. Turkeys were still sitting on their roosts. Raccoons made a shuffling sound as they worked their way through the woods, and this was a stealthy step, and then another, not raccoon-like at all.

I leaned my head back and tried to ignore the sound and suddenly it came again. This time it sounded like it was just few feet behind the tree. Then I could hear a quiet breathing sound, too. My heart was beginning to hammer, and I was listening so hard that my ears began to hurt. Then I heard a sound like a low hum. Like a cat purring!

I sat perfectly still, and my mind began to play tricks on me. I was sure that there was no danger from anything that lived in the woods, except maybe poison ivy or a very seldom seen rattlesnake, but I was sure that if I turned my head and looked over my shoulder, I would be staring face to face with a cougar. The sound came again, and this time it was right behind my tree.

I began to breathe in little gasps, and my heart was racing. I looked over at Thunderfoot's tree and he hadn't moved. His fanny pack was still laying where it had been. He was probably asleep. The thought went through my mind that it was good that he wouldn't see his hunting buddy torn limb from limb if he was sleeping.

I decided that I had to turn and look. I moved my head to the right and leaned out to see around the tree. As, I cleared the tree, there came a scream, "Yeeeeeeooooooow!" and Thunderfoot pounced on me! I tipped over and almost had a heart attack. He was laying on top of me, laughing like a maniac.

"You little fool, are you trying scare me to death?" I whispered.

"You, ha, you, oooh, almost, ha ha!" He was having some kind of fit. Finally he calmed down and sat up. "I thought you said that a cougar wouldn't come near us. You sure were scared of something."

"You maniac, what did you think I would do? You're lucky I didn't take my gun off safety and blow your fool head off."

He lapsed into fits of laughter again.

"How did you get back there in the first place? I didn't see you walk past me," I said.

"Of course, you didn't see me. You were sleeping like a hibernating bear, only you sounded like a fog horn. I just got up and walked right past you, oh mighty hunter."

Hmm, maybe that drowsy spell I had was more than I thought.

"Well, now that you've had your laugh for the day, would you mind sitting yourself down and shutting up, so we might have a chance at a turkey?" I said.

"Yes, Bwana," he said, and he got to his feet and walked back to his tree. As, he went past me, I gave him a punch in the leg.

"Snot!"

He sat down, got situated and things quieted down. I settled down and began to doze off again, when I heard the purring sound. I opened my eyes instantly and looked over at him. He was sitting there, shaking with laughter.

"Here kitty, kitty," he whispered. Sometimes he could be such a wise guy.

Thanks, Thunderfoot.

Never a Borrower Nor a Lender Be

I'm one of those people who take good care of their stuff. I have a place for everything in my home and keep my things in their proper places. I take good care of my guns, cleaning them after each use, and storing them in a gun cabinet to keep them safe, free of dust and dirt. Most of all, I take especially good care of my fishing equipment. Rods and reels are cleaned and greased as needed. New line is almost a religious experience. I check my line after every fishing trip and any that is frayed or looks bad is replaced. My thinking has always been that no matter how much money you spend on tackle, the line that attaches you to the fish is the most important part of the whole system.

Thunderfoot, on the other hand, is about the most careless person I know when it comes to taking care of his equipment. You can always pick out his rods and reels. They are the ones with a dehydrated gob of night crawlers still on the hook from the last trip. Most of his walleye jigs have a desiccated minnow still hanging grotesquely on the hook. His rods are missing guides. He has one that has about four inches broken off the tip, but he still uses it, and uses the first guide as a tip. His reels are full of sand and most of them will only cast a short way because they have such little line left on them. He never replaces his line and after a time, he doesn't have enough to make a decent cast. Usually I can't stand it any longer and I fill his reels with new line.

Tackle boxes are a whole story by themselves. My lures are cleaned, dried, and sorted into their assigned little cubicles after each fishing trip. Hooks are sharpened, line is snipped from the eye of the lure, and bent or damaged hooks are replaced. There is no reason for Thunderfoot to own a tackle box. Tackle boxes have little compartments for lures; he stores everything in the bottom of the box in a big gob. His lures are all tangled together in a big cluster. Most of the hooks and baits have pieces of line hanging from them, and every hook he has still has dried worms or dehydrated minnows still hanging on them, looking like a little collection of miniature mummies. Lures, twister tails, and bobbers all are thrown together in a large tangled mess. For him to get something out of his tackle box, everything comes out at once. And, the bottom of the box has things in it that I wouldn't even touch without rubber gloves. All in all, it's a disaster area.

He calls me a "neat freak," and I may be, but there is order in my fishing, and I want to keep it that way.

Hunting isn't quite as bad. He does wipe down his guns with an oily rag after most trips, but full cleaning isn't such an important issue with him. "They'll only get dirty again when I shoot next time" is his philosophy. Of course, his boots and other gear are normally just strewn around until we get ready to go hunting, and then he has to tear the house apart to find the things he's looking for.

Once, a few years ago, he came over and asked me if I could take a look at his shotgun, which had a crack in the stock. I said sure, bring it over. He walked in with his gun in a cloth gun case, which looked like it contained a hockey stick. When he took the gun out, the stock was bent off to the side at about a thirty-degree angle from the centerline of the gun.

"What in the world did you do to this?" I asked.

"Well, I went up to my grandpa's farm, and we were hunting, and I got back to the truck first, so I just laid my gun in the grass. You know it's against the law to lay it against the truck. So, then I took a little nap, and when grandpa came to the truck, he got in and we left. When we got back to his house, I remembered my gun, and when we went back to get it, we found it. But it looks like he ran over it when we left."

I took the butt plate off the gun and got a wrench on the screw that held the stock on. It was a struggle to get it off, and when I did, we found it was bent beyond fixing. The stock was broken too badly to repair, and the forearm was crushed. I looked in some gun books and found a replacement stock and forearm and ordered them for him. Then we had to call an 800 number to order another bolt for the stock. A week later, we had all the parts and he had a new gun.

So, to say he was careless about equipment wouldn't be an overstatement.

I was thinking about all of the wrecked gear he owned as we fished for walleyes along the rocky rip rap that ran along the railroad tracks on the Mississippi River. In late summer, the rocks were walleye magnets. There were many aquatic insects among the rocks, and they drew in the small fish and minnows that feed on insects. Of course, small fish and minnows attract predator fish, such as walleyes and bass, and the rocks were the best place at that time of year for us to spend a day fishing.

We would go to the upper end of a long stretch of riprap and then position the boat about ten yards from the shore and cast crank baits toward the shore. You had to almost get the bait on dry ground, as the fish were right up in the shallow water waiting for some minnows or crawdads to feed on.

I was using a level wind bait casting rod and reel. The advantage of this type of reel over a spinning reel is that I could put my thumb on the spool and stop my bait just where I wanted it. With a spinning reel, you often cast too far, and your lure ended up on the bank in the brush. That was the problem Thunderfoot was having, and he had just lost his last crawfish colored lure.

"OK, that's it. I need to borrow a lure from you, and unless you want me to lose all your lures, you better lend me a bait caster, too," he said, matter-of-factly.

"If you'd take care of your stuff, you'd have a bait caster of your own.

What happened to the one I gave you last year for your birthday?"

"You know exactly what happened. It fell overboard when that monster fish grabbed my lure last spring."

"And why weren't you holding on to it?"

He looked at me with a peeved look. "I forgot to reel it up all the way, and it fell in. Are you happy now?"

"So, now you want to use one of mine?"

"Wow, Sherlock, you figured that out really fast," he said, grinning. I wasn't sure I wanted him to use one of my good rods and reels, but it was that or give him an endless supply of crank baits that he would throw up into the brush, so I relented and gave him one.

He grinned from ear to ear as he tied on one of my baits and began casting toward the rocks. He was good at it, especially with a rod that had all the guides and a reel that was full of good line.

"Hey, this works better than the one I had," he said.

"That's what happens when you take care of your gear," I said. "Mine just gets worn out faster because I catch a lot more fish than you do," he said. "I'm just ... whoa," he said, as he set the hook into a fish that grabbed his lure. "Holy cow, this is a good one," he said.

I watched him fight the fish for a minute or so and then moved to the back of the boat with the landing net. The water boiled next to the boat as the fish was almost at the surface. Thunderfoot raised the rod again and up came a really nice walleye. "Get him, get him!" he shouted.

I slid the net under the fish and hauled it into the boat. It was a dandy, probably about seven or eight pounds.

"Let's get a picture of him," I said, laying the net and fish in the bottom of the boat. I went forward and grabbed my camera. Meanwhile, Thunderfoot was getting the fish and lure untangled from the net.

"Leave the lure in its mouth and hold it up," I said as I knelt in the bottom of the boat. Thunderfoot stuck his first three fingers under the gill flap of the fish and held it in front of him.

"Say cheese," I said as I snapped the picture.

"Cheeee." Just as I snapped the shutter, the fish took a violent shake, and Thunderfoot lost his grip. His hand came out of the gill flap, the lure swung around and one of the treble hooks sunk into his thumb. The fish fell to the floor of the boat with Thunderfoot attached to the back treble hook.

"Yeeeeeooowww, the hook's in my thumb! Help! Help!" he yelled. The fish was thrashing around in the bottom of the boat, and Thunderfoot was trying to subdue it and keep it from jerking on the hook that was imbedded in his thumb.

I grabbed the fish and tried to quiet it. "Get the fish off the bait," he said, through clenched teeth.

The other hook was still deeply into the fish's jaw, so I had to lay it down to go get my needle nose pliers. The fish started thrashing again, and Thunderfoot went to his knees on the bottom of the boat.

"Hurry up, hurry up."

I found the pliers and grabbed the fish and removed the hook.

Then I lifted the fish and slid it back into the water.

Thunderfoot looked at me in disbelief. "You let my fish go."

"We aren't going to kill that big fish. We'll keep some small ones to eat, you know that."

"Well, you could have asked me first."

"Let me see that hook," I said.

One of the hooks from the treble was sunk into the meaty part of Thunderfoot's thumb, next to where it was attached to his hand. The barb was not visible.

"Ooo, it's past the barb," I said.

"Oh, great. What are we gonna do now?"

"Well, I can try to get it out, or we can quit for the day and go find a doctor."

"Get it out. It's too early to quit."

He turned his head to the side, and I pushed on the hook to see how much it would move. As I pushed, he grimaced and gritted his teeth but didn't say anything.

The hook was just past the barb, so I pushed down as hard as I dared on the shank and then pushed backwards. It moved out past the barb and then popped out of his thumb.

"There, that wasn't so bad," I said.

Thunderfoot was sweating and as pale as a ghost. "Oh, no that was just a lot of fun. I don't suppose it was too bad from your point of view."

"Jeez, I didn't do it to you, you did it yourself. Don't blame me," I said, kind of hurt after my lifesaving surgery.

"Sorry," he said, wiping his forehead and giving me a grin.

I moved back to the front of the boat and positioned it so we could begin fishing again.

I cast to the shore and was retrieving my bait when I heard his reel go "whirrrrr" and then there was a "sploosh" sound.

"What was that?" I said, turning my head to look back.

Thunderfoot was standing there with his mouth hanging open, with his hands out in front of him.

"What was that sound? What fell in?" I repeated.

He looked at me and then at the water. Then I noticed that my rod and reel weren't in the boat.

"My hand is kinda numb, and well, it kinda slipped when I cast and fell in," he said.

I took a deep breath. When I finished my retrieve, I cast again and retrieved the bait again.

Yelling wouldn't bring the rod and reel back; it could be replaced. Thunderfoot felt bad already and it wouldn't serve any purpose to make him feel worse. "Grab another one out of the rod box and try again."

He stood there a minute and then came forward and got himself another rod. He tied a lure on and then punched me in the shoulder as he went back to the back of the boat.

I turned and grinned at him and he said, "Next big one, you hold it. I'll take the picture."

Gladly.

Thanks, Thunderfoot.

Heave Ho

Thunderfoot picked up the phone on the first ring. "Yo."

"Geez, that's a nice way to answer the phone. Did you ever hear of saying hello?"

"I knew it would be you," he said. "Just how did you know that?"

"Because it's Thursday, and we always plan what we're gonna do on the weekend on Thursday night."

He knew me pretty well. "OK, smart guy, what do you think I've got planned?"

"I hope it's going to Lake Michigan and catching some salmon," he said expectantly.

I had been cooking up a trip to the big lake with a friend of mine who had a brother-in-law who lived on the lake and had a big boat for salmon fishing. Thunderfoot knew that we had a chance to go and was waiting for the call.

"We leave at 3 a.m. Saturday morning."

"Three! That's the middle of the night. Will there be any place open that early for breakfast?"

"We'll take some donuts and then stop later so you won't starve." That seemed OK to him, and he said he'd be over in a minute to get things planned. Since we didn't need to take anything with us except a lunch for on the boat, it didn't take long to get ready.

Friday afternoon, he came to my house right after school and we made sandwiches and packed cookies and chips and fruit for the next day's fishing. That evening he stayed over and we both went to bed early. My alarm woke us at 2:30; it took a little coaxing to get Thunderfoot out of his warm bed.

"You know, these salmon will average over ten pounds," I finally said after having little luck getting him motivated.

"Average? You mean there might be bigger ones than ten

pounds?" he said, sitting up in his bed.

"Some over twenty, but if you don't get your lazy butt up, we'll miss the boat and have to fish from shore and catch perch."

He was out of bed like a shot and after a trip to the bathroom to get "civilized" he was ready to leave. We stopped at my friend's house and picked him and his son, Travis, up and off we went toward the big lake.

The two boys were in the back seat and soon we could hear paper rattling as they dove into the sack of donuts. They each ate three or four donuts, leaving us with one each, and guzzled in a couple of quarts of milk. Then it got quiet and they both were slouched down in the seat sleeping.

"It never fails," I said, "ten miles into the trip, nap time."

We drove for another three hours and pulled into a truck stop for breakfast. The two sleeping beauties took a little rousing to get awake, but as soon as the smell of food from the exhaust fan in the restaurant got to them, they were up and ready for some breakfast.

"I need a lot of vittles to give me strength for hauling in those big old salmons," Thunderfoot said as he perused the menu. "I believe I'll have a large stack of pancakes with bacon and a large milk." He looked up at the waitress and gave her one of his famous smiles. She took our orders and in a short time we were all digging into huge plates of food. We finished breakfast and went looking for our host, whose boat was tied up at a slip down by the lake. It was just getting light as we pulled in and met our captain, and it only took a few minutes to load our lunches and get the boat untied and off into the mist that hung over the water.

We motored slowly down the river that led to the big lake. As we did, Thunderfoot was asking the captain lots of questions about all the fish we were hoping to catch. The captain explained that we would be about three miles from shore in two hundred feet of water. Thunderfoot's mouth dropped open at that comment. "How we gonna pull them up from so deep water?" he said.

The captain explained that our baits would be up higher and that the fish would be suspended above the bottom, so it wouldn't be that deep where we were actually fishing. Once we got to the open lake, the captain opened up the throttle and we took off out into the huge expanse of water. Thunderfoot was watching the depth finder, and it kept dropping and dropping and soon it read two hundred feet.

He looked at me with a kind of worried look on his face. "It's mega deep here."

We slowed the boat and the captain asked my friend to take the wheel and keep the boat going in a straight line, and then showed the rest of us how to rig the lines and let the baits back to the correct depth. We began setting the baits and rods in their trolling positions. Each bait was let back a certain distance and then the line was hooked into the clip of a downrigger and lowered to a measured depth. It was all quite impressive.

"Pretty scientifical," Thunderfoot quipped.

Once we had the four lines out, the captain took the wheel and we began trolling.

"We should decide who takes the first fish," I said.

It was decided to draw straws, so we cut four toothpicks into four different lengths and took turns picking them for the order in which we would take turns fishing. Longest went first, and then on down the line.

Thunderfoot drew the longest toothpick. "All right, let me at them."

About ten minutes later, one of the lines popped out of the downrigger and the pole began bucking. "Fish on!" yelled the captain.

"Take him," I said to Thunderfoot, but he just looked at the bucking rod and shook his head no. "You take the first one."

There wasn't time to argue, so I grabbed the rod and began playing the fish, which was about three hundred feet behind the boat. The rod doubled over and the fish fought like a whale. In its first run, I thought it would pull the rod out of my hands or me overboard, but I managed to gain line slowly but surely and in five or six minutes we could see the fish shining like a silver-blue streak in the water behind the boat. My friend grabbed the long handled net and when I brought the fish to the surface, he skillfully slid the net under it and lifted it into the boat.

"Whew, that's a beauty," Thunderfoot said, admiring the nice salmon.

"It should be yours," I said. "Why didn't you take the rod?"

"I guess I was just kind of wanting to see how it was done first.

You know, these things are pretty big and I thought they might pull me overboard, and the water's too deep for me."

"They're strong, but not that strong. You take the next one. You'll be fine."

It didn't take long for the next fish to hit, and this time Thunderfoot grabbed the rod and began fighting the fish as soon as "Fish on!" was yelled. He did a good job and after a good fight, he raised the fish to the net and it was in the boat.

"Whoa, that's the biggest fish I've ever caught," he said, admiring the salmon that would weigh close to twenty pounds. I grabbed the camera and took his picture with the fish; then we heard another "Fish on!" It was Travis' turn.

The next three hours were almost non-stop action. We would barely have one fish landed and another would be on. At one time, we had two fish hooked at once but, with all the confusion, lost both of them.

The boys were having a great time and were consuming the entire lunch, bit-by-bit, between their turns on the rods. As the sun got higher, the wind began to pick up, and by the time we were getting close to our limit, it was getting pretty hard to stand in the boat without holding onto something.

The lake was getting rough, so our captain suggested that we begin to work our way back to the harbor. We made a wide turn and began trolling back into the big rolling waves. Up we went, down we went, up we went, down we went.

Thunderfoot and Travis were sitting on the bench at the side of the boat and had suddenly become quiet. They were both holding onto the railing and had a definite pale look to their faces.

"Are you guys sick?" I asked.

"No, we're fine," Thunderfoot said. "I think we ate too much lunch, and maybe we've got a little upset stomach."

As he said that, Travis bolted to his feet and hung his head over the side and "prayed to the lake god." When Thunderfoot saw his pal hanging over the side, he suddenly turned green and joined him. I walked over and held onto both of the boys' belts to keep them from taking a swim. After a short while, they both stood up, shakily.

"You didn't bring a gun along, did you?" Thunderfoot asked.

"No, why?"

"I thought if you did, you could just shoot me and put me out of this misery," he said, as he leaned over the railing and said another prayer to the lake god. Travis followed him.

The boys "prayed" a couple of more times each, and then were done for. They both went down into the cabin and sprawled out on the bunk. The rest of us, who hadn't consumed enough food to feed a gang of lumberjacks, were feeling fine.

We worked our way back to the harbor and then to the slip. When we got there, we loaded the fish into our coolers and got the boys from their deathbeds. We all thanked the captain for a great fishing trip, and took off for home.

The boys were still kind of groggy, but as they got their land legs again, they began to come around.

"Holy cow, that was fun. Well, all except the sick part," Thunderfoot said.

"It's a lot different than what we usually fish for, isn't it?" I said. "No kidding, and the lakes we fish don't get so bumpy either. By the way, when are we gonna stop for something to eat?"

"As sick as you two were, I didn't think you'd want to eat anything."

"Obviously you didn't notice that our donuts, breakfast and lunch are floating in the lake. We're faminished."

Of course, how silly of me.

Thanks, Thunderfoot.

Just Like a Cannon Ball

"Go and look in the hunting closet," I said to Thunderfoot. He was in need of some old shoes to use for helping me with some roof repair. His feet were as big as mine, so I thought he should use some old castoffs instead of getting tar all over his good shoes.

"Jeez, there's a lot of junk in here," he said. "I thought we cleaned this out a while ago."

"About three years ago," I replied.

"Whoa, what's this? You got a bowling ball? I didn't know you could bowl."

"I can't; that's why it's in the closet," I said.

He came into the living room carrying my bowling bag and sat down and opened it and took the ball and shoes out. "Hey, this is cool. Why don't you bowl anymore?"

"Remember golf?" I said. "I was the same with bowling. At first I wasn't any good at it, then I got fair and then got pretty good. Then, I couldn't get any better than I was and started getting worse again. Rather than take all that frustration, I quit bowling. I should have thrown that ball in the river and forgot about it."

"No way, this is cool, and I like these white shoes, too. Quite snappy," he said, grinning from ear to ear. "Let's go try it out."

"No way, you remember me throwing a golf club into a corn field? I don't think I want to take the chance of throwing that bowling ball through the wall of the bowling alley when I do poorly."

"Oh, come on, let's go tonight. We can take Scott along; he's a real bad bowler so you won't be worst," he said, speaking of his buddy Scott who often went along with us.

"Oh, so Scott is worst, and does that mean that you're a good bowler?"

"Well, of course, I hate to brag, but I have been known to throw a few strikes," he said as he puffed up his chest and rolled an imaginary ball through the living room.

"OK, smart guy, we'll see. Call Scott and tell him we'll pick him up at seven."

He was grinning like Sylvester the cat after he had popped Tweety into his mouth as he called Scott.

We got the roof tarred and had some lunch and then I took a little nap so I'd be ready to show these two kids how to bowl. We picked up Scott and drove to the bowling alley, and the boys rented shoes. But I, the old pro, had my own. We went down to the alley and changed shoes and then the boys picked out a house ball while I got out my ball and polished it up. I felt pretty smug with a couple of rookies like these two, and didn't think I would have any trouble beating them.

"Can we take a practice roll first?" Scott asked.

"Sure, go ahead," I said.

Scott stepped up, put his toe on a dot on the floor, raised his ball to eye level, concentrated for a second, took five practiced steps and rolled the ball down the lane, right into the pocket and smashed the pins. "Strike!" he shouted.

He turned around and walked back and sat down. "Go ahead," he said to Thunderfoot.

Thunderfoot stepped up, put his toe on the next dot over, raised the ball, took his five steps, and rolled another perfect strike, the twin to Scott's. "Steeeeerike," he said, grinning like mad.

"Your turn," he said to me as he walked by.

Suddenly, my haughty air was gone. I was pretty stunned by the form and ability of these two kids. "Where did you learn that?"

"Learn what?"

"How to bowl like that."

"Physical Ed class, they teach us the way to do it and we just do it," Thunderfoot said matter-of-factly.

Oh, boy, I was in trouble. I picked up my ball and put my toe on my spot and sized up the pins. Being left handed, I had a natural curve, so I had to throw the ball real close to the left gutter to keep it from going too far to the right and missing the pocket. I took a deep breath and started my steps. One, two, three, four, and Bang. My right foot slid out from under me at the foul line just as I let the ball go. I landed on the floor on my butt, with my legs sticking over the line, and the ball bounced down the gutter and into the back of the lane. BZZZZZZZZZZZ went the foul buzzer.

I got to my feet as quickly as I could so the whole bowling alley wouldn't see me laying on my back and turned to go back to the seats. Thunderfoot and Scott were doubled over with laughter, tears running down their cheeks. As I approached the seats, they both got up and scurried out of the way.

"Maybe, you better, he he he, check your shoes, he he, they seem to be a bit slick," Thunderfoot managed to say. Scott was speechless, laughing too hard to talk.

My butt hurt but my pride was much more highly damaged, but I tried to put on a good game face. "Well, at least I got that over with so now we can bowl," I said.

"Don't you want another practice?" Thunderfoot asked before falling over with laughter again.

"Just bowl!"

Well, after the first disastrous throw, I did quite a bit better. I threw a couple strikes and picked up a few spares. The boys were a little cooler, too, both bowling pretty well but not running away from me. By the time we got to the eighth frame, Thunderfoot was leading Scott by eleven pins and me by eighteen. He threw a strike in the eighth and so did Scott, so I had the pressure on me. I took extra long to get ready and as I was thinking about my shot, I could hear Thunderfoot whispering in the background. "Don't choke."

I took my steps and threw a perfect ball and got a strike. As I turned around, I gave him a "did you see that" look. He was impressed by the look on his face.

In the ninth frame, Thunderfoot had a bad ball and left himself with a spare. He took careful aim and picked it up. Then Scott threw a split and missed picking it up, so I had a chance to catch up a bit. I got as serious as I had ever been about a non-fishing event and threw another strike. As I got back to the boys, sitting on the bench, I raised my hand for a high five, but they weren't in the mood apparently.

Frame ten, Thunderfoot stepped up and threw a bullet that turned into a smashing strike. His second ball picked up only eight pins, and then he picked up the other two. Scott split again and was done. If I struck out, I could win, but I had to strike out. The first ball went into the pocket like it had radar and made a perfect strike. Thunderfoot was noticeably shaken. "Don't choke," he whispered. I ignored him.

My second ball was a twin to the first, and all the pins flew like leaves in a fall windstorm, except for the ten pin which stood there and teetered back and forth. "Fall down," I shouted, and the pin tipped over.

Now Thunderfoot was really worried. His lead had vanished, and if this ball struck, I would beat him. In fact, I only needed eight to tie and nine to win.

"You better check your shoes again," he said. "I'd hate to see you fall on such a crucial shot."

I ignored him. I got ready for my shot and took a deep breath.

"The shoes are fine," I thought to myself "Don't worry about the shoes."

I started my steps, and as my fifth step came in contact with the lane, my shoe slipped out from under me. My ball went down the alley much too far to the right and as my butt hit the alley, the ball hit the ten pin.

BZZZZZZZZZZZ went the foul buzzer.

I had done the splits when I threw the ball and as I got up, I could feel a draft and reached around to feel the seam in my

166

pants. It was split from the belt loop to the bottom of the zipper. My plaid boxers were now in view of everyone in the alley.

I would have done anything rather than turn around and see the whole place snickering and laughing, but there was no place to go but back toward Thunderfoot and Scott, who by now were both laying on the floor clutching their stomachs.

I sat down to cover up my exposed backside and began to take off my shoes.

"What, don't you want to play another game?" Thunderfoot cackled.

"This is quite enough for one night," I said, as I packed my shoes and ball into the bag. "If you guys are riding with me, you better get your shoes changed. I have a stop to make on the way home, and I want to get there quickly."

They changed their shoes and we got into the truck and headed out.

As we got close to home, we started across the bridge that crosses the Wisconsin River on the way into town. I stopped the truck in the middle of the bridge, put on the flashers, and got out, taking my bowling bag with me. I walked up to the railing of the bridge and zipped open the bag, took the ball out, extended my arm out over the river and dropped it. Kersploosh!

Then I picked up the shoes and bag and dropped them over the rail, too. I got back into the truck. The boys were dumbstruck.

They sat there looking at me like I was insane. "Go ahead, say it, and no, I'm not crazy. I just don't want to bowl ever again, and without that miserable ball and shoes, I won't be tempted to do it again."

They never said a word. We finished driving home and dropped Scott off at his house. He thanked me for a nice time and walked slowly to the house, probably thinking that I had finally lost my mind.

When we got to my house, Thunderfoot got out and stopped.

"Are you mad at me."

"No, not a bit."

"Well, I don't want us not to be pals," he said.

I put my arm around his shoulder and gave him a hug. "That's not gonna happen over some silly game. Don't worry about it. It's water under the bridge, so to speak."

He grinned at that. "More like bowling ball under the bridge." At least it wasn't cluttering up the closet anymore.

Thanks, Thunderfoot.

Close Quarters Camping

The summer was almost over, and Thunderfoot and I had decided to go on a camping and fishing trip over the Labor Day weekend. I called ahead to a campground and made a reservation for a campsite and we were in the backyard, getting things ready.

"First, we've got to dean up the pickup," I said.

Thunderfoot was busy unrolling the hose, and I went to the house for a bucket of soapy water so we could wash all the dust and dirt from the box of the pickup. I had an old topper shell, and we were going to put it on the pickup box and use it for a place to sleep. A double mattress fit just perfect in the box, and this would eliminate the need for a tent and all the extra work that was involved in setting it up and then having to sleep on the ground.

"This will work great and give us more time to fish instead of working at setting up a camp," I said.

Thunderfoot dove right in and soon we had the truck sparkling clean. We waited for it to dry out and then put the topper shell on and damped it down. We took the mattress off the bed from Thunderfoot's room, which used to be my spare bedroom and outfitted it with some sheets and blankets and pillows.

"Wow, that's cool," Thunderfoot said as we finished up the bedroom in the back of the truck.

We packed a cooler with some food and pop and loaded up a few pots and pans for cooking, some lawn chairs for lounging at the campsite and the dogs' dishes and some dog food. We had decided to take Katy and Kirby along, and they were frantic when they saw their dishes going into the back of the truck, knowing that they were going along. We finished loading and backed the pickup up to the boat and hooked it on, and we were ready to leave.

About an hour later, we pulled into the campground and I went to the office to find out where our campsite was. Thunderfoot hooked the dogs up to a couple leashes as required by the campground and took them for a short walk while he waited.

When I got back, we drove down the crooked road that roamed through the park to our site and looked it over. There was a picnic table and a fire pit and not much else at the site. We had everything else that we needed, so we just set our cooler and box of groceries on the table and went down to the boat landing to unload the boat. After I unhooked the straps from the boat and backed it down the ramp, Thunderfoot jumped in and started the motor and drove it off the trailer. I went back to the campsite and unhooked the trailer and left it parked there, while the dogs and I waited for Thunderfoot to pick us up. Our campsite was right on the water's edge, and in a couple minutes, he pulled up along the shore and I carried each dog through the shallow water and put them into the boat. Then I climbed in and we took off for an afternoon of fishing.

It was a glorious fall day and we had great luck fishing, catching many walleyes and some northerns and bass. The dogs lounged in the boat and barked at the other dogs in passing boats who had the nerve to be on 'their' lake, and all in all it was a great day. By late afternoon, Thunderfoot was getting "faminished" so we went in for something to eat. We pulled the boat up and tied it up to a tree, unloaded the dogs and started a fire in our fire pit. We had a little grate to put over the fire and soon our potatoes were sizzling and the beans were boiling. Thunderfoot was grilling two hot dogs on his weenie stick that he had cut from a nearby tree.

The dogs were waiting for their share, and we cooked and ate for quite a while to get everyone filled up.

"Give the dogs their dog food, too," I said, "and I'll make sure the boat is secure for the night."

When I got back, the pans and plates were all taken care of, and the two dogs were snoozing by the fire. It was getting dark by now, so we sat in our lawn chairs and talked and visited with some people who passed by.

About an hour later, Thunderfoot was rummaging around in the back of the truck. "What are you looking for?" I asked.

"My Jiffy Pop. There's nothing like fresh popcorn around a campfire," he said, emerging from the truck with two Jiffy Pops in his hand and a grin across his face.

He took the paper off the first one and held it in the fire. It didn't take long until the pan began sizzling, but he kept pulling it out of the fire because the wire handle was getting too hot to handle. "Jeez, this thing gets hot all the way up," he complained. Then he got an enlightened look on his face and took off his shoes and socks. He put a sock on each hand and used them as potholders. He turned to me and grinned at his own brilliance.

"You better hold that thing back a little, you'll burn it."

"I've done these a hundred times. The secret is to get them hot and then they pop better."

OK, who was I to argue. In a little while, the popcorn began popping and soon smoke began to billow out of the growing aluminum balloon on top. Thunderfoot pulled the popper out of the fire and shook it, trying to keep the corn from burning, but by the time things cooled down, most of the popcorn in the pan was a tan color and smelled pretty smoky.

"Ooch, this one got a bit hot," he said, handing it to me. "Here, this one is yours."

He ripped the paper cover off the second one and held it back away from the fire farther, and soon it began to pop and of course, it turned out beautifully.

He opened it and began eating the corn as I picked through the burnt hulls in mine.

"Sorry, I got yours a bit hot. Too bad I didn't bring another one along."

I tossed my cremated corn into the fire and took a handful of his. He started to protest but thought better of it.

We sat for a while and then decided it was time to go to bed.

I let the tailgate down and we lifted the dogs up into the back of the truck. Then we climbed up in and raised the tailgate. Then I lowered the door of the topper and there we were, a truck full of dogs and people. Thunderfoot and I were trying to get out of some of our clothes and to get under the blankets, and the dogs were trying to find a good place to curl up. We finally got everyone situated. Thunderfoot was on the right side of the bed, I was on the left, Katy was between him and me, and Kirby was curled up by our feet. It was a tight fit.

"This is a pretty cool camper," Thunderfoot said. "What do you think, Kate?" he said as he patted Katy on the back. Katy grunted her approval. "Well good night all," he said.

The campground was settling down for the night and most of the noise was dying down. I was almost asleep when I smelled the most awful smell. I raised my head just as Thunderfoot sat up in bed. "Holy cow, you stink."

"That wasn't me. Don't try to blame me for your smell," I said. "Whew, I can't breathe," he said, turning the crank on the louvered window on his side of the topper. "Open your window." I opened mine, too, and soon the breeze carried the malodorous smells out into the night.

Just as I was drifting off again, there came another blast of the same smell. "Come on, quit that," I said.

"Me? Me? Don't blame me. I didn't do that," he protested.

Just then Katy groaned in her sleep and let one go. "Oh, no, it's Katy," I said.

Another blast of dog essence filled the camper. "Holy cow, why is she doing that?" I said.

"Umm, maybe it's the beans," Thunderfoot answered.

"Beans, what beans?"

"Well, after supper, I gave the dogs the leftover beans. They liked them."

"Oh, great, pretty soon Kirby will start, too. We'll be gassed before the morning gets here."

Just then Kirby let one go.

Thunderfoot started cackling with laughter and soon I joined in.

The dogs looked at us like we had gone insane.

We settled down again and began to drift off to sleep but left the windows open, just in case.

About midnight, I woke up and had to go to the bathroom. I tried to go back to sleep, but there just wasn't any way I was going to be able to hold it until morning, so I decided to get up. Of course, I was pinned down by Katy on one side of me and Kirby on the other, laying on top of my blanket. I managed to move them, amid much protesting and yawning, and made my way to the back of the truck.

The latch on the tailgate had been broken earlier in the summer when Thunderfoot dropped an anchor on the metal handle, so it wasn't easy to open it, especially from the inside. I raised the topper door and decided to crawl over the tailgate. I straddled the tailgate and swung one leg over. Just as it got on the other side of the gate, the back of my thigh muscle cramped up.

"Ooohf," I said, trying to get my leg straightened out, and in doing so, my other leg cramped up, too. "Arrrrgh, oh, uh, ahhhh!"

Here I was, one leg on each side of the truck tailgate, and each had a cramp in the back of the thigh. I wallowed around like one of those big sea lions crawling up onto a rock and managed to fallout of the truck onto my back. The grass was all wet with dew, and I stretched my legs as best I could and finally got the cramps to loosen up. I was panting like I had just run a marathon and all wet from rolling around in the grass when I heard a chuckle.

I looked up and there was Thunderfoot resting his chin on the tailgate with Katy on his right and Kirby on his left. All three were watching me like I was some circus act.

"Uh, what exactly are you doing out there at this time of night?" he said, grinning from ear to ear.

"I had to go to the bathroom and got a cramp," I answered.

"I thought we were having an earthquake," he said. "Do you need some help?"

"No thanks, I'm all right now. Go back to bed."

I walked over to the toilets and got my business done and then returned to the truck. I carefully climbed back in and worked my way through the dogs who had taken over my bed while I was absent. I got snuggled down again when I heard a distinct noise coming from Thunderfoot's side of the camper.

"I heard that. Whew, now I smell that. You're rotten," I said.

I could feel the truck shaking from his laughter. "Katy, shame!" he chuckled.

Katy, indeed.

Thanks, Thunderfoot.

No Fool Like an Old Fool

Thunderfoot was trotting across the backyard as I put my .22 rifle in the back of the truck. We had made plans to do a little squirrel hunting that afternoon, and he had just called to see if I was ready. To be honest, I was sitting in my recliner having a nap when he called, but it didn't take me long to get my gear out and get ready, and I was waiting as he put his gun into the back of the truck.

"Let's be off then," he said, grinning at me. "OK, boss, where do you want to go?"

He thought a while and then suggested a farm that we hadn't hunted yet this season, so off we went. When we got to the farm, I drove past the house to an old logging road that was about a half mile farther down the way. Thunderfoot got out and took his gun from the back of the pickup.

"What are you doing with that shotgun? I thought we were after squirrels," I asked.

"Just in case I see a grouse, I want to be ready. Besides, I'm such a good shot, I can put nary a BB in anything but the squirrel's head." I didn't want to argue, so I told him I'd go back and park at the farm, then take the trail down the valley and meet him up on the ridge somewhere. That was fine with him and as I pulled out, he was sauntering down the logging road towards the woods.

I watched him go and had to remember back to our first squirrel hunting trip, many seasons earlier when he managed to step on every stick, rock and leaf on the road, earning him his nickname of Thunderfoot. Now, he walked along confidently, silently watching ahead and looking for movement that would give away the position of some unsuspecting squirrel. He had come a long way since that first trip.

I drove back up to the farm, crossed the fence and followed a well worn deer trail down into the valley. At the bottom, there was a nice open woods where several wild apple trees stood, and often you could find a free snack of an apple or two that the deer weren't able to reach. This time the majority of the apples had already been harvested by the deer. Tracks and deer pellets were everywhere.

I continued on down the valley, and the path crossed a dry creek bed. I carefully worked my way down the steep side of the ditch and stopped in the bottom to look at the smooth washed stones that littered it. I wondered how often water actually ran down that ditch. As I was standing there thinking about it, I looked up to see a ten point buck walking down the trail from the other side of the ditch, right at me. He had his head down and was sniffing the ground as he got to the edge of the ditch. He looked up and there I was, standing less than six feet away. I was looking up at him, my head being about level with his knees.

He stopped and stared at me, not knowing what this thing was that was standing in his path. My heart was beating so fast I was sure he could hear it, and I was holding my breath, so as not to let him see me move. It seemed like an eternity as he stood there, watching me for movement. Then, he raised his right foot about a foot up in the air and stamped it hard on the ground. I kept completely still. He raised his foot and stamped again. Nothing. He looked at me for another minute and then turned his head to the left and took a step that way. Just as soon as his left foot touched the ground, he turned real quickly to look back at me. I stood stone still. Then he took another couple steps and turned again, trying to catch me moving, but I was onto his game and kept still as a statue. Finally, he gave up the game and walked off through the woods.

I let out a breath and found that my knees were shaking like I had just run a marathon. That was the closest I had ever been to a live buck, and it was a pretty awesome experience. I continued on down the path and worked my way up on the hillside where I found a nice place to sit, and sat down for a rest and to watch for squirrels.

Now, if the truth be known, I really hoped I wouldn't see any squirrels. Not that I had anything against hunting them, I just liked it better when Thunderfoot did the shooting. After all, I fed the little critters at home in my bird feeders, so I wasn't too excited about finding any.

As I sat there, I could hear a squirrel barking up on the hill above me. He barked almost constantly, and I listened for quite a while before I decided to try to sneak up on him. I wasn't sure if I would shoot him or not, but it was good practice to see if I could get close enough, without being seen or heard.

I worked my way slowly up the hill and toward the barking squirrel.

He was having a good time, making lots of noise, so it was easy to tune in to the area where he was. As I got closer, I expected to see his tail jumping up and down as it usually does when a squirrel barks. The barking not only gives their position away, but the tail action usually pinpoints them.

The barking was plenty loud and seemed to be just ahead, but I couldn't see the squirrel. I figured he must be on the other side of the tree, so I snuck up close and began to look real hard. I leaned back against a big oak tree and looked up into the trees around me, looking for the now silent squirrel when suddenly there was an explosion in the tree above my head! Leaves, branches and bark, came raining down on me. Startled, I jumped away from the tree and stepped backward, and fell over a pile of brush onto my butt. I was laying there looking up into the tree, trying to figure out what had happened when I heard the snickering and sobbing coming from my left.

I couldn't see him, but Thunderfoot was over there someplace, and I could hear him laughing and choking.

"He he, uuu, he he, cuu, mmmfff, he he."

"You little snot, where are you?" I said, as I got to my feet.

"Ohohohoh, he he, jeez, whoooo, he he."

I walked over and there he laid on his back in the leaves,

tears running down his face, laughing his fool head off. He couldn't talk but held up a little wood tube with a rubber bulb on the end. A squirrel call!

"Oh, you little devil. You almost gave me a heart attack," I said, now grinning at my own foolishness.

"Oh, man, that was so funny, he he he, you were looking up at the trees and almost walked right up to me." More fits of laughter.

He had let me get right next to him and then shot his shotgun into the tree above my head. I was completely fooled by his squirrel call and walked in like a rat to a cheese baited trap.

We sat there a while and he finally calmed down enough to show me the call. It sounded pretty good, and after I inspected it, I put it in my pocket.

"Hey, give that back."

"I will, when we get home," I said. "I just got stared in the face by a huge buck and almost scared to death by a little brat, and I don't think my old heart will stand any more pranks. So I'll keep it until we're safely out of the woods."

"OK, my stomach hurts too bad from laughing to do any more stuff to you anyway."

Good, I had enough fun for one day already.

Thanks, Thunderfoot.

Not the Way to Start the Day

When we built our first duck blind several years ago, it was standing in the cattails at the edge of the pond. We had been able to walk right up to it and climb a little set of steps and we were ready to hunt.

Over the years, the beaver who shared the pond with us had built a dam at the lower end. The pond had grown by almost a third. Now, our duck blind was about twenty-five feet from the hard ground and we had to wade through mud and water to get to it.

"You know what we should do," said Thunderfoot, "is build a bridge to the blind, so we don't have to get wet when we go out."

It sounded like a good idea so we began to scrounge around for some material to build the bridge that wouldn't cost us, or rather me, a lot of money. We happened to be driving past the hardware store, when Thunderfoot yelled for me to stop. "Look there, those pallets. Do you suppose they'd give us some of them?" he said, pointing to a huge stack of used pallets that the store had out back.

"Let's go see," I said, and we went inside to ask. The storeowner was happy to let us have all we wanted, so we loaded up the pickup with as many as we needed and went home to do some preliminary work on the bridge project.

We got the chainsaw out and cut each of the pallets in half, making them just about two feet wide and about four feet long. Then we removed some boards from one end of each pallet, so the one before it would slide inside the end of the second one, and the two could be nailed together, one after another after another. We then got some wooden posts and a few two by fours to make the base. Our bridge was ready to install.

"Cool, we got most of the work done already," Thunderfoot said as we drove though the woods to the river bottoms. We parked the truck in our parking spot on the high bank.

"Now, if we only had all of this material out there in the marsh, we'd be in good shape," I said, looking at the hundred yards or so that we had to haul all the material.

"Oh, it won't take long," said Thunderfoot, as he hoisted a bridge section out of the truck and took off for the swamp. I followed with another and we made about six more trips each before we had all the lumber at the edge of the pond.

"Whew, that's it for me," I said, panting. "We'll come back tomorrow and do the building. I'm pooped."

Thunderfoot didn't argue, as he too was tired out from all the work. The next morning he was waiting for me in the kitchen when I got up. "Thought we should get an early start, right after some eggs and bacon?" he said, nodding his head up and down.

"Don't you have eggs and bacon and a frying pan at home?"

"Yeah, but you make them so much better than I do."

Big grin.

I made us some breakfast and then off we went to the swamp. We carried a saw and a bag of nails and a couple of hammers with us and began constructing the bridge. Actually it went together much faster than I had anticipated, and in a couple hours, we were done.

Our bridge snaked its way through the cattails from dry ground right up to the blind. We had attached a full sized pallet to the side of the blind by the door, for a kind of porch, and from that we could just walk on a dry bridge back to the hard ground. It was really nice and would make it easy to get into and out of the blind without getting wet and muddy. Plus, we could sneak into the blind quietly and not disturb any ducks that might be on the pond when we got there.

"A masterpiece of engineering," Thunderfoot exclaimed proudly as he looked over our creation. I had to agree and couldn't wait to try it out the following weekend.

The weather turned decidedly colder that week and on Saturday morning, there was a good coating of frost on the windshield as we started up the truck for the trip to the marsh. Thunderfoot scraped the windshield and as soon as we could see through it, we left for our blind with Katy, my golden retriever, sitting between us on the seat. We gathered up our gear and walked out across the marsh to the pond.

As we got to the bridge, I stepped up on it and it was covered with frost. My foot slid off into the water. "Wow, this thing is slippery, be careful," I said, as I stepped back on and slid my way out toward the blind. Thunderfoot came along behind me, walking carefully and Katy followed him.

We slipped and slid our way to the blind and when we got to the little porch, I unhooked the door to the blind and stepped to the side to let him and Katy into the blind first. He preferred the right side of the blind, so it was easier if he got in before me. As I took the step to the side, my foot slid off the edge of the porch, and in trying to recover my balance, lover did it and lost my footing on the other foot and in an instant, I was going over the side, into the water, head first!

I hit the ice-cold water and went straight down, about to my waist. My feet were up in the air and tangled in some button ball brush that grew next to the blind. I began to thrash around like a wildebeest caught in the jaws of one of those huge Nile crocodiles. I was running out of air and was trying to get my head above water. Finally I got my feet loose and flopped over on my back into the ice cold water. I tried to get up and out of the water as fast as I could, so I wouldn't soak through, but I'm just not the most graceful person and by the time I was able to climb back up onto the bridge, I was wet from head to toe.

I knelt there gasping for breath and dripping like a drowned rat for a while and then stood up. Thunderfoot looked dumbstruck. He stood there with his mouth hanging open with the most stupid look on his face. "I'll put out the decoys," he said as he climbed down the ladder into the canoe, which was parked in a little blind of its own. I nodded OK and climbed up onto the porch and stumbled into the blind and sat down.

My gun had gone into the water with me, so I opened the chamber and looked down the barrel to see if it was full of mud or grass. It was OK, so I loaded it and stood it against the front railing of the blind. Then I took off my hat and wrung the water out of it and turned down my hip boots and emptied them out. I took off my jacket and wrung as much water out of it as I could, just as Thunderfoot came back from putting the decoys out on the water.

He climbed back into the blind and edged past me to his side and sat down. He looked out over the pond and to the sky and didn't look my way at all.

There was complete silence, not a bird, not a duck, not a sound.

I began to shiver, and the blind began to shake. Thunderfoot was still looking toward the end of the pond, away from me.

I stared at him; he didn't look my way. Katy was sitting looking out the little dog hole in the front of the blind, and she didn't look at me either.

"Go ahead," I said.

"What?" he said, still looking away.

"Go ahead and laugh. I know it's killing you."

He turned and the tears were running down his face, and he began to laugh and laugh and laugh. "Holy cow, that was the funniest thing I've ever seen you do. Jeez, your feet were flying around, it looked like somebody had killed a moose or something." Tears were running down his face, and he was having a wonderful time telling me how stupid I looked upside down in the water. "I thought you were gonna knock the whole bridge down."

I let him have his fun for a few minutes and actually joined in.

I could just about imagine how it must have looked with me standing upside down in the mud.

"I'm sorry, did you get hurt any?" he finally said, wiping the tears from his face.

I showed him my right hand, where I had torn the skin off the palm when I made an attempt to grab the blind. "Just tore the bark off my hand. I think I'll live."

We sat there for a while and I began to shiver. The cold was beginning to go deep into my body.

"You're froze, aren't you?"

"Yeah, I'm getting pretty cold."

"Let's go home, and get you dry."

I didn't argue, and stiffly got to my feet and shuffled off the bridge while he picked up the decoys and closed up the blind.

We walked back to the truck and by the time I got there, I was feeling a little better, being warmed up by the walk.

As I got to the side of the truck, I could see my reflection in the window. My face was almost black with mud, and my hair was standing up straight on top and out on the sides, stiff with dried mud. "Jeez, I look like the Creature from the Black Lagoon," I said.

Thunderfoot cracked up again.

"You know, it might be better if you rode in the back of the truck and let me drive. You'll have mud allover the truck," he said, trying to suppress a grin.

I agreed that he was right and climbed into the box of the pickup for an undignified ride home.

"And, you know what? When we get home, I think we should get some more boards and put a handrail on that bridge."

I could hear him chuckling as we drove off.

Thanks, Thunderfoot.

Patience, My Boy, Patience

Thunderfoot and I had been scouting for our deer stands the previous weekend and had decided to hunt the woods on the high bank above our duck hunting marsh. Nearly every time we drove down the dirt road to the marsh, we had seen deer in one of the two fields that bordered the road, so we felt pretty confident that we would see some during deer season. At least, I felt confident. Thunderfoot wasn't convinced that we would see anything, but we enjoyed hunting in the area so he went along with the idea.

The woods that we were hunting were an impenetrable jungle of berry briars, prickly ash and scrub oak. It was a great place for deer to hide, and a terrible place for a hunter to walk. That's why I chose to sit in the edge of the fields that bordered the woods. We found two deer trails the came from the woods into the field on the west side of the lane and placed Thunderfoot's stand in between them, right at the fence. I went on the other side of the lane and decided on a stand under a huge pine tree in the corner of the field. It afforded a good view of the land, and was only about a hundred yards from where I would park the pickup, which was an added bonus.

"If you sit and stay put, I guarantee you'll see a deer," I told Thunderfoot.

"Yeah, but will it be during this season, or do I have to wait many years?"

My young friend wasn't the patient type. "Just be patient, you'll see," I said. "Years ago, I decided to sit in the same spot until I got a deer, and I did it. It took six days, but he came along finally. Then, after that, for the next ten years, I got a buck in the same spot every year. It's just a matter of waiting. One will come along, if you wait long enough."

I could tell he wasn't convinced, but he agreed to give it a try. On Friday before the season opened, I got all our gear out and ready. When he came over after school he couldn't believe

184

his eyes. "What's all this stuff? We going to the moon?"

"This is all essential stuff. If you're comfortable, you'll sit longer," I said. He began sorting through the two piles of gear. I had a folding lawn chair for each of us, and a duffel bag full of food and other essential things. He began unloading the duffel bag. "The food I can understand," he said, "but what's all this other stuff?"

"The hand warmers, for your hands, foot warmers, same but for your feet, rope, obvious, knife, same, shells, obvious, paperback book, something to pass the time, and toilet paper, again, obvious. Plus the salted in the shell peanuts, to pass time."

"Pass time?"

"Yeah, they give you something to do to keep you alert."

He just shook his head. "Do we really need all this stuff?"

"Leave it if you don't want it. You only have to walk a couple hundred yards across a flat field, and it'll make you more comfortable."

That night, Thunderfoot spent the night and we made sandwiches for the next day and then turned in. The alarm went off at 5 a.m., and we soon were driving down the road to the woods. It was still dark as midnight, but I wanted us to be on our stands and ready when it got light, so we walked down the lane until we came to the spot where we went different directions and as we parted to go to our stands, I whispered, "Good luck."

"You, too."

I crawled under my big pine tree and set up my chair and put my gear in strategic places on the ground around me. That way I was ready for the day and wouldn't have to do a lot of moving around for whatever I might need. As the daylight increased, I could just begin to make out Thunderfoot's orange jacket over on the other side of the field across the lane. He was right where he was supposed to be.

Dawn turned to day and morning turned to midday. We heard some shots in the area, but not a deer showed itself in either of our fields. I settled back and "rested my eyes" for a couple minutes and when I opened them, I just got a glimpse of a deer between two trees on the other side of the field I was watching. That was it, the only deer action we had for the day.

At closing time, Thunderfoot came walking across his field toward the truck. "Boy, this is a good spot. I saw lots of squirrels, but, oh, that's right we're DEER hunting."

"I never said we'd see one the first day," I said. "There's always tomorrow."

He just rolled his eyes and crawled into the truck.

The next morning we got up and began getting ready to leave.

"We're gonna do the same thing again?" he asked.

"Be patient, you'll see a deer." I could tell his patience was getting pretty thin.

We deployed as we did the previous day and the morning dawned and the sun rose and warmed things up and it was a gorgeous day. At about eleven o'clock, the clouds began to roll in and I saw Thunderfoot moving around and gathering up his gear and soon he was at my stand. He unfolded his chair and sat down next to me. "Did you miss me?" I said.

"No, you said if it started raining, I should come over here and we'd go home."

"Is it raining?" I asked.

"Yeah, it is out there," he said, pointing to the field, "but not under this big tree." I hadn't noticed the rain because of the big pine tree I was sitting under.

"Fine, you watch, I'll read for a while," I said, and opened my book. "Don't you think we'd see more deer if we took a little walk through the woods?"

"Nope, you remember what this woods is like? Prickly ash and berry briars are not my idea of a stroll through the woods."

"Do you think there's a deer within two miles of us right now?"

"Yup."

"Do you think there's a deer within a mile?"

"Yup."

"A half mile?"

"Why don't you shut up and let me read. Be patient, there could be a deer laying right over there in that little patch of brush right now. Just watch and suddenly there'll be a deer, I guarantee it."

"Yeah, but when? Today, next year?"

"If we sit here long enough, there'll be one."

"But ..."

"Shut up, and watch."

I began reading and looked up every couple of minutes to see if anything was happening. Thunderfoot had slid back in his chair, watching, but with little enthusiasm.

I had just turned the page when I heard him say, "Holy cow, there's some deer!"

I looked up and there, about twenty yards from us, was a doe, followed by a nice buck, trotting right toward us. "Shoot him!" I whispered. Thunderfoot raised his gun and aimed. "Shoot him!" I dropped my book and reached for my gun. When I did that, the deer saw me move and began trotting across the corner of the field, away from us.

"Shoot him!" I said, getting my gun up and aiming at the deer.

Thunderfoot was still aiming, so I took a quick aim and shot. The deer began running then, and Thunderfoot ran out into the field after him. "Get back! Get out of the way!" I yelled, as Thunderfoot ran between me and the deer. "Shoot him!"

Finally, he shot, and the deer fell down. "You got him!" I shouted, but the deer got up and ran off into the brush between the fields. Soon he appeared in the field that Thunderfoot had been watching and ran across the end of it and disappeared into the woods on the deer trail that Thunderfoot would have been sitting by, had he been patient and stayed on his stand.

"Oh, no, he got away!" he said.

"Let's see if we can find blood. I think you hit him."

We walked to the field and searched and searched but found no blood. The field was full of mole burrows, and the best that we could figure was that the deer must have tripped in one of them and had just fallen down. We found where he had crossed the lane and found no blood, nor did we find any along the deer trail that he had escaped on.

"Well, he got away clean, at least," I said. "I'd have hated to wound him and let him get away."

Thunderfoot was still dumbstruck, not saying two words since the deer had run in front of us.

"You OK?" I asked.

"Jeez, they just popped up like ghosts. I can't believe it."

"I told you that's what would happen, didn't I?"

He nodded his head. He hated being wrong.

"What took you so long to shoot?"

"I was aiming and he kept moving and I don't know what I did. I guess I got too nervous."

"Why didn't you shoot again, when you were out in the field?"

"I forgot to eject my empty," he said, sheepishly.

I began to laugh. "Well, we really did a good job of that. One reading a book, with no gun in his hands, the other with buck fever. Any deer that crosses in front of us is pretty safe."

"Yeah, you and your book."

I looked at him, and he grinned. "Of course, you may remember that I wanted you to sit right over there, about twenty feet from where the deer went into the woods. Had you been patient, he would have run right up to you."

He just shook his head and sat down. "I'm gonna hold my gun in my lap from now on. Do you think they might come back by again?"

"I doubt it, but there could be another any minute."

"Yeah, yeah, I know, be patient, be patient."

He was learning.

Thanks, Thunderfoot.

Here Yogi

"You know, this is the last year that you can just go buy a bear hunting license. Next year you have to start applying for them with a lottery type drawing, so it might take a long time to get one," Thunderfoot said, as we drove down the road toward the river. "1 read about it in the paper the other day."

"So, why do I care? We're not bear hunters," I said.

"We could be," he said. "My uncle has a cabin up in the north and he has bears there all the time, and he said we could go up there and use his cabin if we wanted to, so it won't cost any money for a place to stay and we can hunt right from the cabin and don't even have to drive some place to hunt, and it's a real cool place."

"You've been rehearsing that little speech for a while haven't you?" I said.

"Well," he grinned, "yeah, but it's still a good idea, huh?"

"Bear hunting? You've seen bears, right, those big black things with lots of teeth? They're not like ducks and squirrels. They bite back."

"Yeah, but think how exciting it would be to get one. We could bring it back and drive around town and let everyone see it. Way cool," he said nodding his head up and down.

"I'm not sure I want to shoot a bear; they never did anything to me," I said.

"Yeah, but this will probably be our only chance to ever go, and you wouldn't want me not to ever experience the glory of an autumn day in the north woods, hunting for bear."

He was sitting there with a miserable look on his face.

I just shook my head. "You poor, pitiful little thing."

He grinned; he knew he had me.

"When does the season open?" I asked.

"Next weekend, and I called Uncle Jim and nobody's gonna use the cabin and we can have it; in fact, I've already got the key," he said, digging in the pocket of his jeans and producing a key to the cabin.

"You were pretty sure I'd go," I said.

He just grinned; he knew I was easy.

The rest of the week we read up on bear hunting, watched some videos that we rented about bear hunting, and by Friday noon, we were loaded and on our way north. It was about a five-hour drive to the cabin, so we would probably get there after dark and not be able to scout, but we figured we could worry about that when we got there. On the way, we stopped at several sport shops to buy a bear license but were always told we had to get farther north because they didn't sell them. Finally we got to a shop that had the licenses and we both got one.

The terrain changed from steep hills and deep valleys to flat, low rising swells in the landscape. The north had been flattened by the last glacier and all of the hills had been ground down to little low rises that undulated along like the swells on a lake.

The last time we had come this way, we had seen a large bear lying alongside the road that had been hit by a car. As we drove past the place, Thunderfoot kept a sharp watch out just in case another one was in the area. "Could be a crossing," he said.

We got to the little town near the cabin and turned off on a county road that ran north toward our destination. The county road turned to a town road that was just gravel and not too wide, and then we came to the end of the dirt lane that ran to the cabin. "Just turn in here and we follow it for a while till we get to the cabin," Thunderfoot said, reading the directions on the slip of paper he was holding.

I turned down the dirt road and we drove for almost a mile and came to a fork in the road. "Which way?"

"Hmmm, the paper doesn't say anything about a place like this," he said.

We looked at the roads and they both looked about the same, so we flipped a coin and took the one to the right. Of course, it went about a quarter mile and ended at a cabin that looked as if it hadn't been occupied for many years. "Well, now we know which road to take," Thunderfoot said merrily.

We got turned around and backtracked to the fork. We took the left fork and went another mile or so and there was the cabin. It sat in the middle of a large clearing in the woods, was built of logs and was quite a nice place. It had a well cared for lawn and there was a shed next to it that housed a gas generator and a water pump and stored firewood for the huge stone fireplace. "Wow, your uncle has a nice place here," I said.

"Yeah, he has a guy who lives up here take care of it, so when he comes up he doesn't have to work all the while he's here."

We unloaded the truck and went into the shed to start the generator and soon had the cabin unlocked and the lights on and a fire going in the fireplace. It was furnished like most cabins, with a couple of couches that opened into beds, a kitchen table that served as a dining table and a place to play poker on a cool fall evening. There were two bedrooms, and each had a set of bunk beds in it, so with the couches opened, eight people could sleep comfortably there. We put our stuff in one of the bedrooms, unloaded our food into the refrigerator, and then sat in a couple of big comfortable chairs by the fireplace. I slid off my shoes and was toasting the bottom of my feet when Thunderfoot went over by the big picture window that looked out over the lawn and stopped by a light switch.

"Watch this," he said. "Uncle Jim said to turn this on after it gets dark, and we'll see some cool stuff"

He flipped the switch and a spotlight burst to life that was aimed at a shallow hole in the ground about a hundred feet from the cabin. Mineral salt had been dumped into it for years, and there were nine deer at the salt lick, digging and pawing and not paying any attention to the light. "They're used to it," Thunderfoot said, as we watched the deer. Most were does but there was one huge buck and a couple smaller ones. All seemed to be taking turns enjoying the salt and were oblivious of us watching them.

"We better get some supper and then get to bed if we're going to hunt in the morning," I said, and we began fixing some food. We hadn't planned anything fancy, and I opened a can of stew and put it in a pan to heat. We got out some bread and butter to go with it and soon we both were full and ready for bed.

Dawn was about six the next morning, so I set the alarm for five to give us time to get a little breakfast before we left. We got up, ate some eggs and toast and soon were walking across the lawn toward the woods. The wind had come up during the night and there was a distinct nip in the air. We followed a fire lane for a while and soon it intersected another.

"Why don't one of us stay on this lane and the other go down that one?" I said, not having the faintest idea of how to go about hunting bears in the north woods. "If you can find a good looking spot, sit for a while and I'll do the same. If you find any sign, like bear poop, that's probably a good thing."

"Do they always poop in the same place?" Thunderfoot asked, grinning.

"No, dummy, but it means there was one there and he might still be around. How do I know, you're the expert here."

We separated and walked off, each down our own fire lane and soon I was all alone in a forest that probably ran for a hundred miles in any direction, in a gale force wind, without the faintest idea of what I was doing, looking for a bear. What was I thinking?

A short way down the fire lane, I ran across a deer path that crossed the lane. I was looking at the tracks in it when I realized that I was looking at a bear track in the middle of it. There was another and another, and they were following the deer trail into the woods to my right. Hmm, maybe this wasn't going to be so hard after all. I followed the trail into the woods and I had only gone ten feet when I began to feel closed in. There was no open area to see what was ahead or to the side of you. The trees and brush were so dense that you could only see a foot or so in any direction around you. These woods weren't like the ones I was used to at home. There we had big trees and some underbrush, but the woods were open, so you could see for a long way. Here the trees were all medium size and real close together, and so dense that you could only see a few feet ahead of you. I followed the trail for what seemed like a long way, and suddenly came to an area that was fairly open, compared to the rest of the woods. Here I could see, maybe, twenty feet around me. The trail went on into the thick stuff again, so I decided that this was where I was going to make my stand. I moved off the trail and found a stump to sit on and sat down. If the bear was planning on going past on the deer trail today, I'd be waiting for him.

I sat there trying to hear any movement, but it was almost impossible because of the wind. The trees swayed and danced and leaves flew like yellow snowflakes. Many of the trees were aspens and birch, and their leaves were flying through the air like a yellow and brown snowstorm. If a bear came by, he was going to be right next to me before I had any indication that he was coming. I was not very comfortable with my situation, and was thinking of getting the heck out of there, when I heard a noise right behind me that sounded like a large animal crashing through the brush. The hair on the back of my neck stood straight up and I whirled around to meet the charge. All I could see were the trees and bushes swaying in the wind. No more sounds came but, suddenly, there was a crackling and breaking of brush from the other side of the clearing. "Oh, my God," I thought. "He's charging from the other side."

I spun around to meet the charge and, again, no more sounds came from that direction. "I must be losing my mind," I thought.

By now I was thoroughly spooked and decided that this was insane.

I really didn't want to shoot a bear anyway and wasn't going to sit here any longer and end up being a meal for an angry bear, so I crossed the clearing and followed the deer trail back to the fire lane. When I got to the open lane, I felt much safer and stopped to catch my breath. I looked down and saw a familiar foot print in the soft sand next to mine where I had been following the bear print. It was Thunderfoot's boot track, and it was following mine into the woods. The little fool had followed me into the woods and was sneaking around pretending to be a bear!

I was about to yell at him when I had a better idea. I took off running down the fire lane back towards the cabin. I ran into the cabin, picked up the duffle bags, still empty, and ran from the cabin and threw them into the back of the truck. Then I jumped in the truck and flew out of the driveway and down the lane spinning gravel and making a huge cloud of dust.

I drove till I was out of sight and then parked the truck and snuck back up the road toward the cabin. As I got near, I could see Thunderfoot pacing back and forth in the front yard, obviously thinking I had been so scared that I had left him behind. I snuck around the shed and got as close as I dared and then let out a loud ROAR!!!! He almost jumped out of his boots and spun around in mid air, with his gun pointed at me.

"Whoa, whoa, I surrender," I said, raising my hands above my head. He dropped the gun immediately and stared at me. "You, uuu, you, I thought you dirty bugger. I don't believe you did that."

I was laughing myself silly by now. "What, can't take your own medicine? I knew that was you in the woods. You sneaky little snot."

He began to grin. "Yeah, you knew, my foot. You were ready to pee yourself. You were jumping around like a scared chicken. How did you know it was me?"

"Your foot prints on the deer trail. Do you think I'm blind?" "Darn, never thought of that. What do you think of this bear hunting? Man, I got into those woods and couldn't see anything, so I came looking for you. Want to keep at it?"

I turned my thumb down.

"Me, too. You know, that stream over there is full of trout and I saw a monopoly game in the cabin."

"Good idea," I said. "Tell you what, you hike down the road and bring back the truck and I'll make us some lunch and then we'll just take the rest of the weekend and relax and let the bears alone."

"Sounds cool to me," he said and began walking toward the truck.

"Hey Yogi, hey Booboo, don't worry, you're safe," he yelled.

Thanks, Thunderfoot.

Yo Quero Taco Bell

Thunderfoot and I had been planning this trip for many weeks. We were in Escanaba, Michigan, on Little Bay de Noc, which was a part of the upper end of Lake Michigan. Several weeks earlier, we had watched a TV show that showed the host catching walleye after walleye on the bay, and we had decided it was worth the six-hour drive to give it a try.

We arrived on Friday afternoon, checked into our motel, and then went down to the waterfront to look over the lake.

"Wow, that's big," Thunderfoot said. "A little bigger than what we're used to fishing."

"No kidding," I said. "You can barely see the other side. You think we can find walleyes in all that water?"

He looked apprehensively at me, but grinned. "Why not? If those TV dudes can, why can't a couple of experts like us do it, too?"

I hoped he was right. We went back to town and decided to stop for something to eat before we headed back to our motel.

"Let's stop at the Taco Bell," he said, pointing to the restaurant on the left.

"No way. Tacos will keep me up all night. I want something that's not so spicy."

He grumbled and griped a while, but we settled on a mom and pop cafe. We had a good supper and then went back to the motel for a good night's sleep.

Next morning, we stopped at a bait shop and got a map of the bay and some advice, and soon we were motoring across the big water. Thunderfoot looked a bit uneasy as we got farther and farther from shore.

"Boy, I hope we don't get lost out here," he shouted over the noise of the motor.

"Don't worry," 1 said. "I set the boat landing as a way point on my GPS. We just have to tell it to take us to number one and it will point the way, just like a video game."

He perked up at that bit of information. "No kiddin', it can do that?"

"Yup, you just push this button, and it remembers the latitude and longitude of the spot and stores it for you. Then when you want to go back there, it shows you the pathway from where you are, to the spot. We can lock in spots that we find fish, too. It's a cool gizmo."

Thunderfoot was fascinated and seemed to feel a little less apprehensive about being on such big water.

We checked out some reefs and sandbars on the map and soon found one that was full of walleyes. It didn't take long for us to catch several nice ones. "Let's lock this in on the GPS and go look for some other places," I said. "I hate to catch too many and have to quit so early."

Thunderfoot agreed and we took off down the lake for another spot on the map and some more walleyes. We kept it up all day and soon had about four really good spots locked into the machine.

"So, tomorrow we can just push number three and come back here?" he asked.

"Yup, tomorrow I'll show you how it works," I said.

We went in and cleaned our fish and went back to the motel and put them in the freezer, and then cleaned up for a trip to town and some supper.

"Hola, senor. Tengas un Taco?" he said as we approached Taco Bell.

"Excuse me?"

"I'm taking Spanish at school, you know. I asked you if you had a taco." He grinned.

"You're gonna pester me till I stop at Taco Bell, aren't you?"

"Si, senor," he said, grinning.

We turned into the Bell and went inside. As I looked over the menu, Thunderfoot got into line and began ordering in Spanish.

"Want me to order for you, too?" he asked. "Yeah, go ahead. But don't get me anything too spicy." What a bad mistake that was.

He picked up the tray and I paid, as usual, and we went to a table and began to eat. The food was good, but way too spicy for an old guy. But I was too hungry to be sensible, and I ate my share of the tacos, refried beans and whatever else he had ordered. We hadn't even left the restaurant and I was already feeling the aftermath of the food.

"Oh, I'm gonna regret this," I said, finishing off my last taco.

We went back to the motel and watched TV for a while and then went to bed. I had hardly laid my head down when I felt the first wave of heartburn and had to get up for some Turns. That went on all night, up and down for Tums and Alka Seltzer. By morning, I was more tired than I had been the evening before and worn out from all my traveling between the bathroom and my bed.

Thunderfoot was smiling and real chipper, ready for a big greasy breakfast as I staggered from our room to the truck.

"Boy, you look like crap," he said cheerily.

"Thanks, and thanks for talking me into those tacos. They almost killed me during the night."

"What a weakling."

We had breakfast and took off for the water. We motored up the lake and stopped at our first waypoint and found our reef real easily. We began to catch fish right away.

"Wow, that thing works pretty darn good," Thunderfoot said as he reeled in a nice walleye.

We fished at the first place for a while and then continued along our path of waypoints and caught fish at each of them. As the day wore on, I could tell that I was going to have to pull into shore someplace for a bathroom break before long. The tacos had worked their way down to the lower part of my system and were going to be parting company with me soon.

"We're gonna have to go in pretty soon; I'm gonna have to visit the latrine," I said.

"What? You're surely kidding. Do you know how far that is? We'll waste a whole hour going all the way in."

"Well, I'm gonna have to go and pretty soon, so get ready," I said. "What you gotta do? Can't you just do it over the side?"

"It's not that. I've got to sit to do this."

"Oh, no! Why didn't you do it before we left?"

"I did, and I did it all night, thanks to you and your tacos, but I have to go again and pretty darn soon, so you better reel up," I said, feeling a particularly bad cramp coming on.

"Oh, man, what a baby. Sit on the back of the boat and let her rip," he said.

Suddenly I had another cramp, and I knew he was going to get his wish. There was no way I was going to make it all the way to the shore.

"OK, you win. Get in the front and keep me pointed away from the other fishermen," I said. I squatted down and lowered my pants and carefully sat on the back edge of the boat, next to the motor.

Thunderfoot was sitting on the front seat, running the foot control electric motor and began turning the boat so the back end was facing toward a bunch of boats off on the other side of the submerged reef.

"Hey, quit that! Turn us back the other way," I said.

He began laughing and kept turning us so my bare backside was going to be shining in the direction of the other boats. "Hey, you little snot, turn us back the other way," I said, as I tried to pull my jacket down to cover my obvious asset, and in doing so, lost my grip on the motor. In less than a second, I went over backward into the lake. Now, it was bad enough to fall into Lake Michigan, into water that was about fifty-five degrees, but it was even worse with my pants around my ankles.

I did a somersault as I hit the water, and when I came to the surface, I grabbed the back edge of the boat. I couldn't see Thunderfoot sitting on the front seat, but could hear him laughing from the bottom of the boat. He was laying in the bottom, clutching his stomach and laughing crazily.

"I'm gonna drown you, I said."

"Oh, ho, ho, not if you can't get in the boat, you're not," he laughed.

"Come here and help me in."

"No way."

"Come on, this water is cold as heck. I won't do anything to you. Promise."

He came back and grabbed the back of my shirt and pulled as I gripped the motor and lifted myself up. As I cleared the water, he began howling again as my bare butt came up into view.

"If the other boats didn't see your butt when you fell in, they sure do now," he said, laughing and crying.

Right then I didn't care; I wanted to get out of that cold water and back into the boat. I finally made it in and flopped on the floor of the boat like a harpooned walrus. Thunderfoot scampered past me to the front seat and began to fish, like nothing had happened.

I crouched in the bottom of the boat and got my pants up and everything situated and then stood up. The people in the other boats all began applauding.

I felt pretty foolish, but what the heck. I took a graceful bow.

The sun was out and it didn't take me long to dry out, so we fished for several more hours before we loaded up for the trip home. As we were driving through town, we were coming up to the Taco Bell, which was just on the right ahead of us.

"Ahhh, senor " he began.

"What's the Spanish word for 'no way'?"

"Hmmm, we haven't learned that one yet."

"Well, I'll use English then... no way. Que Pasa?"

"Si, senor."

Gracias, Thunderfoot.

In the Heat of the Night

The thermometer outside read 96 degrees, and it was only ten O' clock in the morning. We had been having a hot spell that was about five days old, and I was planning on taking it easy for the day and sitting in the air conditioning with a good book when the phone rang.

"Whatcha up to?" It was Thunderfoot.

"Staying cool. Have you been outside yet?"

"No kiddin', it's like the desert out there. Say, you wouldn't want to give me a ride to the appliance store later, would you?"

"What are you buying?"

"Well, Mom ordered a new air conditioner and they called and said it's in, but she's gone for the day, and I want to get it and cool off the house and surprise her when she gets home."

That sounded like a noble idea, so I got some shoes on and went out to the van to go pick him up. It was like a sauna in the van, but it cooled off fast as soon as I turned on the AC. The pickup didn't have air, so the van was much nicer to drive in the summertime. Thunderfoot was waiting and sprinted out to the van as I pulled up. "Whew, it's nice in here," he said.

We drove to the appliance store, which was just down the road in the next town. As we drove along, we passed a roadside fruit stand and there was a big pile of watermelons on a cart in front of it. "Yum, those look good," Thunderfoot said.

I had to admit that a nice slice of cold melon would be nice, so we made a U turn and went back to get one. Thunderfoot thumped and shook about a dozen melons and pronounced one "perfect" and picked it out of the pile. He was standing with it balanced on one hand on his shoulder while I paid for it. "Be careful with that thing," I said. "If you drop it and bust it, you bought it."

He looked at me with a mock worried look, and started back to the van. I talked with the melon salesman about the weather for a bit and then went back to get into the cool van, which was idling so the AC would keep it cooled off. Thunderfoot was sitting in the back seat. I opened the door, and there, sitting on the front seat, was the watermelon, strapped in with the seatbelt!

"Is that safe enough for you?" he said, chuckling from the back seat. "Oh, real funny," I said. "Put this back there and come up here."

I had to laugh even though he was being a smart butt.

We got back on the highway and soon were at the appliance store.

His mom had paid for the air conditioner so all we had to do was pick it up. I backed up to the delivery door, Thunderfoot put it in the back of the van and we turned around and headed for home.

When we got to his house, I asked him if he needed help unloading the AC and installing it. "Nope, I can do it just fine. You go put the melon in the fridge and I'll come over and sample some of it when I get done here."

That was OK with me, and I drove home, put the melon away and settled down for a nap in my recliner. A couple of hours later, I was awakened by the noise of the refrigerator door being shut. I looked into the kitchen and there was Thunderfoot with a huge knife, carving at the watermelon.

"Man, you were snoring up a storm," he said.

"Have some melon," I said.

Big grin. "Thanks, I think I will. Can I cut some for you?"

He cut me a slice, and we sat at the table and enjoyed the cold melon. His hair was all wet and his clothes looked damp, too. "Did you just shower or are you still sweating?"

"I'm sweating. It's still really hot in the house; the new air conditioner doesn't seem to work very well."

"Really? It sure looks big enough. Are you sure you installed it right?"

"What's to install? You plug it in and it's installed."

"Yeah, but did you seal it up real well around the window?"

A stupid look came across his face. "Window? What do you mean?" "You have to put it in the window and then seal up the space around it so hot air doesn't come back in."

He chomped down his melon and headed for the door. "I'll be back later."

I was curious about what made him leave so fast, so I put away the melon and dishes and walked over to his house. As I walked up to the door, I could see Thunderfoot measuring the window in the living room, and the air conditioner, sitting on a small table, in the middle of the room, running.

He looked up and saw me staring at the AC and shook his head.

He knew he was in for it.

"Uh, I know what to do. You go chill the melon," I snickered. "I'm so smart, you don't have to tell me anything."

"Oh, man, you can be so sarcastic sometimes," he said.

The house was as hot as an oven, so we unplugged the air conditioner and opened a window. Then we put the unit in the window opening and slid the little accordion-like things on the top and bottom out to fill the open space. We plugged it in and soon nice cool air was filling the room.

"Hmm, it seems to work pretty well now," I said.

He just looked at me. "OK, for once you're right, but once in a while you're bound to be right. It's just the law of averages."

Sure, sure, but it was sure nice for a change.

Thanks, Thunderfoot.

You Should Model For Calvin

"Let me use it. Please, please, please," Thunderfoot pleaded.

"It's the last one left, and I paid for them, so ..." I said.

"Oh, come on, that's my favorite bait in the whole world. I'll be careful with it, I promise. You can use it after I catch a couple on it, honest."

We were arguing about our last Mississippi Swamper. It was new bait that we had found earlier that summer that we had been having fantastic luck with. It was a soft, plastic bait that had a great wobbling action as it came through the water, and drove northerns and bass wild. I had bought a half dozen of them and this was the last one. The only problem with them was that since they were made of soft plastic, the teeth of a northern ripped them up and after a while, they fell apart. Also, we lost them more than regular baits, because we didn't use a steel leader with them. The action wasn't as good with a leader, and the teeth of a northern often cut our lines, so the life expectancy of a Swamper was kind of short.

I knew Thunderfoot would bug me all day if I didn't give him the bait, so I tossed it to him in the front of the boat. "Now be careful with it."

He was all grins as he tied it on and cast to an opening in the weeds. He had hardly taken two turns on his reel when a fish hit and took off toward the weeds. He set the hook and the line went limp. The northern had cut his line. "Oh, no, the Swam- per!"

Our last Swamper was gone. Thunderfoot was looking pretty dejected. "We might as well go home," he said.

"Oh, come on, don't be such a baby. We've got other things that'll catch a fish."

He tied another bait on but his heart just wasn't in it. The Swampers were his favorite, and others just didn't give him any confidence. We fished another couple of hours and only caught two small fish. "See, we need some Swampers," he said.

We pulled the boat out of the lake and went back to town to look for Swampers. There were none to be found, so we went home for the day. The next day I was driving through another town a few miles away and happened by a sport shop, so I stopped in to see if they had any Swampers. Much to my surprise and delight, they had two left, so I bought them both.

When I got home, I went to the boat shed and tied one on Thunderfoot's rod, which he had left in the boat. I tied the other on my rod. Then I went into the house and called him. "Hey, it's a nice day. Let's go down and see if any northerns are hungry."

"Yeah, I suppose. I'll be over in a minute," he said. He didn't sound too enthusiastic.

We put the boat in the back of the pickup and drove down to our favorite slough and carried it down over the bank. When he went to get in the boat, he saw the Swamper on his pole. "Holy cow, you got some! Oh man, let's get on the water." He was in a much better mood now.

We pulled out onto the lake and began casting. On his second cast, Thunderfoot put his Swamper right in the top of a tree that hung out over the water. "Oh no!" He jerked and twitched and did everything he could to free the bait but it was wrapped around a limb and was a goner.

"You might as well kiss that one goodbye," I said.

He shut his eyes and wrapped his line around his sweatshirt sleeve and began to pull. Suddenly with a crack, his line broke and fluttered down into the water. His Swamper was hanging in the tree, probably forever.

"Oh, that's it. Take me home," he said.

"No way. We're gonna fish for a while now that we're here," I said. We fished toward the middle of the lake and I swung my rod back for a long cast. As I threw it forward, I got a backlash and my Swamper flew about forty yards, hit the end of the line, snapped off and landed in the water, not attached to my pole anymore.

"Holy cow, you lost yours, too," Thunderfoot said, kind of happily.

"I watched right where it landed," I said. "Let's see if we can get it."

We paddled the boat over to the spot and suddenly I could see the Swamper laying on a clump of weeds under the water.

"There, I see it," I said, pointing down into the water.

"Oh, yeah. I can reach it, I think," Thunderfoot said.

He pushed up the sleeve on his sweatshirt, laid over the side of the boat, and reached down. Soon he came up and pushed his sleeve up as far as it would go. Then he laid down and reached and reached, and went in too far and got his sleeve all wet. "I'm so close," he said. This time, he hung over the side and put his head and shoulder into the water. He almost tipped the boat over trying to get back up. No lure.

"I can see it down there; I'm just a little short of getting it."

"Well, let it go then," I said.

"No way," he said. He was wearing bibbed camouflage overalls, and he then stood up and took them off. "What in the world are you doing now?" I said.

"Maybe I can get it with my toes. My legs are longer than my arms, and my pants are already wet."

He sat up on the side of the boat and put his feet into the water and fished around, trying to get the lure. "Darn, can't grab it," he said, sliding back into the boat.

"Let it go," I said.

"No way. I'm all wet now, I might as well go in after it." And, with saying that, he took off his sweatshirt and jumped over the side.

The water was about mid-chest deep, and he stood there on the bottom for a few seconds to let the mud and debris clear so he could see the bait, and then went under water. A half a minute later he came up, with a huge grin on his face, and then held up the Swamper. "See, I told you I'd be able to get it."

He put the lure in the boat and I sat on the opposite side to balance the boat while he climbed back in. Thankfully, it was a nice warm sunny day, because he had gotten every stitch of clothes he had with him soaked in the process of retrieving the lure. There he sat on the front seat, grinning from ear to ear in his underwear, holding his prize Swamper.

"Well, I have to give you an A for effort. You're persistent," I said. He grinned and began tying the Swamper onto his line. "Hey, what are you doing? That's my Swamper," I said.

"Oh, really? Apparently, you don't know about the maritime salvage laws, do you? It would appear that I have salvaged this bait from the deep, and it is now my property."

"Oh, really?"

"Yeah, really," he said, defiantly.

"Well, if you want to be that way, fine with me," I said.

"Thank you very much. Now will you row me over there? I think there's a hungry northern laying there with my name on it." Huge grin.

Oh well, what the heck, I guess he did deserve it. There wasn't a northern in the whole lake that would make me get into that cold water.

Thanks, Thunderfoot.

A Typical Day in the Marsh

The early duck season was in full swing, and Thunderfoot and I were in our blind, planning on hunting all day long. We had grassed our main blind, carried the canoe and the decoys out the previous week, and had just settled down for the day's hunt. We had the decoys out, and Katy was sitting by the little dog door in the front of the blind, waiting for us to shoot a duck so she could do her job. I had made a sack full of sandwiches and had packed cookies and some chips to keep Thunderfoot happy. The early flight of ducks was just starting, and we were ready.

"There's some, over by the woods, and some more. Cool, here comes a couple from the lake," Thunderfoot said as he watched the skyline, looking for birds that might be interested in our decoys.

A minute later, a pair of ducks came by and we stood and shot at them, missing both cleanly. "Well, that's the way to start," I said, laughing. "We educated that pair, so we won't have to worry about them coming back here for a while." Less than a minute later, a small flock of mallards looked at the decoys but weren't convinced, and decided to go on down the marsh.

There were small flocks of ducks everywhere and it was hard to keep track of them. Suddenly, a flock of about twenty teal came right in, low over the grass and were setting their wings into the decoys before we even saw them.

"Holy cow, look," Thunderfoot said as he stood up to shoot. The teal saw him instantly and began to rise up instead of dropping onto the water, and the flock quickly turned into a whirlwind of darting and wheeling birds, making for a getaway. Meanwhile we each tried to pick one duck from the mass and shoot at it. We both shot all three of our shells, and one duck fell from the flock over at the right end of the pond. Katy had been watching the fracas and jumped out of the blind and went back toward the dry land behind us.

"Kate, no, go fetch," I said as I pointed to the end of the pond.

She stopped and stood a minute and then went to where I was pointing, sniffed out the duck and brought it in. Then she took off for the back of the blind again. "Kate, no, come here." She stopped and stood for another minute and then obeyed me and came back to the blind. "Good girl," I said, patting her on the head. She grumbled a bit and then lay down.

"That was some good shooting," Thunderfoot grinned. "At this rate we'll need about twelve boxes of shells each for a limit of ducks." Oh, well, so what; shooting was the fun part anyway.

The next hour or so was pretty busy, and we shot at a couple dozen more ducks without taking so much as a feather from any of them. Things started to slow down as it got mid-morning, and soon I needed to make a trip back to the bushes to say hi to Mother Nature.

"Go way back," Thunderfoot said as I climbed out of the blind.

I was back about a hundred feet from the blind when I noticed a hawk, hovering over the right end of the pond. As I watched it, I began to believe that it was a peregrine falcon because of its size and shape. I had only seen them on TV; but a friend of mine was a birdwatcher and he had recently told me that he had seen one in this general vicinity a few weeks earlier. As I finished my business, I began walking back through the willows and tall grass and as I got near the pond, I saw a lone blue wing teal coming from the left. It was just skimming the tops of the grass and came across the end of the pond going about sixty miles per hour. Thunderfoot saw it just as it got even with the blind and jumped up to shoot, but by the time he got his gun to his shoulder the teal was at the other end of the pond. It started to rise up to clear the grass, and the falcon moved to its right, so quickly that I wasn't sure if I had even seen it make the move, and caught the teal in mid air! There was a puff of feathers, the teal's head flopped over and the falcon carried it off down the marsh.

I got in the blind and Thunderfoot was still sitting there with his mouth hanging open. "Did you see that duck run into that hawk? It got killed and the hawk carried it away."

"That was a peregrine falcon, and we just saw something that probably very few people in the whole world have ever seen."

"How do you know it's a falcon?"

"They're the only hawk-like bird in our area that can catch a duck in mid-flight. And, it's the right size and shape, and I heard there was one around here, so I'm pretty sure."

"Wow, cool. He sure was quick, a lot quicker than me. I didn't even get my gun off safe," he grinned.

Well, that had been an interesting event, so we sat and chatted about it for a while, and Katy began whining to get out of the blind. "Maybe she needs to go potty," Thunderfoot said.

"Yeah, she hasn't been out, since we haven't shot any ducks. Come on, Katy, go potty," I said, opening the door.

Instead of going potty, Kate took off for the brush behind the blind. "Kate, where are you going?"

"Sometimes, I think she's not so smart," Thunderfoot said, shaking his head.

"No fooling. Come on, Kate, get in here." I couldn't see her but the weeds and grass were moving where she was fooling around.

"Kate, get back over here!" I yelled, getting impatient.

Soon we could see the grass moving as Katy came back toward the blind, and when she got to the edge of the pond, we could see she was carrying a dead teal in her mouth. "Holy cow, she's got a duck," Thunderfoot said.

Katy brought the duck into the blind and laid it down next to the one we had shot from the flock of twenty that had come by a couple of hours ago. She looked up at us, gave us a grunt and then lay down to watch out of her door.

Thunderfoot looked at me. "You suppose one of us got that

bird and didn't see it fall?"

"Probably, and Kate saw it and didn't forget. Hmm, makes me feel a little stupid for yelling at her." I gave Kate a pat on the head and she grunted back at me.

Mid-day was pretty slow for duck action so we just sat in the sun and enjoyed the beauty of the marsh. A couple of ducks had landed in the pond just west of us and Thunderfoot was bound and determined to go over there and see if he could get them. "Leave them. It's too soupy over there; you'll just get stuck and all full of mud," I said.

A while later, a small flock of mallards landed in the same pond, so now there was no stopping him. He took Katy with him and began sneaking up to the pond. I could tell he was having a tough time going, because I could see his head and hat above the grass and it wasn't moving very fast. He made slow progress toward the pond, and all of a sudden, I could see him standing on top of the tall grass. When he stood up straight, the ducks flushed and he shot a drake mallard as it cleared the marsh grass. I could hear Katy sloshing through the water and heard Thunderfoot say "good girl" as she brought him the duck. He turned to me and waved. I still couldn't figure out how he got up high enough that I could see him. The grass was at least five feet tall and with his feet in the mud, he wasn't much taller than five feet himself Suddenly he disappeared and then I could see his hat coming my way just above the grass again.

When he got to the blind, he proudly held up his mallard. "A beauty, huh?"

I congratulated him on a nice duck and then said, "How did you get so tall over there?"

"There's an old hay rake sitting there in the mud. I climbed up on the seat and I could see everything in the marsh."

"A hay rake? I heard there was one out here somewhere, but never have seen it. So that's where it is."

"Yup, sitting there like somebody is gonna make hay tomorrow, but they'll have to put inner tubes on the tires, because there's water all around it. How did it get way out here?" he asked.

"In the old days, before the beaver got so thick in these river bottoms, this was all dry ground around these ponds and they used to make marsh hay to use for bedding for the cattle. I suppose it got left one year and never got back to high ground."

"A 'one of these days' things that never happens?" he grinned.

"Probably."

We sat for the rest of the day and didn't fire another shot. All the ducks were flying too far away for good shooting, and they didn't seem interested in our little spread of decoys.

"Well, I guess I'll go out and pick up the decoys," I said, and I got up and stepped into the canoe.

"I'll get the rest of the stuff ready," Thunderfoot said.

By the time I had the decoys in the canoe, he had walked back to dry ground with Katy and was waiting for me. The sun had just about set and the western sky was turning a beautiful red. We stood there for about ten more minutes and watched the red fade and night begin to fall on the marsh. Soon the evening star, actually Venus, began to shine low in the ever-darkening sky.

"Well, we didn't get many ducks, but it was a pretty interesting day," Thunderfoot said.

"Yeah, no kidding. Better than chasing around after girls, right?"

"Ummm, I'm gonna have to think about that for a while," he said with a big grin.

The boy was growing up.

Thanks, Thunderfoot.

Where the Wild Goose Goes

It was getting close to the end of the goose season, and Thunderfoot and I had decided to make a trip to the Horicon Marsh for some late goose hunting. We had been to the marsh many times before, during other years, and always much earlier in the season. This was the first time for us this year, and we had waited until nearly the end of the season. We called our farmer friend with the goose blinds, and he told us we were lucky because he had just had a cancellation and we could have the number one blind.

In the part of the Horicon Marsh designated as the Intensive Zone, hunters must hunt from a blind. This rule is in effect to help the farmers who surround the marsh to recoup some of the money they lose to the hundreds of thousands of geese that feed from their cornfields during the fall. Each farmer is allotted a certain number of blinds according to the acreage he has, and hunters must rent these blinds to be able to hunt. Some farms have elaborate blinds, but most have a plywood structure that is four feet by eight feet and four feet high. There is a little wooden bench and that's about it. Some make their blinds out of bales of straw or hay, but basically they are just a place to sit and hide while waiting for geese to fly in or out of the marsh.

We were pretty excited because the number one blind is the prime blind on the farm where we hunt. It is about one hundred feet from the boundary fence of the marsh, where no one is allowed unless he has geese for parents. The blind is on a knoll overlooking the marsh and is nothing more than a hole dug in the top of the knoll, with a wooden bench in the bottom of it. Actually it looks like a foxhole from WWII. But, what it lacks in accommodations, it makes up for in being in the prime spot on the farm.

Normally, we get one of the blinds that is in the fourth or fifth tier of blinds and have to work our way up, as other hunters fill their limits, until we get to the front of the pack and get some good shooting. We had never gotten the best blind, so we were really excited about having it for the day's hunting.

It was still dark, and the wind was whistling out of the north across a frozen landscape. We didn't have much snow yet, but what little there was lay in little drifts behind clumps of corn stubble and clods of frozen dirt in the fields surrounding the blinds. We stopped and talked to our farmer friend and paid for the blind use, and he told us to drive out through the pasture and park by the cornfield so we wouldn't have such a long walk to our blind.

I drove through the darkened barnyard and down a lane past some cattle to the iron gate at the pasture fence. Thunderfoot hopped out of the truck and went up to the gate and took the chain off from around the fence post and swung it open. I drove through the gate and stopped to wait for him to close it and get back in the truck.

He was pretty groggy yet from the long nighttime drive, and as I watched him, he trudged over and took hold of the gate and swung it back to the closed position, took the chain and wrapped it around the post and clipped it shut, and then looked up with a look of confusion on his face. He was on the wrong side of the gate! He had closed it and stayed on the other side. I was laughing, watching him in the rear view mirror. He stood there a second and then realized what he had done, and then looked up at the truck to see if I had seen him.

He shook his head as he saw me laughing. He was caught doing something that I would surely never let him forget. He climbed over the gate and came to the truck. "I don't want to hear about it. Kindly drive us to the cornfield and shut up," he said. I could see him grinning, even though he wanted to try to keep a straight face.

I never said a word. We drove to the cornfield, parked, got our guns and gear from the back of the truck and started out across the picked corn stubble to the blind. The north wind bit into our faces and stung our ears as we crunched across the frozen snow and corn stubble. We finally got to the edge of the knoll and found the blind. "Wow, this is cool, like in the movies, a foxhole," he said, surveying our little hiding place. He raised his gun and began softly going "tchu, tchu, tchu" like someone firing a machine gun at the enemy. "Take it easy, John Wayne, you'll scare all the geese. They're just down there on the other side of the fence," I said.

He grinned and sat down on the bench, loaded his gun, and then stood it against the front of the embankment. "Ready and able, sir," he reported. I shook my head; he'd been watching too many war movies.

The wind continued to sting our faces and redden our cheeks, and soon the darkness began to fade into grayness as dawn crept over the marsh. In a few minutes we could hear an occasional honk of a goose or a "whaaa, whaaa, whaaa" of a hen mallard. The silence of the night began to give way to many bird calls, and the sounds soon rose in intensity to a quite loud noise. "Wow, they're making a lot of noise. Sounds like there's still a lot of them in there," Thunderfoot said.

Pretty soon a small flock of geese rose from the marsh like a puff of gray smoke drifting up from a campfire, slowly formed a loose V shape and began moving north toward a far off cornfield that was to be their breakfast. They were going to be too far out for us to shoot at, but soon more began rising up and flocks began forming all over the marsh. Soon one of these flocks was headed our way. "Get ready, and don't forget to lead them," I said. Thunderfoot nodded.

The geese crossed the boundary fence and continued on in front of us. "Take them!" I whispered, and we both stood up and picked out a goose and shot. I aimed at the lead goose and hit the second one back. Thunderfoot shot at, well, I'm not sure what he shot at, but nothing happened. We both were using our single shot ten-gauge shotguns, so one shot was all we had. Actually, that was good because a box of shells lasted a lot longer when you used them one at a time.

"Wow, you got one," Thunderfoot said, as he jumped to his feet to run out and gather up the downed goose. He raced to the pasture and brought my goose in for me. I put a sticky tag around its neck and laid it in the bottom of the blind. "That was almost too easy," I said. "My aim was a little off, though. To be honest, I was aiming at the lead goose and got the second one."

Thunderfoot looked at me. "How far are you aiming ahead?"

"Oh, I don't know, maybe fifteen or twenty feet."

"Oh, come on, twenty feet? You gotta be kidding me."

"No, I'm not. Those are big birds and they look like they're going slow, but they're not. You have to shoot a long way ahead of them."

I knew he wasn't convinced so I didn't push the issue. In a short time, another flock came in range and we both shot again, and this time I got the lead goose. Thunderfoot, again, missed. He ran out and picked up my goose and brought it back. I tagged it and I was done for the day. I had my limit.

"Well, I guess I'll put my gun away and watch you," I said.

"That's what you get for being such a smart pants. Now you have to just watch," he said.

The next flock started our way, and I said to Thunderfoot, "Now, be sure to just pick one bird. Don't flock shoot and then lead him."

He nodded and aimed his gun. He was leading the first bird in the flock, and I watched from behind him as he led the bird and then shot. The fifth goose back, ducked his head back as the shot buzzed past his nose.

"You were way too short on your lead. Did you see that other goose duck his head?"

"Jeez, I can't believe I was that short. Are you sure that was me that made him duck?"

"Pretty sure. You see that log laying on the ground over there?" I said, pointing to an old fence post. "That is about seven or eight feet long. Shoot about three logs in front of the first goose."

He shook his head but agreed to try it. The next flock started drifting our way and he got ready. "Now remember, three logs," I said.

I squatted behind him and watched as he got a lead on the lead goose and then swung the gun ahead and pulled the trigger. The second goose back from the lead dropped from the flock and crashed onto the frozen pasture. "Holy cow, will you look at that?" he said, as he climbed over the edge of our foxhole and ran out to pick up his goose. He held it up proudly and then came back and tagged it and laid it in the bottom of the blind with the others.

"As much as I hate to admit it, you were right," he said, grinning.

"As usual," I said.

"Don't wrench your arm patting yourself on the back."

We let a few questionable flocks go by and soon another lowing bunch was coming right toward us. "Well, here comes the last shot of the season," he said. "I calculate them at about 3.25 logs." He took aim, swung ahead and dropped the lead goose.

He turned to me with a huge grin on his face. "Old dead eye strikes again."

Then he jumped over the side of the blind and ran out to get his goose.

I would have liked to stay and sit and watch the geese fly for a while, but there were other hunters in the back blinds who were waiting for their turn in the front blind. "Man, this is a good place to hunt," Thunderfoot said. "Now I see why people try to get it all the time."

"Yeah, it's almost too good," I said. "We got done pretty fast."

"Well," he said, "the way that wind is freezing my ears, I'm kinda glad, and besides, my belly is calling for some pancakes, and sausage, and maybe a couple of eggs for a kicker."

As usual he was faminished.

"Well, let's go then," I said, and we carried our gear back to the truck. The group in the blind behind us waved as they moved up, and the group behind them moved up to their blind, to wait for them to finish.

When we got to the gate, I stopped and Thunderfoot sat in the truck instead of getting out to open it. "What are you waiting for?" I said.

"Aren't you gonna make some smart remark about being on the right side when I close it?"

"Who, me?"

Thanks, Thunderfoot.

Black powder hunting had been gaining in popularity for the past few years, and Thunderfoot had been pestering me to get a black powder gun so we could hunt the extended deer season with our muzzleloaders. I finally broke down and bought one, and he had conned his grandpa out of one, so we now had an extra week to hunt.

I bought my gun a few weeks earlier and had been going to the range to learn how to load it and figure out which type of bullet and how much powder made the best shooting load. Thunderfoot already had that worked out for him by his grandpa, so he came along to shoot and to practice with his gun, too. These modern guns were pretty accurate, and with the invention of the new powders and bullets, were safe and effective for killing a whitetail deer, moose, elk, or even a bear. The only drawback was that you had only one shot, so you wanted to make that one shot count.

Boom! "Whooie, that was a good one," Thunderfoot said, as he fanned the huge cloud of smoke away from his shot. We looked through binoculars and saw that he had hit almost dead center in the bull's-eye that we had painted on the side of a cardboard box that was sitting about fifty yards away. "Give yours a try and see if you can do that."

I aimed, touched off the ignition cap, and half a second later there was a boom, and the gun recoiled and smoke bellowed out of the barrel. After the smoke cleared, we looked down range and saw my bullet had hit within an inch of Thunder foot's. "Not bad for a rookie," he said, grinning.

"Well, I've put about a hundred practice shots through my gun now, so I feel pretty confident that I can hit a deer with it," I said.

"I know I can," he said, matter-of-factly.

We went home and cleaned the guns and made them ready

for the next day, which was opening day for the muzzle loading hunt. His grandpa had invited us to his farm, and Thunderfoot was going to stay the night at my house so we could get an early start in the morning. We made our mandatory lunch and packed it before we went to bed, and what seemed like a very short time later, my alarm was beeping. I went to the spare bedroom and woke Thunderfoot, who grumbled about being awakened until it dawned on him that he was going hunting and not to school. We had a quick breakfast and headed out for grandpa's farm.

I had been at the farm before, so I knew the lay of the land. I was going to go up to the left side of the valley and sit until a couple hours after dawn. Thunderfoot was going up the right side to a stand that his grandpa used for the regular deer season. It was a really luxury stand. It was built about ten feet up in the lower limbs of a huge dead oak tree and was like a little house with a window cut into each side. The windows were just window holes, with no glass, so the hunter could shoot right through them. It had a corrugated tin roof and a couple of chairs inside for the hunter or hunters to sit in while they watched the end of the valley. There was a nice ladder permanently attached to it so even an old, not so agile guy like me could get up with ease.

Thunderfoot was going to sit in the little house and after I got cold, I was supposed to work my way up the left side of the valley and then walk slowly toward him, possibly chasing a deer or two toward the house.

We parked in the farmyard and crossed the gate behind the barn. The valley was about a mile long and pretty narrow. There had been a cornfield in the bottom of it all summer, but that was now picked and grandpa had about fifty head of beef cattle in the valley to clean up the missed corn and use the pasture on the sides of the hills.

"Good luck," I whispered as we parted and each went up one side of the valley. "You, too," he said.

It was a cloudy night, so there was no moon or starlight, and it was as dark as it could possibly be. I could just make out the forms of the lighter colored cattle moving ahead of me and almost bumped right into a big black one. She mooed at me and I said, "so boss" quietly, so as not to alarm her. I crossed the valley floor and started up the side of the pasture on the hillside. It was pretty steep, but I was going across pasture so it was easy walking.

Suddenly, in less time than it takes to tell, both of my feet were in a fresh puddle of pasture pudding, which was as slick as a puddle of fresh oil but smelled a little more fragrant. Both feet went out from under me so fast that I didn't even have time to put my hand down to stop my fall. I was carrying my gun in the crook of my left arm and when I hit the ground, my arm came up and my forehead crashed down on the gun with a crack. I don't know if the crack was audible or just inside my head, but it was real loud and I hit my head real hard on the gunstock.

The next few minutes were kind of fuzzy. I don't know exactly how long I laid there, but the next thing I knew, I could hear a soft, "mooooo." I raised my head a bit and stared right into the wet nose of one of the black cows. She was standing over me, probably trying to figure out if I was alive or dead. It was somewhat light now, so I figured I must have laid there for a while.

My head hurt like crazy and I tried to get up, only to have my feet slide again in the same pie I had slipped in in the first place. Well, actually it wasn't a pie anymore; I was wearing most of it on the front of my pants and coat.

My guardian cow moved back when I began to move and I finally staggered to my feet. Now I could see much better and could see what had happened. The pasture was like a minefield with meadow muffins everywhere. It was a wonder that I had made it as far as I did without stepping in one and sliding on my face.

I continued up to the edge of the woods and sat on a stump for a while to watch for a deer. After a while I began to get cold, so I thought I'd take my little trek up the hill and around the end of the valley to where Thunderfoot was sitting in his nice little house.

It took me about an hour to make the hill trip and soon I could see Thunderfoot sitting, looking out the window of the house on the tree. He waved, held up a sandwich for me to see and motioned for me to come up and join him.

I walked across the end of the valley and climbed up the ladder into the house. "Holy cow, what happened to your head?" he said.

"I fell down in some cow poop," I said.

"Whew, I guess you did, you're wearing most of it. Did you know you've got blood allover the side of your head?"

"No, is it still bleeding?"

"Nope, it's all dried. You look like heck."

"Thanks."

"Want a sandwich?" he said, offering me the last sandwich.

"What, you're not hungry? What happened to the other five of them?" He just grinned and patted his belly.

I opened a can of pop and took the sandwich, and we both sat down in the chairs. I was telling him about my adventure in the pasture when suddenly he began looking really hard at the hillside across the valley. "There's a deer coming down the hill," he whispered.

I looked and, sure enough, a nice buck was working his way down a trail on the side of the hill. "Don't move, or he'll see you," I said.

Thunderfoot nodded, and raised his gun slowly. I was just about to say, "Don't shoot it inside the house, stick it out the window," when he touched it off. Now, to say it was loud is the understatement of the year. Imagine setting off a huge firecracker in your bathroom and that might be close. The muzzle blast displaced a huge amount of air and made the leaves and debris on the floor fly around the house like a hurricane had hit. Then the smoke from the gun filled the little house, and I couldn't even see Thunderfoot three feet away from me. "Holy cow, my ears are deaf!" he said.

My ears were ringing like mad, and I could barely hear what he had said. I waved the smoke away with my hat and soon the wind cleared it enough so we could see each other.

"I was going to tell you not to shoot inside the house," I said, shaking my head.

"Good idea," he said, nodding his head. "I wish you would have said it sooner, so I wouldn't be totally deaf now."

Despite our hurt ears, we both began to laugh. "Whew, that was loud," he said.

"Hey, did you get the deer?" I asked.

We both looked out the window and, sure enough, there laid the deer.

"Cool, what a marksman I am," he said.

"Well, you better go field dress him and we'll get him tagged," I said.

"Eh? Can't hear you."

"I said ... " Then I saw him grinning and handing me his knife.

"Could you, just this one more time?"

Oh well, at least I wouldn't be able to hear him pestering me for the next couple days to do some other fool thing.

Thanks, Thunderfoot.

Wisdom From Thunderfoot

When Dan nicknamed me Thunderfoot many years ago, I never dreamed that we would become such good friends and have so much fun together. I think maybe I was lucky to have a friend like him, but he always says it's him who was lucky to find a hunting and fishing buddy like me. Who knows, maybe we were meant to meet and have all these great times together so we could share them with you.

I've been places, seen things I never thought I'd ever see.

And I've done things, wow, so many things, that I never ever dreamed I'd do. Sometimes I almost wish I hadn't done some of them, because at the time, they weren't too much fun, but after we got dry or washed the mud off of us, we thought they were pretty funny.

We've had lots of fun and done some pretty crazy things, but most of the time we just ~ere doing something that many people do, enjoying the outdoors. No matter how normal your plans are for a day, there are lots of things that can happen to make a little fishing trip or hunting trip into a day you'll never forget. Especially when you hunt and fish with someone who never forgets a thing, like Dan. He seems to be able to remember every time I made a mistake or had a little accident. And, of course, I think he makes it look like most of the things that went wrong are my fault. Of course, I'm totally innocent of all such charges.

And I've learned so much. I've not only learned to catch a fish or shoot a duck, I've learned about life and, of course, death, and friendship. I wish I could count the times we just watched a deer or duck or squirrel and never even shot at it and still had the fun of being there. Or, the hundreds of fish that we caught and then put back, to fight again. And, the sadness of Lucy leaving us, and the funny feeling in my stomach when I've shot a nice deer or duck. It's a feeling that I am happy that I got the game I was after, but also the feeling of sadness that I took the life of such a beautiful thing. Of course, death is part of life, and also part of hunting.

And the friendship. I don't know how many people have a friendship with another person like we have. I can't imagine how many hours we've been together in a cold duck blind or an ice shanty. Or the hours we sat under the hot sun in the boat. The hundreds of sandwiches and cookies we shared; the hours just sitting quietly watching for game to come to us; enjoying every minute of it. We have a bond that has lasted many years and hopefully will last for many more.

No matter how cold or hot or bored you get, being with your best friend makes it enjoyable. And, we've sure enjoyed a lot of those special times.

Dan keeps complaining that he's getting too old for some of these little adventures we go on. I keep telling him that as long as he is still upright and breathing, I expect him to keep going with me, and he said he thought maybe he could. So, we're looking forward to lots more fun in the outdoors.

I thank you for reading this book and hope you had a laugh or maybe a tear. If you enjoyed reading about us, just think how much fun it was to be there. So many memories, and hopefully so many more coming in the future.

We'll see you on the water or in the woods, and as always, I'll be the one with the grin on my face.

Your Buddy, Thunderfoot

About the Author:

Dan Bomkamp is an avid outdoor enthusiast. He grew up along the Wisconsin River and has made his home there since his college days at UW-LaCrosse. He has been involved in the sporting goods industry for many years and began his writing career by writing short stories for outdoor magazines in the early 1980s. He has hosted 30 foreign exchange students from 11 countries and has traveled to Europe to visit many of them.

His other books include: *The Adventures of Thunderfoot; Thanks Thunderfoot; Voyageur; The Gosey; Big Edna; Lost Flight; and Tag.* He lives in Muscoda, Wisconsin with his Boston Terrier, Buster, and his cat, Tigger.

You can contact the author at *danbomkamp@live.com* or visit his website, *www.danbomkamp.com*.